Books in print by the same author:

DRAMA AND INTELLIGENCE
A Cognitive Theory

DRAMA AND FEELING
An Aesthetic Theory

The Director's Shakespeare Series:

SHAKESPEARE'S WORLD OF WAR
SHAKESPEARE'S COMIC WORLD
SHAKESPEARE'S WORLD OF LOVE
SHAKESPEARE'S WORLD OF DEATH
SHAKESPEARE'S PROBLEM WORLD
SHAKESPEARE'S MASKED WORLD
SHAKESPEARE'S TRAGIC WORLD
SHAKESPEARE'S MAGIC WORLD

PLAY, DRAMA AND THOUGHT:
The Intellectual Background to Dramatic Education

RE-PLAY:
Studies of Human Drama in Education

RE-COGNIZING RICHARD COURTNEY:
Selected Papers on Educational Drama
Edited by David Booth & Alistair Martin-Smith

The Birth of God

American University Studies

Series XXVI
Theatre Arts

Vol. 26

PETER LANG
New York • Washington, D.C./Baltimore
Bern • Frankfurt am Main • Berlin • Vienna • Paris

Richard Courtney

The Birth of God

The Moses Play and Monotheism in Ancient Israel

"We are rediscovering that a holy theatre
is still what we need. So where should we
look for it? In the clouds or on the ground?"
—*Peter Brook*

PETER LANG
New York • Washington, D.C./Baltimore
Bern • Frankfurt am Main • Berlin • Vienna • Paris

Library of Congress Cataloging-in-Publication Data

Courtney, Richard.
The birth of God: the Moses play and monotheism in ancient Israel/
by Richard Courtney.
p. cm. —(American university studies. Series XXVI, Theatre arts; vol. 26)
Includes bibliographical references and index.
1. Bible as literature. 2. Drama. 3. Moses (Biblical leader). 4. Jews—Kings
and rulers. 5. Kings and rulers—Biblical teaching. I Title. II. Series.
BS535.C64   221.6'6—dc20   95-43349
ISBN 0-8204-3055-2
ISSN 0899-9880

Die Deutsche Bibliothek-CIP-Einheitsaufnahme

Courtney, Richard:
The birth of God: the Moses play and monotheism in ancient Israel/
by Richard Courtney. –New York; Washington, D.C./Baltimore; Bern;
Frankfurt am Main; Berlin; Vienna; Paris: Lang.
(American university studies: Ser. 26, Theatre arts; Vol. 26)
ISBN 0-8204-3055-2
NE: American university studies/ 26

The paper in this book meets the guidelines for permanence and durability
of the Committee on Production Guidelines for Book Longevity
of the Council of Library Resources.

PREFACE

The concept of one God was born in the time of Moses and it happened in a ritual play. The earliest human societies were infused with drama. Whether they were of hunters as in the paleolithic period or, later, of farmers in the first civilizations in the Near East, made a difference to *the style* of performance, but both used dramatic action to control their world.

The infusion of dramatic action in daily life also applies to contemporary tribes when they are remote from Western cultures. They too use performance to understand existence and try to control it; e.g., Amerindians and Inuit, Australian aboriginals and those in the highlands of Indonesia and Southeast Asia, and others high in the Himalayan mountains or deep in the African forests.

Peoples perform ritual dramas at life and social crises: birth, puberty, marriage, death, or events that threaten society. Tribal people see even the smallest event as dramatic. So American Indians on remote parts of the Northwest Pacific coast perform simple rituals when they catch their first salmon of the season, just as those people in remote corners of the Congo perform simple rituals as the dawn rises each morning. Both these people perform their actions "on behalf of" the other (the salmon, the sun) to renew them. This indicates the person's "power," brought about by drama.

*****

In this book, I examine ancient Israel. The first *historical* fact of which we are certain happened c.1250—the conquest of Canaan by Joshua and the Israelites. Events before that time, from the Creation to Moses, are known as "legendary history." It may surprise some readers to know that even the Exodus from Egypt and the flight across "the Sea of Reeds" are supported by no historical evidence. So what really happened?

Unfortunately the Bible, as it exists today, is only of little use to us. The original Moses–Exodus story was written c.950–900 B.C., much later than the events—about the time of, or a little later than, Solomon. It was not liked when the Jews returned from the Babylonian Exile, centuries later in 587 B.C.

So it was suppressed. To know what really happened as Joshua led the Israelites across the Jordan, we must return to the remnants of *The Book of J* that were left in the Bible, often by mistake, by the new authors and editors.

What we discover is that Moses and Aaron, and probably the biblical characters before that—from the creating God to the Prophets—were figures in a ritual drama.

My perspective in looking at these issues is dramatic. That is, I am neither a biblical scholar, nor an historian of ancient religions. My viewpoint is that of a theatrical critic who examines ancient ritual drama, and my primary emphasis is practical—on what was *done*. If readers and reviewers understand this, they will not mistake my intention.

*****

Most quotations from the Bible are from the Authorized Version. The modern translation of *The Book of J* by David Rosenberg is indicated by round brackets.

I am very grateful for the work of modern scholars in anthropological, biblical and Hebrew studies whose research has proved invaluable to me. I owe a great deal to the works of Harold Bloom, James W.Flanagan, Theodor H.Gaster, David Rosenberg, Victor W.Turner, J.M.N. Wijngaards, and others referred to in the book. I have followed them closely although I have specifically focused on dramatic events. But I do not wish to implicate any of them in my mistakes, nor any other person to whom I am also grateful: Dr. Robert J. Landy of New York University for some helpful suggestions; Rt Rev. E. J. Burton and the late Professor G. Wilson Knight for their constant support of my theatrical work; those who worked with me when I was directing folk and ritual drama in Yorkshire, Smethwick and Stockport, England (1955–67); Professor David Booth and Dr.Bernie Warren; a number of my doctoral students at the Ontario Institute for Studies in Education, and at the Graduate Centre for the Study of Drama, The University of Toronto, for their insights into ritual drama—Dr Robert Gardner, Dr Belarie

Hyman-Zatzman, Dr Bat-Sheva Koren, Dr Peter McLaren, Dr Alistair Martin-Smith, Dr Helen E. H. Smith, Dr Alexander Tumanov, Dr Michael Wilson, and, particularly, to Sandra L. Katz who first suggested to me that such a study was possible; to Peggy Nicolle for the initial typing, to Bob Borbas for help with computerization, to David Beneteau for reproducing the map and help with the manuscript, to my secretary Sandra Burroughs for preparing the manuscript; and to my wife, Dr Rosemary Courtney, for her expert editing and the index.

R.C.

Jackson's Point , and

Toronto, Ontario, and

Elephant Butte, New Mexico

1984–1995

CONTENTS

FIGURES

		ISRAELITES	NEAR EAST
LEGENDARY	1800	Abram/Patriarchs in Canaan	Hyskos in Egypt
	1700	Descent of Israel into Egypt	Egypt: New Kingdom
HISTORY	1300	Israelites forced labour in Egypt	Rise of Hittites
	1280	Exodus/Moses	End of Hittites

HISTORIC	1250-1200 Conquest of Canaan				
	The Judges			Assyrian domination	
PERIOD	1040	Samuel/Saul			
	1000	David			
	961	Solomon king			
	950-900 *The Book of J*				
	922	Death of Solomon			
	922	*JUDAH*	*ISRAEL*		
		Rehoboam (-915)	Jeroboam (-901)		
		Abijah	Nadab		
	900	Asa	Basha		
		Jehoshaphat	Elah/Zimri		
		Omrii Samaria			
	850-800 *E revision of J*		Ahab	Elijah	
			Ahazia		
		Jehoram	Jehoram	Elisha	
	842	Ahazia/Athalia Jehu			
		Joash	Johohaz		
	800	Amaziah	Jehoash		
	750	Uzziah	Jeroboam II Amos Hosea		
			Zechariah		
	745	Jotham	Shallum/Menahem		
	735	Ahaz	Pehahiah		
		Isaiah	Pekah		
		Micah	Hoshea		
	722		Samaria falls	Sargon II	
	715	Hezekiah/Manasseh			
	650-600 *Deuteronomy*				
	642	Amon			
	640	Josiah Nahum			
	612			Nineveh falls	
	609	Jehoahaz			
	600	Jehoiakim Jeremiah		Babylon domination	
		Jehoiachin			
	598	Zedekiah	Ezekiel		
	587	Jerusalem falls		The Exile	

Figure 1: Chronology: Patriarchs to the Exile

DATE	ISRAELITE		NEAR EAST
B.C.			
950-900	*The Book of J*		
587	The Exile		
550	*The P text*		Cyrus of Persia
539			Babylon falls
538	Return of exiles. Zerubbabel		Edict of Cyrus
522			Darius the Great
515	Second Temple rebuilt	Haggai Zechariah	
500	Malachi		
490			Battle of Marathon
458	Ezra's mission		Artaxerxes I
445	Nehemiah arrives		Aeschylus' Oresteia
431	Walls of Jerusalem rebuilt		Peloponnesian War
400	*The Redactor*	Socrates dies	Artaxerxes II
350			Alexander the Great
333			Defeat of Darius III
323			Ptolemy I of Egypt
			Rome conquers Italy
312			Seleucus I
250-100	The Septuagint		
200	Judea under Egyptian rule		
167	Temple profaned		
166	Maccabean revolt. Judah		
160	Jonathan		
142	Judea autonomous. Simon		
134	John Hyrcanus		
64			Pompey in Syria
63	Pompey takes Jerusalem.	Judea a Roman province	Seleucid Empire ends
48			Caesar defeats Pompey
37	Herod the Great		Rome defeats Egypt
27			Emperor Augustus
6	Birth of Jesus ?		
A.D.			
14			Tiberius
26	Pontius Pilate prefect of Judea		
37			Caligula
66	First Jewish War		
68	Destruction of Qumran		
70	Dispersion		

Figure 2: Chronology: From the Exile to the Diaspora

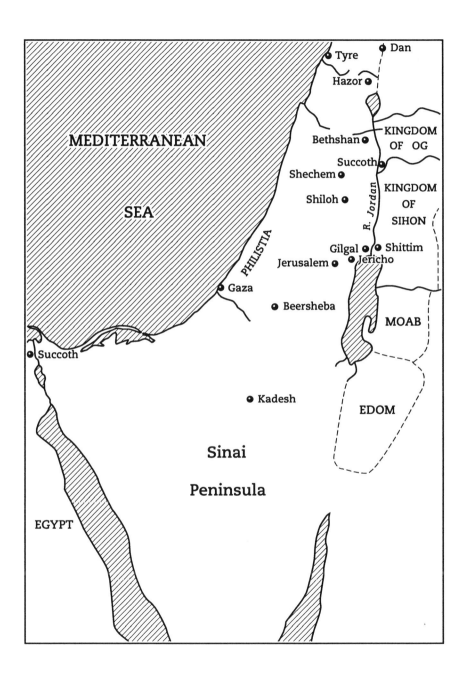

Figure 3: The Sinai and Canaan

B.C.	
c.1250	The Conquest of Canaan
950-900	The Book of J
850-800	E revision of J
650-600	Deuteronomy
550	The P text
400	The Redactor
250-100	The Septuagint
90	Canonization of the Hebrew Bible completed
A.D.	
400	Saint Jerome's Latin Vulgate translation of the Bible
1530	William Tyndale's Pentateuch
1534	Luther's Bible (Old Testament)
1535	Miles Coverdale's Bible
1560	Geneva Bible (Shakespeare's Bible)
1611	King James (Authorized Version)
1952	Revised Standard Version
1966	Jerusalem Bible (Catholic)
1970	New English Bible (Protestant)
1982	New American Jewish Version

Figure 4: Biblical Text Chronology

DEFINITIONS

Bible	from *ta biblia*, Greek for "the books"; suggests diversity.
The Book of J	the oldest strand in the Pentateuch, probably composed at Jerusalem in the tenth century B.C.; most suppressed.
Court Historian	wrote most of what we now call *2 Samuel* at the same time as *The Book of J*.
D	the writer or "school" of *Deuteronomy* c.650-600.
E	Elohist; biblical author.
Hebrew	now the language of contemporary Israel; anciently, the Old Canaanite language of the Bible.
Hebrews	term for the ancient Israelites (now defunct).
Israeli	a citizen of the post-1947 state of Israel.
Israelite	the people of ancient Israel to the Return from the Exile.
Jew	from the Hebrew *yehudi*: a Judahite (Judean), descendant of Judah, Jacob's (Israel's) fourth son (heir), historical carrier of the Blessing of Yahweh, first given to Abram.
The Jews	the Israelites from the Return until the present moment.
liminal	the ritual state between separation and re-aggregation.
P	priestly author of the Bible.
Pentateuch	derives from a Greek term, *hê pentateuchos biblos*, "the book of the five scrolls."
R	Redactor, biblical author.
Schism	split of Solomon's Empire into Israel (Jeroboam) and Judah (Rehoboam).
Sea of Reeds	correct translation of "The Red Sea" at the Exodus.

for

the late ALEC BARON

and other theatre friends in Leeds

and

my Indian friends on Vancouver Island

INTRODUCTION

THE BIBLE

It will be startling to some readers to find that the *evidence* we have of the Exodus of the Hebrews from Egypt, together with the characters of Moses and Aaron, come from the performance of an ancient play—a ritual drama.

We must distinguish, first of all, history and religion. History provides us with *evidence*, but religion gives us *belief*. Whatever we believe of the Bible, the historical facts are clear: Joshua became the first known dramatist when he created a ritual play performance for the new nation—The Moses Festival Play about the Exodus. In contrast, we have no *evidence* that there was an event in history called the Exodus, nor that Moses and Aaron were historical personages. Nor is there any evidence, historical or archeological, that Saul or David ever existed.

Yet this does *not* mean that the Exodus did not happen, or that Moses and Aaron, Saul or David, did not exist. They may well have done. *Whether these events and people were real or not, however, is not the issue addressed in this book.*

The first fact of Israelite history occurs when they crossed the Jordan into the promised land. History, the study of authenticated past events, begins for Israel at that moment in time. Simultaneously it is likely that there were migrations into Canaan and the peasants rose up in revolt. All the Hebrew past up to that point, from the Creation to Moses, is known as "legendary history" because it cannot be authenticated apart from the words of the Bible.

The reader may well *believe* that Abraham left Ur, that Moses changed his staff into a snake, or that God wrote on stone with fire. Nothing in this book should disturb the faith of this reader: the fact that the events of Moses' life (as written in the Bible some centuries later) came from a ritual drama, does not affect faith. Indeed, this book can be read by those who do, and those who do not, believe in the authenticity of Moses. After all, the ritual drama had to come from somewhere.

The people who crossed the Jordan had a past—what was it? Whatever the answer, it does not affect the fact that Moses' ritual drama is the basis from which the first writer of the Bible created Israel's history.

In the ancient Near East, Festivals celebrated major religious events, particularly the annual New Year—an intercalary period of several days. As major events in life altered (a conquest, a new king, etc.), so did religious events and the nature of the Festival. The ritual dramas in these Festivals are called "plays," but they were not plays as we know them today. They were huge, sprawling events lasting many days during which the myth of the god ruling the city was acted out in ritualized fashion among a host of other rituals. The local king acted as himself in some rituals, and as the god in the ritual dramas. Priests, priestesses, and acolytes played other roles in the ritual drama.

These Festivals were common in every ancient Near Eastern state. Until recently, however, Biblical scholars have denied there was such a ritual drama in Israel; and Biblical literalists today, who think every word in the Bible is literal fact, deny the existence of The Moses Play. For them, Moses was a real person who led his people out of Egypt and travelled with them to Canaan, but died before he could enter the promised land.

Modern scholarship, however, demonstrates that the Israelites had their Festivals, too. Indeed, we may assume the sequence of *at least* three main Israelite Festivals:

* *The Yahweh Festival* : A Pre-Canaan event
         Celebrating agriculture and Yahweh
* *The Moses Festival* : As Canaan was occupied
         Celebrating the promised land, Moses, and Yahweh
* *The Royal Festival* : A Post-David event
         Celebrating the House of David and Yahweh

Between these Festivals, changes occurred. In the reign of Solomon, The Royal Festival was held as the writer of *The Book of J* began composing the

Moses Play; and with the later Schism there were other variations which we will examine.

Readers of this book need to put themselves back in time: a great writer and scholar wrote *The Book of J* probably as Solomon lay dying and into the first years of the Schism. He did not write about the Play being performed in his own time (that was the David Play), but about the Moses Play which was performed as the Israelites entered Canaan centuries before. At the time he was writing, he lived in the events of the Schism and so he included oblique comments about the events of his era. Given that *The Book of J* was largely expurgated centuries later when the Israelites returned from the Exile, it is no wonder that so little has been known of it until recent years.

PART 1:

BACKGROUND

Religious Festivals began with hunting tribes and expanded with the great agricultural civilizations. They were of several days in length, in intercalary periods, and they included all kinds of dramatic performances to celebrate the Divine and Creation.

The most significant of these performances were the ritual-myths which changed as society altered. In ancient Israel these were performed in specific ritual dramas: [1] the Festival Plays of Moses and the Land-giving; and [2] the David Play. Remnants of these are to be found embedded in the early Books of the Jewish Bible (the Old Testament).

Human performance is as old as Homo sapiens *and Part 1 of this book will examine the necessary background.*

1
DRAMA IN THE ANCIENT WORLD

Ritual drama was common to all ancient religions; they were dramatic even in remote pre-history. The worshipper entered the religious action directly; by experiencing it, he or she took on the role of the Divine. This religious *doing* (action, role-play) then affected each person's daily life. The "power" of the Divine was the model not only for religious experiences but also for social life.

THE HUNTERS

In the Ice Ages, the Neanderthals and *Homo sapiens* both demonstrated extraordinary dramatic traits.

The large-brained Neanderthals,[1] hunters of huge Arctic animals, had burial customs showing a belief in life after death. Most remarkably, in the Shanidar cave (Kurdistan) the dead were buried with colourful flowers meant to restore their health in the afterlife—very like laying flowers on modern graves. Archeology can tell us little about a Neanderthal ritual drama based on the now extinct giant cave bear (*ursus spelacous*), but we may glimpse it in bear rituals today from Finland to Japan.[2]

Paleolithic hunters[3] also dramatized their existence in their masterpieces of painting and sculpture, found deep in caves used for ritual drama and dance. The Divine was a universe of spirits: "the upper world" of the air and the sky; the everyday world where people were "spirits in the clothing of men," and "the lower world" in the earth signified by the caves—the model for the temples of later farmers. The roles of spirits were linked to the dead. A correct burial ritual enabled the dead to travel safely to the spirit world, and stopped them from returning to the ordinary world as ghosts. "Real life" and "fictional life" were two aspects of the same thing.

The person who interceded between the spirits and human beings was the shaman (priest, magician, sorcerer) who worked for the community's good; thus the African witch-doctor tries to "doctor" witches to protect the community from evil powers. In possessed dramatic dance, imitating all the spirits he meets and controls, the shaman ensures the community's health in rain making, fire walking, success in the hunt, or curing illness. To increase the fertility of the cosmos are sexual rituals symbolic of creating life. A shaman, ancient or modern, travels in a trance to the other "worlds" to force the spirits to do his will. All shamans require initiation: a rite of passage is carried out by "ancestor spirits"—a traumatic ritual drama because the person is ritually "killed" as a human and "resurrected" as a shaman. There were two kinds of paleolithic shamans: [a] those in caves worshipped animal spirits; and

[b] those around hearths above ground worked with bird spirits and the Mother Goddess—a spirit of fertility, with massive breasts and hips, who affected all life.

The hunting tribes spread over the globe to create great civilizations, or to continue their ritual life in the most inhospitable places. As they moved, each divided into "secret societies" (moieties): initiated groups based on age and sex, attached to a particular spirit. The moieties performed the death-and-resurrection of their spirit where "good" also overcame "evil." This became another form of ritual drama: the "monster" or "beast plays." Today these are found in Tibet, Southeast Asia, China, Japan, Africa and the Americas. All have specific myths which are acted out in ritual drama.

THE FARMERS AND THE PRIESTS

Mesopotamia

The neolithic revolution brought farming and metallurgy to the Near East as the earth turned warmer. From c.12,000 B.C., crops spread over most of the globe. Mesopotamia developed vast cities, irrigation, complex governments, specialized jobs, and social classes including kings, warriors, and priests. Instead of spirits, farmers had gods; heaven was dramatized in human terms, and liturgical king-priests acted as gods. Everyone else acted as a participating audience in the ritual drama—a central ritual play and hundreds of other rituals taking place all over the city. And these traditions continued for thousands of years, and even into modern Europe where their remnants have become folklore.

The Sumerians descended onto the fertile valleys of the Tigris and the Euphrates c.3500 B.C., overcoming the pastoralists in the valleys—a rivalry of herders and farmers (e.g., Cain and Abel) common in the ancient Near East and today in cowboy movies! The Semitic-speaking Akkadians won control c.2370 B.C. Over centuries, power was taken in turn by the Babylonians, the Assyrians who destroyed the Northern Kingdom of Israel in 722 B.C., and the

Neo-Babylonians who forced the Exile of Judah in 587 B.C. Power was suddenly taken by the Persians in 539 B.C. who let the Jews free.

The focus of Mesopotamian ritual dramas was agriculture: water, sun, earth, plants and fertility—birth, copulation, death and rebirth. After the sacred union of sun and Earth Mother, the seed "died" in winter drought; after rain it was "resurrected" in spring—sacred plants sprang from the body of the Goddess. In a communal meal humans ate the divine. Many rituals occurred at key seasonal moments: cosmic life was cyclic and was renewed every year at the New Year Festival that spread to farming communities far from Mesopotamia. In these "plays," the king (or priest) impersonated a dying god who was resurrected to conduct a "Sacred Marriage" ritual with a goddess (a priestess). In Sumer the god was Damuzzi and the goddess was Inanna—they were Tammuz and Ishtar in Akkad, Marduk and Zarpanitum in Babylon, and Assur and Ninlil in Assyria. By acting "as if" they were the gods in the *present*, king-priests re-presented the *past* and foretold the *future*—renewed life by reaffirming natural law until the next year. The dramatic act collapsed time. The annual Akîtu Festival of Babylon was performed in the eleven days at the vernal equinox when the cosmos was "between years." Such intercalary periods (like "The Twelve Days" of Christmas) spread widely: the cosmos returned to chaos (was turned upside down) when the ritual-myth re-created the universe. Yet these "plays" were not "theatrical" as in modern Western cultures; they were proto-dramas performed by the king and priesthood *on behalf of* the community, while the people participated directly in many of the actions.

In Mesopotamia existence was seen as dramatic. Human life was dramatized as a mirror reflection of the life of the gods.

Egypt

Despite Egypt's agricultural basis, it was never urban. It remained a rural society based on the Nile where two kingdoms were unified—the north of the delta (Lower Egypt) and the south of the river (Upper Egypt)—a double idea that existed *in theory* throughout Egyptian civilization. This fiction was dramatized by having two of everything—two palaces, two granaries, and so on—so that *all things were thought of as being "double" or multiple.* From the start, Egyptian ritual had two simultaneous meanings: the action itself (water cleansed the temple) and a more significant meaning (water cleansed it in a religious sense). *Yet only one thing was done.* This "double" idea is the core of drama—an actor puts himself in another's place. Egyptian gods were roles of the sun god, Re; and each god was manifest in several roles. Horus could be Re-Harakhte (the youthful sun of the horizon), or a falcon, or other things. The Egyptian gods *dramatized themselves* in many roles.

The ritual-myth told how Geb and Nut (earth and sky) had four children: Osiris and Isis, Set and Nephthys. Osiris succeeded to his father's throne, ruled wisely, and married Isis. The jealous Set drowned Osiris in the Nile and cut up his body, except the hidden phallus. Osiris, with an incomplete body, could not be resurrected and became the god of the dead. Isis bore him a son, Horus, who eventually defeated Set in battle, won back his father's throne and reunited the two kingdoms. Life (corn, Osiris) died in winter, followed by an intercalary period (Set's rule); then came spring and the crops (the rule of Horus). The ritual was unique. Mesopotamian rituals focused on plots and words, but those of Egypt carried their greatest significance in ritual action.[4] Burials included actresses who performed the roles of Isis and Nephthys mourning the dead (Osiris).

There were Festivals of the gods, the king, and the dead. Royal Festivals were specifically dramatic. Egypt had a pharaoh who was a god incarnate, and his rule over two kingdoms was dramatized when he performed each ritual action twice. In a ritual "land" dance, he wore a short kilt with a tail attached and danced twice towards the four directions of the world. He wore "the Sed robe," an archaic costume which symbolized his mediation between the gods and mortals. In Festivals there were ritual battles and circumambulation rites: marched processions around a town or temple dramatizing the pharaoh's command over the land (echoed at Jericho). In many Festivals a pillar was erected, symbolic of Osiris' phallus and dramatized as him (linked to Dionysos in Greece).

In the Osiris Festival, the Egyptian ritual dramas became almost plays as we know them. At Memphis, a Presenter told the plot which the actor-priests mimed; but it lacked genuine dialogue. Nearer to theatre was *The Triumph of Horus*, performed annually at Edfu.[5] The structure is simple and is based only on the latter part of the myth:

* the Prologue praises the king and the Festival;
* Horus (as Upper and Lower Egypt) kills Set, harpoons a hippopotamus and kills snakes;
* rejoicings over Horus' victory; a hippopotamus dismembered twice with parts given to the gods;
* the triumph of Horus, the gods, and the pharaoh;
* a brief Epilogue.

The Edfu actor-priests performed outside among the buildings on multiple acting areas. The participating audience was around them, thousands strong. For the first time in Egypt, language began to have a dramatic flavour. This ritual drama was being performed at roughly the same time that the great Greek tragedies were first presented in Athens.

The Hittites

The Hittites,[6] a powerful Aryan nation in Anatolia (c.2600–1285 B.C.), mixed their beliefs with those of the farmers they conquered. They followed the Aryan theme of the storm god castrating his father and, at Yazilikaya, they had a cult of the dead based on the bull, human skulls, skeletons, and fire cremation.

They also had Festivals based on the seasons with dramatic dance.

The Purili Festival combined an ancient seasonal performance for rainfall, with a ritual battle between the storm god and the dragon, Illuyankas. In other

Festivals, the god Telipinu disappears and all life withers; the gods seek him out and when he is woken, furious, Telipinu destroys all about him but the gods capture his fury and seal it in the earth; he is restored with jubilation, and before him is erected a pole—from which is suspended the fleece of a sheep, various foods, and "long life and progeny." This death-and-resurrection ritual myth concerns a god of demonic fury like Yahweh in Israel, and Shiva and Kali in India; also the pole has links to the ancient shamanic pole (or tree), the Djed pillar of Egypt, the pillar of Dionysos, Jason in Greece, and the maypole.

In the Winter Festival the cosmos was again paralyzed, this time by a winter-death figure, Hahhimas, who was sent back to the Netherworld so that the sun could return and food and drink be provided.

Syria

In Syria, dramatic rituals were an even greater mixture than among the Hittites. Syria lay on the great trade routes between the Hittites to the north, the Egyptians to the south, and the Mesopotamians to the east. As a result, the Semitic peoples of Syria were continually being invaded by warring armies, each bringing their own religious traditions. About 2400 B.C. the Amorite city of Ebla was the basis of a Western Semitic empire. It had a cuneiform type of writing, "Eblaite," which was the forerunner of all Canaanite scripts including Ugaritic, Phoenician and Hebrew.

By the sixteenth century a group of Aryans, the Hurrians, formed the state of Mitanni as a buffer between the three great powers. This allowed the polyglot port of Ugarit to develop the first modern writing—Ugaritic script (a highly simplified cuneiform used alphabetically)—to record its ritual-myths.

In the iron age, Mitanni was destroyed by the Hittites which, with Ugarit, was overcome by the "Sea Peoples"—new groups of sea-faring Aryans, including the Philistines and the Phoenicians. They developed the secular script that is the basis for the modern roman alphabet, and established a state around the Levant ports about the time that the Israelites reached Canaan.

Aryans

Aryans[7] from north of the Black Sea invaded the Near East in groups steadily from the beginnings of Babylonia to the formation of Greece. They were male-dominated tribes governed by hereditary kings or an oligarchy of warriors. Each group and their gods were clearly divided into social classes.

The Aryans were transient pastoralists and herdsmen whose horse-drawn chariots and advanced metal weapons made them irresistible among the sedentary farmers. This revived the ancient rivalry of the herders and the farmers as the old shamanic religions once more mingled with those of agricultural fertility (the Goddess). The Aryans introduced fire for sacrifice and cremation. Their supreme deity was the sky god, male and a father, who was succeeded by his son, a younger storm god linked to fire. The son usually overcame the father by force and bloodshed (e.g., Zeus). Light became dramatized as good, dark as evil; the female deity was evil and was personified as a dragon or serpent—the ritual battle between the storm god and the dragon became the central dramatic symbol for the Aryans in the Near East. It was even incorporated into the Akîtu Festival when the Kassites (an Aryan ruling group) inserted the battle between the god Marduk and the female Tiamat: Marduk killed her, cut up her body, and from the pieces created human beings. These traditions influenced the Israelite ritual drama as we shall see.

Ancient Greece

The birth of ancient Greece occurred after it was invaded by the Dorians, an Aryan people. Zeus and his group of deities inhabited Parnassus while incorporating the Goddess in the rituals of Demeter. The archaic Greeks envisaged the world as surrounded by the mighty freshwater river of Ocean with all springs and streams deriving from him. By the sixth century B.C. dancers in animal masks were performing. Somewhere about 750-650 B.C. Homer created the *Iliad* and the *Odyssey*, oral myths without rituals. Ugarit texts show how writing began to force ritual and myth apart, a process continued by Homer and Hesiod with whom myth developed to story as literature.

The god Dionysos arrived in classical Greece, inspiring frenzied and ecstatic worship, with singing and dancing of the dithyramb (poetry) in the streets of Athens. Once Pisistratus ordered the public reading of Homer's works as martial propaganda in the time of crisis, his myths were re-ritualized into tragedies by Aeschylus, Sophocles and Euripides, and these came to be performed in the Theatre of Dionysos.

CANAAN AND THE ISRAELITES

When the Israelites arrived in Canaan they were set in a dramatic context. They saw life as dramatic: they existed in a "double" world formed through farming and metallurgy—of reality and fiction whereby a comparison between the two provided "truth."

But what ritual drama did the Israelites face in Canaan? Canaanite religion[8] was a mixture of the fertility rites of the Semitic farmers and the warlike divinities of the pastoral Aryans. In the myths, the father god was El ("king," "bull") who had two wives: Asherah, a fertility Earth Mother of great power; and Anath who was related to the Egyptian cow goddess, Hathor. A third goddess, Astarte, was worshipped from Phoenicia to Palestine but she was probably a mixture of one of the Syrian goddesses with an earlier local deity. The young storm god, Baal, took El's two wives from him. Baal combined traits of Damuzzi and Tammuz from Mesopotamia with the Aryan storm god. Dressed in a short kilt and armed with a battle-axe and lightning spear, he had the shamanic horns of a bull on his helmet, and was essentially a warrior. Of the other gods, Yam, the dragon, and Mot ("Death"), challenged Baal for supreme power.

The fundamental Canaanite rituals were those of "the Sacred Marriage," the ritual battle of god and dragon, sacrifice, and the communal meal found in the Bible and the Canaanite ritual-myths. The existing text of the Canaanite

New Year Festival is entirely mythological yet behind it lurk the elements of antique rituals: Baal wounds El who appeals for help to Yam, the dragon; Baal overcomes Yam with weapons made by the divine smith; Baal calms Anath (who has given way to demonic fury like Yahweh, Telipinu and Kali) and the gods build him a palace; Baal goes to the Netherworld to meet Mot and dies; Asherah declares Athar as king in his place but Athar is not big enough to fill the throne (a forerunner of Macbeth); the resurrected Baal (or Anath) then kills Mot in a ritual battle and Baal is declared king forever. It is likely that this poem was recited at the New Year Festival while sections were acted: like circumambulation when Baal travelled around cities; rain-making when Baal opened "the windows of heaven"; a substitute king in the Athar incident; and a banquet at the end of days—common in the Near East.

The text of the incomplete Canaanite *Poem of the Gracious Gods* is in two parts. The first is the scenario of a ritual for the Canaanite Festival of First Fruits which may have been the prototype for the Israelite Pentecost, held at the time of the equinox. Unfortunately we have no information about the nature of the performance. The second is a humorous tale which, while it burlesques El, contains hints of much earlier ritual performances.

Thus the Israelites faced in Canaan a rich ritual-drama tradition, sharing traits with many cultures of the ancient Near East.

The Israelites

The division between story and action also came about with the ancient Israelites. To the peoples who lived around them in Canaan, Israel was of far less significance than the major powers: Mesopotamia, Egypt, the Hittites, and the Persians—even of states that did not last very long, like Mitanni. The culture of early Israel was very similar to that of its neighbours in the Near East. Herders and farmers celebrated the rituals of both, each place mingling them in its own particular manner. What made the rituals of Israel unique, however, was that all were directed to the worship of one God—Yahweh—and the performance of monotheistic ritual myths. Monotheism and the requirements of Yahweh had an enormous impact upon later human history.

The Israelites conquered Canaan c. 1250 B.C., but their rituals were not recorded until *The Book of J* some 300 years later, written in Solomon's reign or just after. By this time, Canaanite and Israelite ritual-myths had mingled.

In 587 B.C., Jerusalem fell and many people were carried into Exile in Babylon. When they returned in 538 they had altered their religious beliefs but met the people who had retained the old ritual-myths. The two groups clashed and those who returned from Babylon slowly weeded out the ancient rituals which were omitted when The Redactor re-edited the relevant books of the Bible by c.400 B.C. He emphasized the mythic level and tried to remove all traces of old rituals.

Modern Jews can be troubled by the problems of historicity. Hebrew Festivals and fasts celebrate particular events in the past. But if modern scholarship shows that these historic events did not take place (or, at best, they *probably* did not occur), what happens then? For example, if the Exodus from Egypt did not take place exactly in the form described in the Bible, should the Passover then be discarded? But such a question will not be asked if we remember that *the historical events supposedly associated with the Festivals are illustrations of their basic themes.* In religious terms, the most important thing is the basic truths which the Festivals exemplify. Whether the events actually took place as the Bible describes them is not as important to religious belief.

The sixteenth chapter of *Leviticus* says that the Israelites annually got rid of their sins by transferring them to a scapegoat. The scapegoat ritual was as old (at least) as the Sumerians and was practised by many ancient peoples in the Near East, as well as the Israelites. As the scapegoat idea is primitive and the ritual is rather crude, should it be ignored? On the contrary, just as the parables of Jesus have genuine significance for Christians in the ideas that lie behind them, so do the ritual-myths to the Jews. Behind the scapegoat lies the valid principle that sin is not just personal; it impairs society as a whole and it cannot take on new life until the taint has been removed. For Jews, this truth is what is significant, not the particular expression of it.

2

PERSPECTIVES ON BIBLICAL RITUALS

Monotheism was a major change in human development. But to say that it grew out of a ritual drama first performed by Joshua and his people as they arrived in the promised land may, at first sight, seem a radical statement. But this is not so when modern biblical research is taken into account.

Different Bibles

The Jews call their Holy Scriptures Tanakh, an acronym for the three parts of the Bible:

[1] Torah (the Teaching, or Law, or the Five Books of Moses, or Pentateuch);
[2] Nevi'im (the Prophets); and
[3] Kethuvim (the Writings).

The Torah, or Pentateuch, will largely concern us in this book.

The Hebrew Bible should not to be confused with the Christian Bible (see *Figure 4*), which is founded upon it, but which is a very severe revision of the Bible of the Jews. To Christians, the Hebrew Bible is the Old Testament, or Covenant, and it is followed by the New Testament. This is unacceptable to Jews, who do not see their Covenant as "old." The Christian work replaces the idea of the Torah with a man, Jesus of Nazareth, as its focus.

The division of the Hebrew Bible into chapters and verses is quite arbitrary and does not reflect the intentions of the original authors. Later Jewish editors divided the verses in a long process that was only concluded in the ninth century A.D. The chapter divisions were made by Christian editors up until the thirteenth century A.D.

The Christian Old Testament and the Hebrew Bible are arranged differently, and that makes a considerable difference to their meanings. The first five books follow the same order in the two faiths but have different names: thus the Christian *Genesis* is the Hebrew *Bereshith*, "In the Beginning"; the *Exodus* is *Shemoth*, "Names"; *Leviticus* is *Wayiqra*, "And He Called"; and *Numbers* is *Bemidbar*, "In the Wilderness." After the Torah, or

Pentateuch, there is little in common between the order of the two works: the
Christian Old Testament ends with the prophet Malachai proclaiming the
appearance of Elijah, who is seen as the forerunner of John the Baptist. But
the Hebrew Bible ends with 2 *Chronicles*, so that the whole finishes with the
Return to Jerusalem and the rebuilding of Solomon's Temple. The Septuagint
is the Greek translation of the Hebrew Bible. It was prepared 250–100 B.C.
in the Alexandrian Jewish community; and it was considered sacred by the
Jews until the Christians used it as their official text for their Old Testament.
The Septuagint began the translations into Jewish vernacular versions; e.g., the
ancient Aramaic Targum Onkelos, the Aramaic Pseudo-Jonathan, the Arabic
version of Saadia Gaon in the tenth century A.D., and the modern American
versions of the Jewish Publication Society (1917, 1985). The American
Jewish versions, despite their accuracy, miss the voice of J and the literary
value of the King James Bible.

The Authorized Version has an extraordinarily unified style, based on the
rhetoric of William Tyndale, the martyred pioneer of English Bible translation,
and of his follower Miles Coverdale—both mellifluous authors. The
Authorized Version is a powerful text that makes it difficult to see that
Genesis, *Exodus* and *Numbers* are a palimpsest. The style became the biblical
style in English, with a strong effect upon writing second only to that of
Shakespeare. The King James Version is essentially a revision of Tyndale and
Coverdale, as was The Geneva Bible (1560), put together by English Calvinist
exiles, the text which was used by Shakespeare and which affected his work.[1]

The Bible has become less authoritative as an historical document in the
twentieth century. Earlier assumptions about authorships and dates have been
denied. The historical foundations for the creations and falls (*Genesis* 1–11)
have been replaced and even "the conquest" of the promised land is in doubt.

Most modern historians do not think that only invading foreigners led by
Joshua brought monotheism to Israel. Even the most conservative critics
consider that invaders, pastoralists, and peasants in revolt co-existed.

THE RELIGIOUS PERSPECTIVE

Yahwism emerged as the Canaan city-states disintegrated at the end of the Late Bronze Age.[2] The two kinds of societies had opposing ideologies, and the tension between land-holding aristocracies and classless peasant groups (Habiru) caused a widespread peasant revolt. If the conquest led by Joshua took place at the same time, then these events are seen as history. But from the religious viewpoint, the monotheistic community began at Sinai with the covenant. This was "Israel believed"—where the *origins of the idea of monotheism began.*

But this was not necessarily its beginnings in other perspectives. For many anthropologists, early Yahwists borrowed a common ancient Near East covenant formula and changed its function to unify the community with Yahweh. Yahwism did not rely upon the law, like a centralizing monarchy; indeed, its opposition to centralism was the religion's fundamental tenet, and it lasted throughout Yahwist history. Canaanite kings claimed divine prerogatives that Yahwists thought were rightfully God's. The contrast can be seen from the myths: myths are ideologies that legitimate power structures;[3] but Israel's religion manifested in the covenant contrasted with the mythic content of its neighbours, despite shared common items.

THE HISTORICAL PERSPECTIVE

The Amarna Letters are remarkable historical evidence from Canaan's Late Bronze Age. Their origins can be identified by locale, even by individual cities.[4]

Several letters from Jerusalem's Abdi-Heba, a soldier who headed a city-state in contrast to the usual succession of a "royal" family, credit his succession to the power of the pharaoh.[5] Remarkably, he sites Jerusalem liminally between the Egyptian and Syrian cultures. As shepherd of the pharaoh, he appeals for protection against other chiefs and the tumultuous Habiru.

The Canaan in the *Letters* was a patchwork of political districts[6] in social chaos: small centralized states were decaying; there was competition among heads of city states vying for their own survival and the resources of their neighbours;[7] and tributes increased as chiefs tried to raise their personal standings with Egyptian overlords.[8] The *Letters* portray a maladaptive system depending on stability and peace which it also disrupted; e.g., when decreased labour was required, lowering marriage ages increased the size of labour pools.[9] But the *Letters* also confirm that the system was religiously legitimated by beliefs in the divine right of power. This picture is a backdrop for the emergence of Yahwism and the formation of the Yahwist state in the land of Canaan.

Two modern schools of historical thought (of Albrecht Alt and William Foxwell Albright) in their different ways view the Bible as *a witness* to history rather than as a narrative text.

THE ARCHEOLOGICAL PERSPECTIVE

But G. E. Wright saw archaeology as *a direct aid* to reading the Bible.[10] To Wright, "valid scientific criteria" seemed a naive application of scientific method,[11] so he used cross-disciplinary methods. Subsequently James W. Flanagan[12] developed a wholistic approach using archeology and other disciplines.

Biblical historians have tried to keep pace with modern archeology. From the 1960s, archaeologists turned away from history and literature towards science. Radio-carbon and thermo-luminescence dating, and trace analysis, brought objective measures that changed the questions asked of history and ways of interpreting data. One important effect of these new methods was to revise the dates and periods of biblical history.

The Iron Age

The Late Bronze Age ended with widespread upheaval: the Mycenaean world broke up as the "Sea Peoples" ran amuck; and the Hittite, Kassite, and

Late Bronze Age	*(1550–1200 B.C.)*
-LBIA	(1550–1500 B.C.)
-LBIB	(1500–1400 B.C.)
-LBIIA	(1400–1300 B.C.)
-LBIIB	(1300–1200 B.C.) [Canaanites]
Iron Age 1	*(1200–918 B.C.)*
-Iron IA	(1200–1000 B.C.) [Israelites]
-Iron IB	(1150–1000 B.C.) [Sea Peoples]
-Iron IC	(1000–918 B.C.)[David–Solomon to 922; then Judah and Israel]
Iron Age II	*(918–539 B.C.)*
-Iron IIA	(918–721 B.C.) [722 Samaria falls]
-Iron IIB	(721–605 B.C.) [612 Nineveh falls]
-Iron IIC	(605–539 B.C.) [539 Babylon falls]

Figure 5: Archeological Dates[13]

Mitannian states and other prosperous societies collapsed, especially along the Mediterranean coastal plains. Assyria was in resurgence. Bronze Age traditions continued into the twelfth century at some sites like Megiddo and Shechem, while others show a complete break.[14] Cultural continuity varied according to place[15] and cultural unity did not emerge, if at all, until the latter half of the 10th century. The area was a conduit for foreign trade[16] so the key concern of the unstable and fluid societies was to maintain security.[17] Over the whole Age, Yahwism came to dominate and Joshua's ritual drama of Moses became that of David.

In Iron 1A, unstable leaderships overlapped the rise of Yahweh. Farmers expanded in the highlands and across the rift into northern Transjordan; yet the Bible shows Yahwism moving in the opposite direction, perhaps due to the conquest mythology and quest for unity in *Deuteronomy*. Benjaminite traditions absorbed those of the Lower Bronze peoples, and towns of the two religions co-existed, as language shows: *nagid* meant a leader with suggestions of kingship while *melek* meant that the nomadic leader was not a king. The saintly Samuel (*melek*) and the chiefly Saul (*nagid*) represented changes in leadership, but it was David who became both *nagid* and *melek*.[18]

Stories of Judah and Transjordan, seasonal shrines, and settlements along trade routes, indicated events. Iron was a luxury item prized, traded, and used for grave goods. Most continuous activity was between the two southern East-West geological depressions (the Jezreel and Beersheba corridors) but it also fanned out North and South in Transjordan. Interaction and variety were everywhere.[19] The festival drama was a mixture of herding and agricultural traditions.

In Iron B, the remains of the "Sea Peoples" show that new societies evolved. Existing Israelites were federated. The Philistines were not and from the coastline they moved overland along trade routes (by the Jezreel corridor into the Jordan and Yarmouk valleys), building small, unfortified villages as buffers between factions and against exterior powers (especially Egypt) by pastoralism, or by terrace farming and storage. Where the Bible blames such changes on invaders from the desert or sea, archeology shows movement from west to east and north to south. Mediterraneans and mercenaries traded new goods with various groups. As smiths they were feared and disparaged. Pillaging, skirmishes, and military threats abounded. They attacked the Israelite federation militarily and symbolically by capturing their symbol of non-centralized unity, the Ark. Iron artifacts, smelters and seasonal shrines at sites like Deir 'Alla, in conjunction with new wares, show the Philistines' threat. Ritual-myths were both of herding and agriculture.

In Iron 1C, the region experienced a complex social growth but pacification and centralization reveal no evidence of conquest, destruction or displacement. New lands became productive, and the increasing population clung to old traditions and transformed them. The variety of ritual myths reflected the forms of subsistence: nomadic and pastoral; semi-nomadic pastoralist and agrarian; sedentary and agrarian; and seafaring, mercenary and trading. Peoples moved eastward along the geographical paths.

Biblical myths place David, the youthful giant-killer and musician, as a warrior in Saul's employ. David's drama was bounded by two of the major East-West geological corridor-depressions and the North-South Jordan valley. He married into noble houses outside these boundaries, moving upward and outward among many segments of society, building a network of alliances which culminating in a Jerusalem-based, increasingly cosmopolitan and centralized state, stable enough to construct monumental architecture; e.g., the temple in Jerusalem.

All kinds of leaders and groups were affiliated to Jerusalem (nomads, pastoralists and farmers) and it became a rather artificial centre, the personal holding of the ruling family.

As a Yahwist nomadic chief and a former Habiru who adapted to all parts of the new system, David legitimated a shared leadership. He then moved to dynastic rule. Solomon moved further away from a nomadic and pastoral base. As a result, the state soon split in two—Israel to the north and Judah to the south centered on Jerusalem. The pharaoh Shishak invaded (c.920–918 B.C.), and left signs of his battles as far apart as the Esdraelon and Jordan valleys.

THE ANTHROPOLOGICAL PERSPECTIVE

Edmund Leach says that the Bible is not history; there is no archaeological evidence that Moses, Saul or David existed, nor any event linked to them;[20] if not sacred, the Bible would be rejected as history[21]—"[it] has the characteristics of mytho-history."[22] To obtain biblical facts, therefore, anthropologists search for human patterns.

The earliest events in the Bible are records of *ritual-myths*. At first the story line (the myth) was performed (the ritual). But which came first, myth or ritual? Some say myth, some ritual, some both, and some say it varies in each case.[23] The early books of the Bible have only myths and we must actively seek the ritual level; the ancient biblical editors had religious motives so there is no "true" interpretation. Some Biblical meanings are found in the structural relations encoded in texts[24] written by the final editor. Those of earlier writers are hidden, buried in those of their successors; and recovering them is much like trying to "unscramble an omelet."[25] Yet three main things can be discovered: [a] the ritual bases within the myth, [b] the structural metaphors, and [c] the changes—the relations of contrasts, conflicts and contradictions in process.

How is this done? The "myth and ritual school" assumes that the Israelites shared common patterns with rest of the ancient Near East. Pieces of history missing in one society are matched from the records of another; e.g., T.H.Gaster and others reconstruct rituals from parallel myths in different cultures.[26] Albright shows that, as all social structures are *organismic* rather than organic, each with its own distinct character and definite life cycle, anthropologists use analogy.[27] Albright seeks *patterns in process*—he compares successive states to discover change.[28] Comparative patterns in archeology can be drawn from anthropology and sociology,[29] and they can be used to inform the life of, say, pre-monarchic Israel.[30]

Biblical narrative contrasts thought with action: the *emic* and *etic* domains, widely used in modern anthropology.[31] This is not an objective-subjective dichotomy. *In both, the observer remains the investigator.*

The actions of social and ritual dramas, although details differ, show Israelite patterns that were virtually synonymous with all Near Eastern cultures.[32] Victor W. Turner saw that groups are in ceaseless conflict with others—then tensions are related to transformations that all societies of the area periodically undergo. Turner claims that social dramas are universal:[33] to describe them he used the metaphor of "social dramas" marking the social changes in a controllable way. They are acts that societies choose to cope with crises. In ritual dramas all over the Near East, a god died and was resurrected at each New Year Festival. A way of life plays itself out in "an endlessly repeated social drama."[34]

Rites of Passage

Anthropologists have developed many ways to analyse social and ritual drama. Edmund Leach seeks the synchrony in texts, the reversals, the sense of *communitas*, and the self-contradictions contained in them.[35] For Rappaport, "certain things can be expressed only in ritual [which is] *the* basic social act"—formal, performed and communicated.[36]

The pattern of Arnold van Gennep's "rites of passage"[37] is often used to analyse ritual transformations. Each rite has a tripartite structure:

* The rite of separation: individuals move from an original aggregated position in which structures and relationships are known and defined.
* The liminal, marginal condition: people feel they are "in between": suspended in time and space—vital to "regenerative renewal."[38]

*   The rite of reaggregation: new statuses and roles are newly defined
        —a move back to the secular sphere.

The meaning of ancient rituals is expressed in many ways: speech, actions,
ritual, ceremony, and "symbols which become indexical counters in subsequent
situational contexts."[39] Processions are rites of passage; e.g., beginning ⇒
process ⇒ end. Moving the Ark gave symbolic meanings—different when
carried into battle from David processing with it to Jerusalem.

Within "rites of passage" Turner found two kinds of connected rites: [1]
status elevation; e.g., David takes over from Saul; and [2] *status reversal*;
e.g., Moses ceases to be an Egyptian slave to lead his people out of Egypt.
These mark the sequential and hierarchical transformations of social change[40]
which are "the patterned arrangements of role sets, status sets, and status
sequences consciously recognized and regularly operative in a given society
and closely bound up with legal and political norms and sanctions."[41]

Changing the cultural models in the minds of the main actors brings *shifts
in paradigms*: sets of socially sanctioned rules that result in sequences of
social action. *Root paradigms* go beyond this to patterns of belief and world
views; e.g., the death-and-resurrection paradigm is vital for both agricultural
societies and Christianity; but it is so alien to other paradigms (e.g., of ancient
Rome) that the conflict can lead to martyrdom. "Through the social drama one
can sometimes look beneath the surface of social regularities into the hidden
contradictions and conflicts in the social system. The kinds of redressive
mechanism deployed to handle conflict, the pattern of factional struggle, and
the sources of initiative to end crisis, which are all clearly manifest in the
social drama, provide valuable clues to the character of the social system."[42]

Typically, social dramas are rites of passage in four phases:[43]

*   *Breach*

        This occurs when: [a] one party publicly disregards a crucial norm
        held by the other; or [b] it is performed by a representative of a group
        (Moses' actions in Egypt)—a "symbolic trigger" beginning the social
        drama (the Exodus).

* *Crisis*

    In mounting crisis the break is either confined to a part of society, or it spreads widely. If the latter (e.g., the Hebrews in Egypt), secondary crises can be provoked causing lasting splits in social relations. Crises are liminal: previous society is in the balance.

* *Redressive actions*

    The offended group tries to limit the crisis: representatives begin informal and formal rituals that vary.

* *Reintegration*

    Reintegration may occur if either of the two groups comes together again, or recognizes the split and legitimates it—a new order is established.

Using these four phases, Turner creates a *processual analysis* that includes the relations among ritual, symbol and paradigm, as well as social drama.[44] He analyses processual units (regularized situations and temporal structures) by looking at them through the symbols that store their meaning.[45] Thus he focuses on the ritual dramas that reveal fundamental social change.

Ancient ritual dramas included their own version of "rites of passage" in the seasonal Festivals. Hunters linked the movements of the sun, moon, and stars to when the animals were on the move, the rutting season, and so forth, so that their cave art was a gigantic calendar used for animistic practices.[46] Crops were linked to the seasons: winter was the death of seeds, spring their resurrection, summer was the growth of plants, and autumn was the conversion to food. The exemplar of the New Year Festival was the Akîtu in Babylon: the whole population (with the king acting as the main god) performed a sprawling ritual drama of eleven days which incorporated many smaller rites.

The huge farming ritual dramas were of two main kinds: the rites of emptying and of filling. These were paired in a quaternity structure: mortification, purgation, invigoration, and jubilation. The god (the king) and the supernatural and natural worlds all performed "as if" they were mortified, purged, invigorated and then jubilant.[47] Joshua's ritual drama had the same structural characteristics.

YAHWIST RITUAL DRAMA

Data from history, literature, archeology, religion and anthropology indicate that, as part of monotheism, the Yahwists celebrated their God in ritual-myths that were similar *in structure* to contemporary Canaanites and other Near Eastern peoples. Post-Exilic Jews found the ritual-myths of these first Yahwists offensive to the changes in their beliefs which had occurred in Babylon, so Yahweh worship was largely expurgated by editors after the Exile. Modern readers of the Bible, however, may not realize the biblical material referring to Yahweh worship must be rediscovered.

Transition

As the Yahwists changed towards the sedentary, agrarian life of the Iron Age, they created ritual enactments to maintain group unity and harmony. Apart from being monotheistic, the structure of the Moses ritual-myth was agricultural like others in the area (e.g., the Akîtu), while many incidental rites were of the herding type. The ritual-myth mixed the subsistence traditions; and the whole culminated with Moses.

As Joshua crossed the Jordan, the migratory groups lost their flexibility to resolve conflicts; they were transferred either to outside the community, or onto a symbolic level through ritual drama that they resolved religiously—thus dual chieftainship for one leader enabled distinct social units to remain intact while integrating Israel with other regions politically. The ritual drama of the Yahwists restored equilibrium and resolved conflicts either directly, or by sanctifying the acts of individuals or groups who maintained order.[48] Although raiding still occurred, opposing groups were also integrated ritually by sharing sacred ideas and actions.

This was not unusual. Archaeology and literature show the prominence of rituals in Iron Age I: seasonal ritual centres like Deir 'Alla; the appearance of iron to manufacture luxury items and grave goods (including ritual objects); small cultic buildings above the ruins of Bronze Age shrines; frequent references to the Ark with its nomad-sedentary symbolism of a shrine attended by Eli and Samuel; the ark's relocation in Jerusalem; and the construction of the temple—all reveal the value placed on ritual.

Ritual items included the mysterious and magical. Meteoric iron, which came from the heavens, was used in rituals and tombs. With forging, transforming metal took on mysterious qualities: symbols of the metamorphoses produced by iron's use in daily life.[49] The social, economic, and political adaptations of iron became symbolically attached to the forging process. This increased the need for sanctification and ritual as new institutions and personalities had to be legitimized.

The sacred beliefs of other peoples' religion were borrowed and given new sanctity. Iron Age Yahwists adapted Lower Bronze Age prototypes, merged northern and southern myths, combined sedentary and nomadic stories, and spread the symbolism of the ark—just as Joshua took over a Near Eastern structure to create the main Yahwist ritual drama. Thus Yahwism spread rapidly among many different peoples.

The Change of Ritual Drama
Soon after Joshua created the Moses Play, it changed. The nomadic people did not develop independent, visible, permanent forms of ritual. There were no goods to spare, so temples and shrines were resisted; thus building a temple was prohibited in the early David stories. But increased productivity raised social expectations and increased ritual specialization. When the Yahwists changed the story it was acted in the rituals which produced other myths, poems, and narratives; it strengthened the bonds of members in a social group; it adjusted inequities by helping to redistribute resources; it sanctified important messages and conventions, linking them to sacred statements; and it associated the leaders in their roles with these beliefs and they achieved sanctity through rituals—as did the ritual's messages.

Several times in the Bible, writers re-played a story to revive its sanctity. They restructured, retold, and rewrote the myth based on the root paradigm— the Yahweh dramatic metaphor that changed from Moses into David.

With David in Jerusalem, the sedentary people began a full ritual system. It was expensive in goods and labour, training specialists, and acquiring prestige items. What emerged was the David ritual drama.

But after Solomon, political ends exceeded economic means. The Schism resulted and there was a partial return to former alliances.

Israel adapted and re-ritualized the adaptations. As a result it became more complex. This was very different from Judah where David's rise had been seen as more straightforward.

PASSOVER AND PERFORMANCE

How does such a reading of the first books of the Bible affect a modern Jew? Today as he celebrates Passover, he recalls the Exodus from Egypt. He brings the Exodus out of the past, and lives within it in the "here and now." He re-plays it and so re-cognizes it. He brings the historic flight from Egypt into the present: by collapsing time, he gives the event deeper meaning. He goes through a dramatic process by putting himself in the place of the historic Hebrew: he imagines *now* what it was like then. In his mind, he *identifies* with that ancient Hebrew and, in a sense, *becomes* him—dramatizes him through identification and impersonation. In so doing, he becomes one with the Hebrews of all times. *The Passover is essentially a dramatic act.*

In all the history of the Jews, the Passover was seen as the foundation of the nation. The Exodus symbolically brought Israel into existence, and it remains the kernel of modern Jewry with (at least) four levels of meaning: [1] historically it celebrates Moses leading the chosen people out of Egypt so that Yahweh could bring the people to Sinai and conclude the covenant; [2] politically it leads Israel from slavery into independence as a nation; [3] seasonally it celebrates the reaping of new grain because it is God who gives the rain and the sun that allows it to grow; and [4] humanly Passover celebrates freedom when people cast aside idols, ignorance and obscurantism.

The original Passover, before the Israelites adopted it, followed the common pattern of seasonal Festivals in the ancient Near East. The Israelites took over this primitive ritual and gave it a new meaning. They transferred their worship from one of the gods to *the* God—the foundation of monotheism. The Bible describes that first ritual in detail.[50]

Today the Passover is much more complicated. On the first two evenings is the traditional Seder service which fulfills the Bible's order to retell the story of the Exodus to one's children[51] as *an experience*. Then the Haggadah repeats the story of the Exodus: "The Haggadah is the script of a living drama, not the record of a dead event, and when the Jew recites it he is performing an act not of remembrance but of personal identification in the here and now."[52]

The fact that the original Passover was a dramatic fiction should not affect modern believers. The Passover was first acted to celebrate the Exodus from Egypt which was incorporated into a Festival play when Joshua arrived in Canaan—and the monotheistic God was born.

PART 2:

RITUAL DRAMA OF MOSES

Part 2 of this book deals directly with the Festival ritual drama first produced by the Israelites soon after they entered the promised land. What bits of the script we have left were written by J some three hundred years after the event. It is difficult to know where the script began. But it ended in Yahweh's triumph, the life of Moses and the gift of the land.

3

WRITING THE TEXT

At the heart of the Old Testament lies a simple story contained in those books which are regarded as the most authoritative by Jewish tradition: *Genesis, Exodus, Leviticus, Numbers,* and *Deuteronomy*—the five together being known as the Torah, or the Pentateuch. Put together in a historical sequence, however, *Joshua* must be added. These six books—the Pentateuch plus *Joshua*—when considered as a unit are called the Hexateuch. As the Hexateuch was first written, much of it was originally based on the ritual drama created by Joshua.

The story tells how God the creator, attempting to redeem human beings from their sin of rebellion against him, chose Abram (Abraham) and his people (Israel) to carry his blessing to all peoples. The first major climax comes with Moses: [1] God's greatest acts demonstrate his saving power by rescuing Israel from Egyptian slavery, [2] in forming them into a nation through the covenant with himself at Mount Sinai, and [3] by giving them a land in which to live, Canaan. The second climax comes with David.

We do not know when the elements of this story were first put into writing. Much later Jewish tradition claimed that Moses wrote the whole of the Pentateuch, but this was not so. While it is possible that Moses prepared a collection of laws, known as the Book of the Covenant, including the Ten Commandments,[1] it is clear that the *writing* was not his. The written tradition of the Hexateuch is, in fact, of a much later date.

The elements within the Hexateuch are many and various. Put together by later writers, the original sources are of different ages. Perhaps the oldest materials were ancient poems like the Song of Deborah,[2] the Blessing of Jacob,[3] the Song of Miriam,[4] and the Prophecies of Balaam.[5] Yet some sources are quite late. One example is an old book discovered in the temple at Jerusalem in 622 B.C. which became the core of *Deuteronomy*.

The sources of *Genesis* we can find are raw bits of story that were common to many cultures in the Near East. In fact, the tale of origins[6] is a creation myth like many others of the region, in which human beings take their place among the generation of gods and cosmic forces. What makes this origin myth unique, however, is that the place of humanity is revealed through Israel's religion. *Genesis* is made up of genealogies and narratives (myth, epic, saga), often well assimilated into one whole but sometimes they are not—as with the sudden appearance of Cain's wife in an inappropriate context.[7]

Biblical (Old Testament) scholars disagree as to the antiquity of the oral tradition upon which the Hexateuch was based. Some consider it built on antique oral sources; others think that nothing is older than the middle of the first millennium B.C.; still others (as in this book) consider the oral tradition that of the Festival play. Yet modern scholars generally agree that the writing of the six books is the result of the work of a series of Israelite scholars[8] as follows: the J tradition, the E tradition, the D tradition, the P tradition, and the work of R, the ultimate Redactor.

Biblical Authors

The earliest and unknown author called J wrote the core of *Genesis, Exodus,* and *Numbers*. The most modern version of *The Book of J* is translated by David Rosenberg, interpreted by Harold Bloom (New York: Grove Weidenfeld, 1990), a remarkable document that provides us with considerable information. I shall rely heavily on this work as we proceed.[9]

Although *The Book of J* is of early history, it was written at a much later date than the events it describes. Joshua and the tribes of Israel occupied Canaan about 1250 B.C., but the event was not written in *The Book of J* until c. 950–900, at the end of the reign of Solomon or shortly thereafter in the Schism. J stands for the author, the Yahwist, named for Yahweh (Jahweh),[10] God of Jews, Christians, and Moslems. We have difficulty in finding the words and phrases of *The Book of J* in the first books of the Bible because post-Exilic scribes edited and changed them in order to match later practices, beliefs and ideas.

At the same time as J, the Court Historian wrote most of what is now called *2 Samuel*. There are several indications that he might have worked in close contact with J so that the two authors exchanged ideas and images.

About 850–800 B.C. there followed E's revision of J. E stands for the Elohist, for "Elohim," the plural name used for Yahweh in that version.[11] E combined J's text with a variety of material, probably from written sources that are now lost. E, a more shadowy figure than J, probably lived in the Northern Kingdom in the ninth century B.C. and, as a result, his was a Northern Israelite point of view compared with the Judah-dominated story of J. E was very conscious of the problems of obedience to God as against idolatry, together with the way God revealed himself to human beings. He re-worked the Binding of Isaac and perhaps Jacob's wrestling with the angel. So began the tradition of reducing the extraordinary J to something more ordinary and normal.

Two hundred years later (c.650-600), the books of *Deuteronomy* were written by D. D was two or three people who focused on the violent moment of King Josiah's puritan reform in 621 B.C. D likely based his work on the discovery of an ancient book in 622 B.C.—the core of *Deuteronomy* which influenced the contents of other books, and was the focus for the reforms of Josiah.

The P text was added to J and E—a major revision—about 550 B.C., after the fall of Jerusalem to Babylon in 587 B.C., and was continued deep into the Exile. P stands for the Priestly Author, or "school," who composed an alternative text—that is, all of what is now *Leviticus* and the larger share of *Genesis, Exodus,* and *Numbers*. P contributed the lengthy legal sections of the Pentateuch, and the creation and flood stories of *Genesis*. He also altered Israel's ancient ritual traditions in order to make their themes fit to the updated liturgy. The monotheism of P was much more hard-line than the earlier J; he reduced the ritual elements of the myths in the ancient story and he contrasted the religion of Israel with those of other local peoples, such as the Canaanites, which he condemned. More than J and E, P thoroughly assimilated his sources and gave them the stamp of a particular vocabulary and literary technique.

Finally c. 450–400 B.C., these first books of the Bible were put together by R (The Redactor), either Ezra the Scribe or a member of the Academy of Ezra. He made the final revision over a century after the return from the Babylonian Exile, and produced the Torah some four hundred years before Christ—probably much as we have it now.[12] From the time of Ezra to the destruction of the Second Temple in 70 B.C., a cultic Yahwism gradually moved to the worship of Torah, and so to the birth of Judaism as a book religion. It was not until 90 B.C. that the canonization of the Hebrew Bible was complete.

But *The Book of J* had been very different. J's idea of heroism was the heroic David. His idea of order was Solomon. Cult and priests meant nothing to J, and Torah worship would have meant even less.[13]

We must always remember that The Moses Play was written by J—not by those of Moses' time, nor by subsequent authors of the Bible.

The Drama of the Festival Play

One difficulty in this brief account is a factor of history. In the period from Joshua to the Exile (c.1250–587 B.C.), the Israelites traced their beginnings only as far back as the Exodus. There were only implications about the migration of Abraham and the other patriarchs. It was later authors who amplified the material about the patriarchs.

The first facts of Israel's *history* occur once Joshua and the Israelites are in Canaan. Everything prior to that—all that is contained in *Genesis*—is generally regarded as "legendary history." The many components of *Genesis*, put together by the biblical authors, were materials shared throughout the ancient Near East[14] and they incorporated traditions of many other peoples. It was the job of the biblical authors to put these pieces together in a way that supported the traditions of Yahweh and Israel. They did so as propagandists: J on behalf of the House of David, E for the Northern Kingdom, D from the point of view of Josiah, and P conservatively represents the priestly and non-dramatic traditions after the nation returned from Exile.

Confusions will arise unless the reader realizes that there are two vital factors of time in this brief account. *The first Festival script was not the same as the script in J.* The text performed varied over time: with Joshua it concluded with the land-giving; but it concluded with David in Solomon's time. After Solomon, and until the Israelites returned from the Exile, we might assume that *The Book of J* included the whole performance. Subsequently, however, *the dramatization in J was mostly expurgated in the final Bible.* The post-Exilic authors (P and R) greatly reduced the importance of ancient ritual dramas and agricultural banquets. After their return to Israel, the priests began to emphasize an overpowering feeling of guilt and sin; and the domination of the priesthood established post-Exilic worship. The natural and spontaneous element of early Israelite worship was suppressed; and the information about popular ritual Festivals became so re-edited that most of their dramatizations were removed.

THE BOOK OF J

The existing Torah is far from J's spirit. *Leviticus* and *Deuteronomy* are distant from J, but even *Genesis*, *Exodus*, and *Numbers*, in their redacted form as we read them today, give us a very different vision than does *The Book of J*. There is a vast gulf between the Yahweh of *The Book of J* and the God of Judaism and Christianity. J's Yahweh is a "fiction," just as his Abram, Jacob, Tamar, and Joseph appear to be very much his own creations. He did not go quite as far with Moses, and yet he is the most vivid of all the Moseses in the Torah. J's characters are all "fictional": that is, they are dramatic personages, and they contrast radically with the figures in the post-Exilic Bible. And yet J is as strict a monotheist as the sages.

Today there is nothing in the Bible that we call *The Book of J*. We find it embedded within other Books. There is no agreement upon the dating of *The Book of J*, or upon its surviving dimensions. Indeed, much about the book is conjecture.

There was no Bible at all until some six centuries after J, and the Bible as we know it was assembled by rabbis after yet another six centuries. J used materials in Hebrew most of which are now doubtless lost to us, but what we have are embedded in J's text or preserved elsewhere—the Song of Deborah and Barak in *Judges* 5—and show that aesthetic writing came before J in Hebrew literature. J is less a historian or a theologian than he is a poetic dramatist. He tells his stories in a bravura style with the flourish of performance, and he combines, for the first time in any language, every genre available to him in ancient Near Eastern literature. J's imagination is not restricted by cult.[15]

Most scholars assume that one Yahwist wrote in the great literary age of c. 950–900. Certainly someone wrote *The Book of J* in the Phoenician-Old Hebrew script. It was probably written in ink with a reed pen on a papyrus, and the sheets were then glued together to make a scroll. But we have no idea who. Whoever he was, he probably lived at the court of Solomon and that of his successor and son, King Rehoboam of Judah, whose kingdom fell apart soon after his succession. Most scholars assume that J was not a professional scribe but rather an immensely sophisticated member of the Solomonic élite.[16]

Structure

The Book of J has the following structure:

[1] Creation to Egypt (introduction that may not have been performed);
[2] the Exodus and the formation of Israel at Sinai (in the Moses Play);
[3] the gift of the promised land (in the Moses Play); and
[4] the granting of security under David (added to later performances).

Above all, J saw Israel as the people chosen of God. This structure is highly original. The Creation and Exodus frame the lives of patriarchs, and J began the Western tradition of fusing myth and history—"The result was a new kind of narrative, closer to Tolstoy than to Homer, and departing radically from the archaic narratives available to J as models."[17] J probably took his work from a script or *scenario,* yet it is the first known work that links a primordial vision (Eden) to the national redemption from Egypt via the patriarchs.

The Book of J has admirable heroines—Sarai, Rachel and Tamar—but questionable heroes in Abram, Jacob and Moses.[18]

Style

The style of *The Book of J* is also unique. It is highly suggestive of the words and language of a ritual play as we shall see. J, like Blake, thinks paradoxically: he is uncanny, tricky, sublime, and ironic. He often juxtaposes differences—contrasts and paradoxes. Although we can find some clues to this style in *2 Samuel*, it was expurgated by P and R and is now most difficult to find. Bloom has shown us that as a writer, J is incisive, economic and bold; yet his elliptical style is very different from any other writer of the Bible. He forces the listeners or readers to participate, to be constantly alert and respond. That is, he leaves something out that allows listeners or readers to contribute to the meaning—a sure sign of writing for performance; e.g., as in Aeschylus, Shakespeare, and ritual dramatists in Asia, as with the Kathakali theatre in India, and the Noh theatre in Japan.

Like most good ritual dramatists, J evades the stock responses of the participant-audience. A good modern example of this strategy is the many ritual animals (dragons, horses, etc.) that "come out" annually in Southwest England, and who use improvisation to keep responses fresh. J provokes the fresh reactions of the participant-audience by dissociative means; and he uses endless wordplay, puns, false or popular etymologies and homonyms.

Bloom also shows that J is virtually Shakespearean in his witty profusion.[19] Shakespeare's text is more readily available to us than is J's,[20] but Shakespeare's originality remains as veiled from us as J's, and for similar reasons. The West has been massively influenced by J and his revisionists, and by Shakespeare: our ways of representing ourselves to others are founded upon J's and Shakespeare's way of creating character through dialogue.

J is also original in having Yahweh as his prime character; that is, the West's major literary character is God, whose author was J.[21] Bloom says: "Perhaps J and Shakespeare resemble one another most in the endless newness of their imaginative worlds. Despite Yahweh's curiosity and his power, his creatures are made free to invent and reinvent themselves constantly, and that is the law of being for Shakespeare's protagonists also."[22]

We go further than Bloom in two ways:

    *   *Dialogue*—J's main style is dialogue (*dramatic speech*).
              Indeed, we could equally well describe Shakespeare's style
              in much the same way.

    *   *Irony*—J is the master of irony: the incongruity between [a]
              an event, and [b] the effect of the adjacent words and actions
              —understood more by the audience or readers than by the
              characters.[23] This is *dramatic irony*, as seen in playwrights
              as distant as Sophocles, Shakespeare, and Synge.

In other words, *internal evidence indicates that The Book of J records the early Festival ritual drama of the Israelites.*

Contemporary Jews from very strict sects may deny this, the reason being that they rely upon P and R while denying the validity of J's work. This is difficult to maintain under the weight of evidence in modern scholarship which we will follow here.

4
WHERE DOES THE MOSES PLAY BEGIN?

Most of the early parts of the story in the Bible (God, the Creation, the Patriarchs) are only available to us now in the P version. J is hardly present. Hidden behind this, however, are various effects from J.

Monotheism first appears in *The Book of J*.[1] Supposedly stated by Abram (Abraham) and repeated by Moses, in fact monotheism lies in the acts of Yahweh and is repeated in the acts of Moses Festival Play created by Joshua—which is in *The Book of J*. Yahweh, like the Egyptian and Mesopotamian maker-gods, shapes man out of the "dust of clay" that has been moistened from the rising of underground springs. But in Babylon the many gods stand in front of a potter's wheel and they fashion man upon it.

Yahweh is different. He is the one and only God. But do J's few remnants from the early stories indicate that he began the Festival play with the Creation or with Moses? Of one thing we are certain—many of the rituals pre-Moses that appear in *The Book of J* are outside the structure of the Festival Play. They are rituals extra to the core of the Festival.

YAHWEH AND CREATION

The Nature of Yahweh

J's Yahweh is more of a person even than the Jesus of the Gospels. The latter does not have the terrifying extravagances that burst from Yahweh.[2] Indeed, *the Yahweh of J is not the God of the later Jews, Christians and Moslems at all*. J's Yahweh comes from an archaic Judaism now largely lost to us. He is not a theological God but a very human character who is violent and unpredictable. As Harold Bloom put it, Yahweh is the hidden King Lear of the Bible. Like Lear, J's Yahweh *is a fictional character*. Both use complex and troublesome extended metaphors or figures of speech and thought. The representation of Yahweh is all too human, even childlike. And the composite artistry of the Authorized Version cannot hide the profound differences in the three books of *Genesis, Exodus* and *Numbers*, particularly when they describe the same event, like the two versions of the Creation.[3]

The Creation

The Redactor began *Genesis* with P's cosmological version of the Creation, not J's irony. Bloom suggests that what is now *Genesis* 1–2:4a was deliberately composed to replace J's extreme vision of an archaic combat myth —Yahweh's battle with the Dragon and the Deep. In J's dynamic version, Yahweh moulds the clay like a child playing at making mud pies. More original and ironic is the creation of woman—there is no similar story in the ancient Near East. J gives six times more space to the woman's creation than to the man's.[4]

J's is not part of the Creation in the Bible, but in other places it slips through into the modern day. There are passages when Yahweh triumphs in a grand fight with a dragon or sea serpent (Rahab, Leviathan), or the sea which opposes Creation. Hidden within J's combat is a Canaanite myth that tells how the storm god Baal and his sister-wife Anat fought Yam, or the sea (chaos)—itself derivative of the Babylonian epic *Enuma Elish*. Every trace of this world-making conflict was obliterated in the Israelite Creation story as re-formed by P and R. But we can find remnants of J elsewhere: "Thou hast made all the borders of the earth: thou hast made summer and winter" (*Psalm* 74:12–17). In an extraordinary metaphor, J identifies the flesh of the slain Leviathan with the manna fed to the wandering Israelites in the Wilderness.

> Thou rulest the raging of the sea: when the waves thereof arise, thou stillest them.
> Thou hast broken Rahab in pieces, as one that is slain; thou hast scattered thine enemies with thy strong arm.[5]   (*Psalm* 89: 9–10)

Isaiah, like the *Psalms*, recalls a more archaic account of Creation even as he equates it with the miracle of deliverance at the Sea of Reeds:

> Awake, awake, put on strength, O arm of the Lord; awake, as in the ancient days, in the generations of old. Art thou not it that hath cut Rahab, and wounded the dragon?

> Art thou not it which hath dried the sea, the waters of the great
> deep; that hath made the depths of the sea a way for the ransomed to
> pass over? (*Isaiah* 51:9–10)

Piecing the bits of J together from *Job, Psalms, Isaiah, Kings, Nahum, Proverbs, Jeremiah* and *Habakkuk* allows scholars to give a composite vision of the archaic cosmogony as follows:

> Yahweh created the Sun, the Moon, and the Stars; he stretched out
> the skies like a tent to shroud the Deep, and placed his secret court
> above the skies, founding it upon the Higher Waters. As he did so,
> Yahweh rode above the Deep, which rose against him. Tehom, queen
> of the Deep, tried to drown out Yahweh's Creation, but he rode against
> her in his chariot of fire, firing at her hail and lightning. Yahweh killed
> her vassal Leviathan with one great blow to the monster's skull, while
> he ended Rahab by thrusting a sword into her heart. The waters fled
> backward and Tehom surrendered. Yahweh shouted his triumph, and
> dried up the floods. He made the Moon divide the seasons, and the
> Sun divide day and night. Observing Yahweh's victory, the Morning
> Stars sang together and all the sons of God shouted for joy.[6]

If J began in this way, it seems obvious why the Redactor chose P's stately vision of Creation.

The stories of the Creation and the Patriarchs were not holy tales for J but simply tales conveyed by ancient ritual: stories of action. J's dynamic Yahweh has little in common with the God of P or Jeremiah; rather he has similarities with the Davidic God of the Court Historian whose sophistication matches J's awareness of Yahweh. Adam's heavy sleep into which Yahweh puts him is J's ironic metaphor for the mystery of love.[7]

In the post-Exilic period, the priests could not allow for theogony.[8] The monster was depersonalized and Creation was consummated by the mere "word" of God in seven days. Israel and Babylon shared the tradition of the Sabbath: in the Exile, they shared the magical qualities in the number seven;

in Mesopotamia the *shabuttu* was a day of penance, while in Israel it was a happy day of rest from work—which became associated with the market economy of Israel.[9]

In creation myths elsewhere, man was created to be the servant of the gods: by Assyrian times he was a slave who gave the gods a dehumanized quality —eventually passed on to Greece. In contrast, P declares (with hints in J) that man is created in the image and likeness of God. Human domination over the natural world is modelled on God's own, of which it is part. While *Genesis* puts its faith in both God and man—an idea unique to Israel—the view of man is an ideal one. The Babylonians had modelled their behaviour on the activity of the gods. But the Israelites of P's time had two models, one God and the ideal man, ultimately derived from J.

EARLY STORIES

The Garden of Eden

Originally this plot consisted of two stories, both of man only: [1] the Creation and the "Fall," and [2] the garden, the tree of life and banishment. J's story hints at an older Judaism where Adam was a lesser Yahweh. There is no "Fall" for J because there is nothing fallen about nature, earthly or human; and J has no split of body-soul, nature-mind.[10]

Eden was "in the East" (the rich valleys of Mesopotamia), while for some it was an ideal garden based on the island of Dilmoon—a Mesopotamian tradition.

The Tree of Life is a metaphor prevalent in the Middle East and derived from the magic shamanic tree, and "the plant of life" of the first farmers. J's Yahweh makes no threat of punishment about the tree, just a statement of the way things are. Human beings, denied access to the tree of life (that is, condemned to face death), became guilty of the sin of disobedience. There was no implication that sex was something morally bad.

The serpent represented Baal, which allowed J to be ironic about the fertility cults of Canaan, whereas P attacked them. The serpent was also an ancient shamanic symbol which carried the performance traditions of "the trickster" (in the biblical "cunning"). His ability to change his skin gave him the secret of immortality, becoming a death-and-resurrection symbol. The charming serpent of J is his most ironical creature.[11]

Cain and Abel

The Cain and Abel story is a fragment from much earlier times. It raises questions; i.e., why is no reason given for God's rejection of Cain's sacrifice?

There are traces of the ancient feud of the pastoralist and the farmer; each carried out his own regular sacrificial ritual.[12] S.H.Hooke has said:

> It is in the field, the tilled soil, whose infertility has brought about the situation, that the slaying of the shepherd takes place, and the suggestion is that the slaying was a ritual one ... a communal ritual killing intended to fertilize the soil by drenching it with blood of the victim; in the words of the narrative, 'the earth has opened her mouth to receive thy brother's blood.'[13]

Cain speaks his infamous denial that he is his brother's keeper; ironically he must now become a nomad—just as his parents were expelled from Eden, Cain is now expelled from the soil. He must settle in the windblown land, where he founds the first city. The urban, for J, is based upon brotherly murder, a murder provoked by the arbitrariness of Yahweh.[14]

It is probable that the Cain and Abel story is a later rewriting of an ancient myth dramatizing a ritual slaying, and intended to secure fertility for the crops. It was followed by the flight of the killer (scapegoat) who was protected by a mark that indicated his sacred character. It is likely that the theme of this ritual was separate from the annual Festival.

In the Israelite ritual of the Day of Atonement, one goat was slain and another (the scapegoat) driven out into the desert.

In Babylon, the sacrificing priest had spread the blood of a beast on the walls of Marduk's shrine and then had to flee to the desert as he had been defiled (the scapegoat). In the Athenian ritual of Bouphonia, an ox was ritually slaughtered by two men who then had to flee.

The Genealogies

In *Genesis* 4: 1, 17–24, the genealogical table which gives Cain's descendants for the next seven generations indicates economic and cultural progress—Cain builds a city and names it after his first son, Enoch. Among his descendants are Jabal, ancestor of the nomad herdsmen; Jubal, father of harp and pipe music; and Tubal-cain, the ancestor of all master-workers in bronze and iron.

Adam and his descendants all have enormous life spans, the oldest being Methuselah who died at the age of 969 and was the father of Noah. Likewise, the records of the Sumerian kingdom of Larsa give a list of ten legendary kings before the Flood who each reigned between 10,000 and 60,000 years. In the ancient Near East there was a common belief that, before the Flood, men lived much longer.[15] After the Flood, the life-span was reduced. Even today, Jews wish each other long life "up to a hundred and twenty years." The life span was steadily reduced until it reached the normal span (and thereby history as such) with the monarchy: "The years of our life are threescore and ten, or even by reason of strength fourscore."[16]

The Flood

The Flood is likely derived from the Babylonian version. Behind an obscure reference (*Genesis* 6: 1–4) lies a ritual myth about a race of semi-divine beings (lesser gods in Babylon, "giants" in the Bible) who rebelled against the gods and were thrown down. The Tigris and Euphrates had many floods: Ur's excavation revealed massive destruction from flood waters.

The most notable Mesopotamian flood story is that contained in *Gilgamesh*. This was taken over by the Canaanites whose mythology was followed by the Yahwist. In contrast to Mesopotamia, flooding was not a major event in Syrio-Palestine.

This same obscure reference contains ancient elements of polytheism and polygamy. The Yahwist shows that God's judgment upon man applies to every human being and, in addition, he condemns the ritual of "the Sacred Marriage"—the ritual intercourse which was widespread in Babylonia and Canaan; it even penetrated later Israelite religion[17] and, from J's viewpoint, had to be stopped.

Author P gives a sacred quality to human blood when he says that "If anyone sheds the blood of man, by man shall his blood be shed" because "in the image of God has man been made."[18] This is a remnant of the Babylonian tradition in the *Enuma Elish* that man was created from the blood of the deity. The tale probably hides a ritual performance of which we now know nothing.

The Deluge over, Yahweh declares that there will be no more mass destructions of people or of animals. The story of Noah's sons seeing him naked has likely been censored. It is probable that the Noah and the Flood story has little or no spiritual significance for J, unlike P's solemn account of the First Covenant.[19]

THE PATRIARCHS

There is no historical or archeological evidence for the existence of the patriarchs. We know them only from religious sources.

The remote legendary history of the Jewish people begins with the ancient Hebrews, or Habiru, a "rabble" according to Bronze Age Egyptian officials. At the start of the second millennium B.C., the Habiru began to move from Mesopotamia westward until they reached the Mediterranean. One group among them was later headed by a charismatic leader, Abram, who as Abraham became the father of Judaism, Christianity, and Islam. It was possibly eighteen centuries B.C. that Abram left Mesopotamia for both spiritual, political, and economic reasons. The "patriarchal period" is not a well-defined chronological entity and history becomes confusing. Rather, embedded in this narrative cycle are reminiscences of centuries-long historical processes that may derive from the West Semitic migrations where tribes made their way west, reaching their height during the first quarter of the second millennium. These extended time spans were telescoped in the biblical narrative into a mere trigenerational scheme—Abraham, Isaac, and Jacob.[20]

J's heroes share some of Yahweh's worst qualities, as well as some of his best. But J at least has heroines—Eve, Sarai, Rebecca, Rachel, Tamar, Zipporah—who are not theomorphic but are sympathetic.[21]

Abraham

Abraham, the son of Terah, was descended from Noah's son, Shem, and was the first legendary patriarch. The name "Abram" in J means "exalted father"; the now more familiar "Abraham," which means "father of a host of nations," was introduced by P.[22]

Terah and his family lived in the Mesopotamian city of Ur where they served the moon god, Sin, somewhere about 2000 B.C.

The Abraham of Jewish legend is very different from J's slim portrait—as a baby he proclaims God; he defies the tyrant Nimrod of Babylon by destroying the king's idols, and survives Nimrod's attempt to burn him alive in a fiery furnace.

There is no richness in J's story which begins with Yahweh's call for Abram to go out, and he obeys Yahweh's words before he is told their purpose. Childless in Ur, in Canaan Abram would be made into a great nation. Terah and Abraham went to Haran, a city in northern Syria linked to the gods of Ur. It also had dealings with the ancient city of Ebla where tablets reveal a deity under the name of Yah or Ya'u—perhaps the origin of the name Yahweh.

The journey from Ur to Haran, and Abraham's subsequent travels (to Canaan c.1800 B.C., to the Negev, to Egypt, back to the Negev, and then to Canaan again) were likely by more than one person. They were probably taken from historical memories of ancient Israelites in Judah and the Negev, condensed through oral story-telling before they were written down.

This can also be seen in the remarkable parallelism in the journeys of Abraham and Jacob[23] which show that the ancient narratives had been standardized even in preliterate times.

The journeys established the Canaanite religious sites of Shechem, Bethel and Mamre as sacred places.

The character of Abraham changed with each writer. For J he was modest and obeyed God implicitly, but for P he was an oriental potentate. Elsewhere he was "Abraham the Hebrew," a local warring chieftain. Yahweh completed a solemn covenant ritual and oath, concluding with a fire ritual, with Abraham; and confirmed his promise of the land to an eventual Israel.[24] To this end Abraham took a heifer, a goat, and a ram, each of which he split in two, and ritually placed each half opposite the other (the concept of doubling)—a graphic dramatization of what would happen to people who failed to keep their oaths. Ritual practices of this kind were common over the whole area.[25] The later covenant made by God that Abraham would be "the father of a host of nations" had, in contrast, no ritual;[26] this covenant led Abraham's aged wife, Sarai, to bear him the son Isaac.

The story of Abraham's sacrifice of a ram instead of Isaac, the so-called E version,[27] represents that author's belief that the Israelites had rejected human sacrifice for ritual purposes—a practice which in reality they continued over many centuries. J's original Binding of Isaac has no trace of J's language now, and it features an Abram who will not do for Isaac what he did for the sake of Sodom. We have no vision of Abram in exile akin to those we have of Jacob, Joseph, and Moses. We do not see in Abram a great agonist, as Jacob will be.[28]

In J, Abram goes down into Egypt even as Joseph and Jacob and all the children of Israel go down after him. Not only is such repetition typical of ritual drama but also the descent into the underworld of Egypt and the return to Canaan is a variation of the ritual of Inanna and other gods and goddesses descending into the underworld, only to be resurrected in their ritual dramas. J has Abram escaping from famine (*Genesis* 12:10–20). Fearing that his wife's beauty will expose him to danger, ignobly Abram is disguised as her brother; Sarai loyally complies, but J clearly suggests that she becomes Pharaoh's concubine, with material gain to her "brother" Abram. This was not a sin to J, who never makes a judgment, here or elsewhere.[29] E tells a similar story about Abram and Sarai with the Philistine king Abimelech (*Genesis* 20), but E is more serious, and Abimelech never touches Sarai. J lets Isaac play a similar trick on Abimelech and his court (*Genesis* 26), but for very little reason beyond ritual repetition. The story must have originated in ancient ritual.

When Yahweh, two angels, and Abram walk down the road to Sodom together, J allows Yahweh to speak to himself in a revelatory monologue:

> Do I hide from Abram what I will do? Abram will emerge a great nation, populous, until all nations of the earth see themselves blessed in him. I have known him within; he will fill his children, his household, with desire to follow Yahweh's way. Tolerance and justice will emerge—to allow what Yahweh says to be fulfilled. (42)

This is not to be taken literally.[30] The essential sin of the doomed towns is inhospitality, always a betrayal of the nomadic ideal. Jewish legend emphasized the wealth and greed of Sodom and Gomorrah as the cause of their savagery to strangers, who were exploited, robbed, starved, and indeed forcibly sodomized. J's instance is when the mob gathers around Lot's house and demands that the family come out to receive Sodom's customary welcome. The angels descend toward Sodom, but Abram faces Yahweh to join in the most remarkable dialogue in J.[31] Yahweh resolves to pull down Sodom because its inhospitality diminishes life and so shows contempt for the creator of life. To tolerate the violent inhospitality of Sodom would be lunatic. Yet Abram engages in humane haggling with Yahweh on behalf of the people of the cities.[32] Buber says that, for Sodom, Abram "utters the boldest speech of man in all Scripture."[33] Abram thinks that Yahweh is in danger of forgetting his promise to Noah after the Flood, and intercedes to remind Yahweh just who Yahweh is, or is supposed to be. J provides a sublime but rather menacing comedy of the wary Abram haggling with the unwary Yahweh, slowly arguing him down from fifty innocents to ten as the number for whose sake the cities will not be destroyed. After Yahweh proclaims, "I will not pull down on behalf of these ten," then "Yahweh, having finished speaking to Abram, went on. Abram turned back, toward his place." (43)[34]

Isaac

Yahweh repeated the Abraham covenant with Isaac at Beersheba[35] which was the place generally identified with the Isaac legends, according to the Yahwist. There Isaac built an altar and dug a well—water was associated ritually with religious places. Isaac's love for Rebecca is seen as a substitute for the loss of his mother, Sarai (*Genesis* 24:67). J's subtle economy is shown in his Rebecca: she says little at the well or afterwards, but enough to show that she too is Yahweh's chosen; she is contrasted with her brother Laban, who carefully neither approves nor disapproves. She has a strong will and her choice of Jacob over Esau is a choice of the present tense, of direct over indirect speech. Esau belongs to the past tense, the cosmos of the hunter and the pastoralist.

Jacob

Jacob is J's fullest portrait among the patriarchs; he and his twin, Esau, are among J's liveliest people. J's Jacob is a man of feeling, endlessly cunning in his quest for the Blessing but unable to realize its fruits.[36] Jacob wins his new name, Israel, as a Blessing from one of the Elohim who wrestles him, and it becomes the name of a people.[37]

The origin of Jacob wrestling with the angel at the Ford of Jabbok[38] may have been the shaman's struggle with the spirits of "the upper world," or related to the folklore tradition of river gods that were propitiated before a river was crossed—an ancient legend that still survives today in fragmentary form in the Near East and Europe. The change of Jacob's name to Israel marks a turning point in the biblical narrative—to win the new name of Israel is also to win a very different Blessing from the one stolen from Esau.

The twin sons of Isaac and Rebecca, Esau and Jacob, were rivals—the hunter and the herdsman. Then the story speeds ahead from the oracle at their birth to their adult life,[39] and the narrative obscures ancient rituals. The theme of hostile twins was common in the Near East and was continued in subsequent myth and folklore. J makes a sharp contrast between the acute sensibility of Jacob and the roughness of Esau.

As Jacob went to Haran to escape the wrath of Esau, he slept over-night at Bethel, already an Israelite sacred site. Resting his head on one of the stones of the shrine he dreamed of a ladder reaching to the heavens, and of Yahweh repeating the covenant he made with Abraham. So he took the stone, set it up as a memorial and poured ritual oil on it—that is, he consecrated a *massebah*, or phallic shaped sacred stone derived from fertility magic, like many subsequent Israelites.

The Canaanite El was turned into Yahweh by the biblical authors with traits only known at a later time.

The Covenant between Laban and Jacob covers an ancient non-aggression pact between Abram and Israel. Yet Jacob, in dividing the herds with Laban, produced spotted cattle by shamanistic magic—manipulating spotted sticks, he used the magical principle of like producing like. His son Joseph was also a magician.

When Jacob returned to Canaan, he stopped first at Shechem where he received instructions from Yahweh to go to Bethel again and build an altar to God.[40] J transformed an ancient pilgrimage ritual: rather than abandoning one set of gods for another, as *Genesis* does, it became a jouzney to avoid ritual contamination. The Israelites left their personal possessions (clothes, ritual ear-rings, and so forth) at Shechem under a sacred tree, purified themselves, put on fresh clothes, and journeyed to Bethel where a religious site was established. This pilgrimage was periodically re-enacted in liturgy as well as at various ceremonies en route—the planting of the "oak of weeping" over the grave of Rebecca's nurse Deborah, the *massebah* planted over the grave of Rachel after the birth of Benjamin, and so on.

The crucial incident for J is grotesque: the proverbial sale of Esau's birthright for a mess of pottage. But just as significant is when Jacob stands at Bethel (*Genesis* 28), suddenly Yahweh stands alongside him, and a particular place, *makom*, is named. Jacob flees from the consequences of his (and Rebecca's) hoax when, in the flight, he receives the reward of his usurpation: Yahweh stands next to him and speaks to him as familiarly as he spoke to Abram.[41]

As Rebecca was first met at a well, so Jacob has a similar first encounter with his cousin Rachel—it is another pastoral idyll, even more charming for revealing the impulsive in Jacob. He suddenly kisses Rachel and bursts into tears (parallel with the tears of Esau). J shows Jacob in the act of falling in love with the woman who will be Joseph's mother.[42]

The tale contains Rachel's finest moment in J—her theft and concealment of the *teraphim*, her father's household gods[43] where she is the equal of her outrageous husband and her sly father.[44] Ironically Jacob, unaware of the theft, urges Laban to search the caravan. By stealing the idols and so cunningly sitting on them, Rachel guarantees the result by playing upon the male awe of a woman's periods—Rachel (and J) frightens off Laban.[45]

In the Israelite ritual of the Day of Atonement, one goat was slain and another (the scapegoat) driven out into the desert. In Babylon, the sacrificing priest had spread the blood of a beast on the walls of Marduk's shrine and then had to flee to the desert as he had been defiled (the scapegoat). In the later Athenian ritual of Bouphonia, an ox was ritually slaughtered by two men who then had to flee, reversing the fooling of Isaac. Jacob is now the deceived in a striking double irony, since only the authenticity of Jacob's passion for Rachel made him ignore all the omens warning him against Laban—although Laban is no match for Jacob.

J uses disguises and deceptions nearly as often as Shakespeare (as Bloom says); these great dramatists are allied in their obsession both with wordplay and the "mask and the face." Reality and appearance are linked dialogically in both J and Shakespeare: there is a bizarre comedy in Jacob's complex trickery of the peeled rods, leading to the hilarious result that all the sturdy animals go to him while only the weaklings go to Laban. Jacob works himself into a classic farce dilemma: he flees from Laban, but only toward Esau, who is accompanied by four hundred men—a typical ritual action.

It is another of J's ironies that Jacob, caught between two possible vengeances, moves into his wrestling match with an angel. The latter J refuses to identify,[46] the whole sequence revolving around the mask and the face, illusion and reality.

Joseph

The story of Joseph—son of Jacob, and the shepherd subservient to his elder brothers—is not directly re-created from bits and pieces of ancient oral tales and rituals. Rather, it is a whole short story: part of the "wisdom" literature of the Near East, probably from even older rituals. Joseph was honoured as a sorcerer (shaman) by the Pharaoh. He interpreted dreams and visions; and he practised divination by hydromancy—revelations by gazing into water.

There is a plausible background to Joseph's story. In the Hyskos period (1720–1560 B.C.) a group of Near Eastern peoples (the Habiru) controlled Egypt; they had among them people with Semitic names who mixed Canaanite with the native Egyptian religion. A Hebrew such as Joseph could have risen to high position. At the return to power of the native Egyptians, task-masters were set over the Near Eastern people left in Egypt. Thus the Hebrews were in bondage at Goshen and the stage was set for the appearance of Moses.

In the story of Joseph, J provides a fine study of the father-son relationship. Jacob, despite his success, is unlucky; Joseph's luck is constant and charmingly outrageous. He is not aggressive or hostile, but is a born politician, clever at getting his way through all means available[47]—a wisdom figure in a purely worldly sense.[48]

J begins as the young shepherd is a spoiled tell-tale hated by his brothers because he is his father's favourite (*Genesis* 37). Jewish legend emphasizes Joseph's personal beauty, which reminds the bereaved Jacob of his lost Rachel. The long-sleeved tunic, the outward mark of Jacob's love, ironically becomes the emblem of the aged patriarch's grief. Mistranslated in the King James Bible as the "Coat of many colours," it was in fact a royal tunic, like that worn by Tamar in the terrible scene where Amnon rapes her (*2 Samuel* 13:18–19).

Like Tamar's, Joseph's garment becomes an emblem of violence and cruelty. The brothers give the tunic to Jacob as legal "proof" that Joseph is dead.[49]

The site of Shechem has complex meanings in J. It was the site of the first Moses Festival performance; it was where Joseph's brothers conspired; Dinah's grief was avenged by the massacre led by Simeon and Levi; and Rehoboam was crowned and then rejected there.

Jacob is now called Israel, suggesting his is the true Israel, not Jeroboam's realm. (The selling of Joseph is thus linked to Jeroboam's disruption of the legacy of David.) Taken down into Egypt, Joseph descends into a cosmos of death (like Inanna's descent to the underworld and in contrast to the liberation narrative of Moses—that is, Jeroboam is the betrayer of Israel.)[50]

As Joseph rises in the household of Potiphar, his attempted seduction by Potiphar's lustful wife is derived from an Egyptian romantic tale. It becomes great comic writing in J—another instance of Joseph's luck. Everything except the lady has been granted him with an authority equal to Potiphar's.[51] A little later, when Joseph is in power over all Egypt, he is reunited with his brothers, and then restored to his father, Israel. In the saga there are frequent omissions of J and substitutions of portions of E by R, sometimes with both J and E versions.

There are two accounts of the brothers descending into Egypt: the second (*Genesis* 43) is by J.[52] The brothers want to take Benjamin with them, but as he is all of Rachel left to Jacob, he resists until Judah promises to forsake the Blessing if he does not bring Benjamin back from Egypt.

The brothers are bewildered when they enter Joseph's house to enjoy a meal with the pharaoh's chief minister. To the steward as they gather round the door, they declare their innocence in finding their money returned to their bags on the way home from Egypt after their first visit. Joseph's steward dryly informs them that their God must have reimbursed them, but that he in any case has been paid.[53]

J's message is that one is always a child, even the grand bureaucrat Joseph, who is refreshingly free of the desire to be revenged upon these who sold him into slavery.

Joseph is like his father in his self-dramatizing tendencies; both express acute sensibility, and they are persuaders of themselves and of others. Joseph reveals himself to his brothers, and flings himself weeping upon his father's neck. Jacob grandly proclaims that at last he can die, having seen that his son is still alive—he is the better performer, maintaining his heroic composure in front of his people. The dying Jacob gives Shechem to Joseph as a personal fief, since Jeroboam was crowned there. There remains the moving account of Joseph's grief for his dead father and the subsequent journey to Canaan to bury him. J ends with the return of Joseph and his brothers to Egypt. The scene is set for the story of Moses and the Exodus.

Joseph and the Self

With Yahweh, Abram, Rebecca, Jacob, Tamar and Joseph, J pioneers the human sense of self. These characters demonstrate what kind of a Yahweh J inherited, and how he is one of the starting points for our sense of ego.[54] J's Yahweh is unique..

Hunting tribesmen, ancient Sumerians and Egyptians had a communal sense of the self. As Egypt progressed mostly in peace, gods and pharaohs had several roles each with different tasks ("doubling"), but their character was communal. However, those in the Tigris and Euphrates basin who faced continual raiding and warfare either: [a] dehumanized the ego (as with the Assyrians), or [b] began to break down the communal self before the beginnings of a tragic atmosphere (Neo-Babylonians) which they passed on to the ancient Greeks. It was Sophocles in *Oedipus Rex* who created the first complete three-dimensional character.

Yahweh in *The Book of J* is an *individual*. He has a considerable feeling for his own Self which strongly influences the patriarchs, particularly Abraham in his conversation with Yahweh about Sodom, and Joseph as David's surrogate. Joseph has an amplified Self that includes Yahweh's relation to vitality—he who will be present *when and where he will be present* is a God of judgment and justice, but he is also a God who has created a vital universe.

The Blessing has clearly more to do with a wholeness of Being than with reason, judgment, or morality. David defines the wholeness of Being; he incarnates the dynamics of change, and those dynamics belong to Yahweh whose *essence is surprise*. Non-believers cannot change; they are fixed stereotypes, with no desire to be helpful to Yahweh. That desire is élitist, and its fullest embodiments are David, and Joseph before him. *Human caprice* is the essence of élitism and helps account for what attracts Yahweh to David and Joseph.

J's major personages, Yahweh included, are remarkably like Shakespearean characters, as Bloom says. This is not only because they are both dramatists and write dialogue, but also because the J portions of the Geneva Bible influenced Shakespeare's ideas of representation. Moreover, the perpetually changing consciousness (the *process of mind*) of J's people is very dramatic; it is different from the Homeric state of mind, and prepares for a similar dynamism in the Shakespearean personae. What is different in Shakespeare is that his characters change by brooding upon what they themselves have said. Shakespeare developed this technique from his profession as a player, his use of the dramatic metaphor ("All the world's a stage"), and hints in Chaucer; and yet, as Bloom says, "even the Wife of Bath and the Pardoner seem less Shakespearean characters than are J's Jacob, Joseph, and Yahweh."[55]

PLAY OR PROSE?

Most of the fragments of biblical stories from the Creation to Joseph in *The Book of J* may have originated in ritual drama. Many clearly did but others, specifically the Joseph story which was a romance, was not the direct recording of a ritual. On the other hand, even J's Joseph story was based on still more ancient rituals.

Some of the stories from the Creation to Joseph may have possibly have been included in the Festival play of Moses. To modern thinkers it is logical that the whole story of the Israelites would be included. But this was not necessarily so as they crossed the Jordan. There is a tradition that the Festival play began with Moses.[56] And it is there that we specifically discover direct speech attached to "witnessing"—a sure sign of ritual drama.

It could be that the rituals from the Creation to Joseph were either a spoken introduction to the Festival or, more likely, they were performed elsewhere in Israelite religious life. For example, Jacob wrestling with the angel at the Ford of Jabbok was probably the mythical level of a ritual performed at a specific place; the ritual battle with Leviathan was fought by the Canaanites and some Israelites in direct contact with them; on the Day of Atonement, one goat was slain and another (the scapegoat) driven out into the desert, but sacrifice and scapegoat were common in the Near East before Abraham; Adam-Eve and Cain-Abel are incomplete ritual fragments from much earlier times. Many of J's heroes, from Abraham to Joseph, have various kinds of ritual embedded in the text.

If these fragments of *The Book of J* demonstrate anything it is that ritual dramas of all kinds were performed in Israelite everyday life. Human existence was understood as dramatic and the Moses Festival Play was the climax of the year.

5

THE EXODUS

At this point, we need to remind ourselves of some basic facts leading to the Exodus. In legendary history, the descent of the Israelites into Egypt was at the time of the New Kingdom, c.1700 B.C.; and their forced labour in Egypt was from c.1300. About 1280 Moses led the Israelites in the Exodus, and they entered Canaan c.1250–1200: the first historical event of which we know.

The Performance of Salvific History

Israel always regarded its salvation as based upon three events:

[1] the Exodus from Egypt,
[2] the travels and events in the desert, and
[3] the gift of the promised land (Canaan).

These three events were performed in, and constituted the most important ritual dramas of, Canaan when occupied by the Hebrews. They were the key ritual performances of the year. The Exodus is the oldest and most significant event in the verbal record of salvation. It was the starting point of Israel's faith and this it has remained. It is the cornerstone of Jewish salvific history.

In comparison, the stories of the patriarchal tradition are late. The desert travels and the Land-giving are so closely allied with the flight from Egypt that at times they seem one. The possession or loss of land was always thought to result from being on good or bad terms with God. Over historic time, the tradition of the Land-giving increased in importance yet it was never as important as the Exodus. The biblical references to the Exodus are twice as frequent as those to the Land-giving.[1]

The sources of J, and perhaps E, were either the rituals themselves or, at least, direct reports of them. Given the ritual traditions all over the ancient Near East, it is likely that these sources were *scenarii*—ancient kinds of "prompt books"—records of the actions and words that were performed in the ritual drama.[2] Among contemporary traditional people, "prompt books" of diverse kinds exist.

The Plot

The Israelite *scenario* was of a specific kind. *The plot of the Exodus that exists in J's words in the Bible, or can be assumed from these, is the record of a performance*—it falls in between the *legendary* history of the patriarchs and the *actual* history of the occupation of Canaan.

It is a mixture of oral, ritual, and literary traditions made at different periods and written from different theological viewpoints. "In addition," says Mircea Eliade, "the influence of several literary genres has been detected. The seeming historicity of an episode became subject to doubt when it was found that the Redactor used the cliches of a particularly literary genre (saga, novella, proverb, etc.)."[3]

This is particularly the case when the genre is seen as based upon records of a performed ritual. In conjectured history, it is most likely that the Joseph-tribes fled from Egypt into the desert. There they travelled for many years, probably linking up with other groups of people, such as the Kenites, before moving into Israel where they met up with still further groups. It was the information about the flight from Egypt and the Israelites' subsequent wanderings that made up the plot.

The Ritual Themes

The people who had lived through the Great Deliverance and the Covenant attracted other Habiru already in Palestine: the sacred community was fostered by the re-enactment of these events in a sacramental experience. Through the dramatic enactment on regular religious occasions at the central sanctuary in the promised land, the historical circumstances of the escape from Egypt and the Covenant were transformed.[4]

The beginnings of the monotheism of Israel are told in *Genesis* 46–50, in *Exodus* and in *Numbers*. They contain a series of supposed historical events, most of which are said to be caused by God. In fact, J derived them from either a performance of the ritual drama or a "prompt book." We do not know for certain how this was displayed but, if it was a *scenario*, it may well have appeared somewhat like the following:

* Jacob's sons settle in Egypt (a possible Prologue).
* Centuries later a pharaoh orders the killing of the Hebrews' firstborn.
  Moses is miraculously saved from the massacre.
  He is brought up at the pharaoh's court.
* Moses kills an Egyptian soldier who was beating a Hebrew.
  Moses flees into the desert of Midian.
* He first meets Yahweh in the "burning bush."
  God's mission is for Moses to bring his people out of Egypt.
  He also reveals the divine name (monotheism stated).
* Yahweh, through Moses, forces the pharaoh's consent by the plagues.
* The Hebrews leave, cross the Sea of Reeds that drowns the Egyptian army.
* The theophany and Yahweh's Covenant with the people on Mount Sinai.
  The instructions about the content of the revelation and the ritual.
* Forty years' journey in the desert, including a period at Kadesh in the
  Negev.
* Moses dies, according to tradition, in the plain opposite Jericho.
* Canaan is conquered under the leadership of Joshua.

But how far did the ritual drama follow the biblical sequence? To address this and other questions, segments of the plot will now be examined.

THE EXODUS IN PERFORMANCE

If a group of Hebrews did settle in Egypt, the most likely time was that of the Hyskos. If so, the Hebrews were in Egypt from approximately 1700–1220 B.C. when the Exodus might have begun.

At about 1550 B.C. the pharaoh Ahmose I overthrew the Hyskos and pursued them into Palestine. For many years, as a result, Egypt ruled Palestine and Syria. From the sixteenth to the thirteenth centuries B.C., the pharaohs used conscripted Syrians and Palestinians for construction work in Egypt, treating them like slaves.

The most likely time for the Exodus was in the reign of Rameses II (c.1290–1224 B.C.). Unfortunately, as no Egyptian records exist to confirm that the Hebrews fled from Egypt, this must remain conjectural. Yet the

Exodus certainly seems to reflect a historical event focused on monotheistic Israelites.

J's ironic humour appears when the Hebrew midwives tell Pharaoh that they have failed to kill the male babies because their mothers, unlike Egyptian women, are so vigorous that they give birth before the midwife reaches them (*Exodus* 1:19).

This humour, like J's comment of genocide through shrewd dealing, frames the birth of Moses[5] and may be the first scene.

Aaron is introduced in *Exodus* 4:14. It is at this time that Moses has a new status in *The Book of J*. Moses has resisted his own election by Yahweh, but Aaron's role seems to remove this block and to release Moses's cunning.

Moses starts by requesting of the Pharaoh not the freedom of his people but a vacation for them so that they can worship Yahweh in the desert. Since Yahweh is unknown to Pharaoh, the request is refused.

This may be the first of a series of scenes featuring both Moses and Pharaoh. Moses and Aaron do not immediately argue with Pharaoh, to whom Moses is an object of scorn. Moses is also cursed by the overworked Israelites, who now must make bricks without straw. Moses is reduced to a pathetic stammering while Yahweh ominously proclaims, "Now you will see what I do for Pharaoh" (124).[6]

Then the great plagues begin. J enjoys the plagues, which Buber calls a "fantastic popular narrative."[7] Throughout the plagues and the dialogues between Moses and Pharaoh, J writes in the vein of the romance of Joseph with pure irony, since J is wholly on Yahweh's side.[8] But the constant repetition of the different plagues clearly indicates a ritual drama.

Moses

P is wary of Moses, E exalts him, while J treats him with irony. J does not write history. His Moses is as remote as the Patriarchs. J's writing is all in a single genre, although it refers to the many genres of the ancient Middle East.[9] The names of Moses and others mentioned in the Bible appear to be Egyptian.[10]

Moses almost certainly existed as a person in history. Yet, because he was a fabulous figure in the Biblical story, the events of his life became mythological and legendary. Like many other cultural heroes all over the world, the historical personality was swamped by legendary material. This was particularly the case with Moses because the events by which we know him originated in the ritual drama performance: the performed Moses was particularly alive because he spoke living dialogue in a living form. In this sense, we can liken Moses to Greek personages (such as Electra, who was probably a real person) whose character differs according to the individual dramatist. In addition, elements of Moses' character come from different performances of the Moses Play which changed over time.

This accounts for two contrasting features of Moses as a character: his magical performances as a shaman, and the likelihood that he originated monotheism in the Moses Festival Play. On the face of it, it is surprising that a shaman should create monotheism. But prehistoric shamanic practices, codified within two agricultural styles (Mesopotamian and Egyptian), were inherited by the Hebrews. Later Jewish traditions classified them as "magic" in opposition to Yahwism proper. But in the early days the people believed in them.

Moses is at first intemperate though wary. Then in *Exodus* 2:11 he is suddenly mature: he knows his Israelite identity, he is fierce to avenge his brothers, and is wary of his exposed situation. After he escapes Pharaoh, Moses again is aggressive against the shepherds at the well, defending the daughters of the priest of Midian. He is again courageous and, in the naming of his son (*Exodus* 2:22), dedicated to his people. But he has qualities that make him unsuitable to lead a people out of bondage—anger, impatience, and a deep anxiety about his leadership. In personality and character, he contrasts with the David of *2 Samuel*.[11]

St. Stephen before the Council proclaimed how "Moses was learned in all the wisdom of the Egyptians."[12] But "wisdom and knowledge" in the Solomonic period could either be intuitive, magical and ritualistic, or rational and ethical (typically Greek). Like many traditional peoples, the Egyptians believed that knowledge of another's secret name (like Rumpelstiltskin) gave power over that animal, spirit, person, or god. In Deuteronomic references (during a strong influence of Egyptian piety) knowledge of Yahweh's name was magical knowledge: "Yahweh, in the epiphany of the thornbush, at first avoids naming his name as did the *numen* with which Jacob wrestled. [Later] Yahweh instructs Moses to call his name. By this means Yahweh was compelled."[13]

J writes for Yahweh and Moses some extraordinary dialogue in *Exodus* 3: Yahweh gives the prelude to the dialogue by blazing forth as the fire in the thorn bush. The dialogue shows Yahweh overcoming Moses by sheer power. Yahweh, who is *in* the fire but is *not* the fire, warns his involuntary prophet not to come too close. Never before has Yahweh spoken of the category of "the holy," invented to keep Moses and the mass of Israelites at a distance. As will become crucial at Sinai, Yahweh seems to need certain defences before he extends his Blessing from one élite family to all of their historical descendants.[14]

Moses was a charismatic leader of a nomadic group, not a state-priest supported by settled institutions. He had shamanistic powers and through him Yahweh repeatedly spoke. Was he, like other shamans who spoke in tongues, also possessed? It seems so as he shatters the stone tablets of the Commandments, or wipes out his nearest kin. The performed sorcery of Moses was mightier than that of the Egyptian shamans, Jannes and Mambres: although each could turn their magic rods (shamanic *batons*) into snakes and bring up frogs onto the land, the Egyptians could not drive them away—they could not compete with the divine power given to Moses.

In the many mutinies against Moses, Yahweh sent fiery serpents,[15] which Moses took away from the people by setting up a bronze snake-image for worship[16]—a talisman as a protection against evil, similar to those of shamans throughout the ages. Snake worship continued on into later Judea.[17] The fact that Moses was a performing snake priest,[18] and that Aaron served a bull god, parallels the two-fold universal shamanic practices—some dancing in caves as animals, others dancing round hearths as birds and snakes—like today's rituals among the Hopi in Arizona. However, with the rise of agriculture, snakes and serpents became increasingly with the rites of the Goddess.

Many of J's women are stronger than the men: Sarai, for example, or Rebecca. Job's nameless wife is bitterly laconic. As the afflicted Job sits on the ashes of his existence and scratches his inflammations with a potsherd, his wife cries out to him, "Do you still retain your integrity? Curse God and die!" Moses' wife, Zipporah, is also bitter in the frightening bridegroom-of-blood episode. Zipporah smears the blood from their infant son's foreskin between the legs of Moses: "Because you are my blood bridegroom." Spoken to a barely conscious, perhaps dying man, this has great force: it is intended for Yahweh, who is so affected by it to withdraw from his murderous attack upon his own faithful prophet.[19]

Monotheism

How did monotheism come about within the Festival Play? It is possible that the Hebrews of Egypt knew of the religious reforms of the pharaoh Akhenaten (c.1,375–1,350 B.C.) who replaced the polytheistic Egyptian religion with the worship of the sun-god, Aten. *But Akhenaten did not begin monotheism*; his reforms combined the many existing gods into one god who had many forms: a religious syncretism that resulted in a peculiar type of monism. This was very different from the Hebrew monotheism which was a unique conception of one "God above nature, whose will is supreme, and who is not subject to compulsion or fate."[20] But religious changes in Egypt, together with the Near East generally in this period, produced an intellectual climate within which monotheism could arise.

The Torah is pervaded by the idea of monotheism, yet this tie between Yahweh and the Hebrew people did not exist with the Patriarchs.

Nor did Babylon, Egypt, Canaan, and the rest of the Near East know of it either. The origin of monotheism is seen to lie within the Hebrew people at a particular moment in time—either in their desert journey, or probably in the remarkable event of the "burning bush." This is accepted by most scholars working today.

It is only with Moses that the contrast between the belief in Yahweh and paganism occurs. Monotheism appears for the first time in the story of the burning bush in *Exodus* 3 and 4: 1–17. This is a unique event in a number of ways: God redeems human beings by commissioning a prophet who then has a mission to a people; God reveals his name to a prophet; and the theophany takes place in the desert with no altar, sanctuary or temple. At the same time, the battle with paganism must have begun in Egypt. Certainly, it ends with the fall of the pagan pharaoh and his magicians whereby, although Egypt is not converted to Yahwism, the Hebrew faith is confirmed.

It is likely that Moses was historically the first to think of monotheism. Although he had the authority of an antique magician, he was also the model for the later Judges. Like Deborah, Gideon, Samson and Samuel, he was a leader with political authority. He wielded this authority all his life: he made his appearance in the time of troubles, and he not only fought idolatry but also punished idolaters. Unlike the Judges, however, Moses came from a family of magicians: his brother was the bull-priest Aaron, and his sister was Miriam, a prophetess and a poetess.

In *The Book of J* Moses grows and changes. When he returned from the desert, Moses was no longer a simple magician: he was the messenger of Yahweh. The message he brought was that of monotheism: there was one God, Yahweh. In the ritual drama, the battle lines were drawn between the God of Israel and his enemies. His enemies were not several gods (as with all the other peoples in the ancient Near East) but heathen human beings. Moses came out of the desert to rouse the Hebrews with the message of the transcendant God who had shown himself in a vision—the burning bush.

The Flight from Egypt

Moses had made a Covenant with Israel on behalf of God: they were now Yahweh's people and he promised them the land of Israel. Thus the Exodus was necessary.

In the account of the miracle of the crossing of the Sea of Reeds (papyrus) —not the Red Sea, as often translated—J's version (*Exodus* 14) is strikingly different from P's, which builds on E's. For P and R the deliverance at the Sea of Reeds was crucial. In P, Yahweh orders Moses to raise his staff up over the sea to create a path between two walls of water. Once the Israelites have crossed, then Moses raises his hand and the waters drown the pursuing Egyptians.

But for J, who had not known exile, the deliverance was a less vital story than either version of the origins, primeval and patriarchal. (The crisis for J's Yahweh arrives at Sinai in his confrontation with the unruly host of the Israelites.)[21] The Israelites follow the lead of the pillar of cloud by day, the pillar of fire by night. Pharaoh and his troops overtake the fugitives at the Sea of Reeds.

Moses comforts the terrified Israelites, and the cloud reverses direction: it ceases to lead and, in a darkened form, comes between the fugitives and the Egyptian pursuers so they must stop. In the darkness, a great Yahwistic wind leaves the seabed bare. J concentrates on the Egyptians, who flee into the full seabed and all of them are drowned.

J also emphasizes the terror of both Israelites and Egyptians while showing Moses at his best[22]—excellent dramaturgy! We may assume J's version was easier (better?) to perform than others.

The flight from Egypt was connected to the Passover, an archaic sacrifice practised for generations among the nomadic ancestors of the Hebrews. By linking it with the Exodus they incorporated it into Yahwism and gave it new life.

Thus *a ritual was interpreted as history*. This tendency became characteristic of Yahwistic monotheism and it was continued by Christianity. As a result, generations of believers have thought that these ritual events and personages were factual whereas they were fictional. Actual events and actual people may have existed but they have been known through their dramatized form.

The Bible states that 600,000 men fled from Egypt, not counting dependants;[23] this, however, was probably an exaggeration—a dramatization, like the life-spans of early personages. It is possible, too, that different groups of slaves fled by various routes. The crossing of the Sea of Reeds probably occurred near the modern El Kantara, on the marshes near the lakes to the north of the Suez Canal. It is likely that the Hebrews crossed the Sea of Reeds over a dry lake bed, parched by a sirocco. Later a rainstorm turned it into a swamp and bogged down the pursuing Egyptians. This became dramatized in a simpler form:

> At the blast of thy nostrils the waters piled up,
> The floods stood in a heap.[24]

It was this ritual tradition that came to be written in *Exodus* 14: 22.

The records of Egypt do not mention the Exodus. This is hardly surprising. The escape of a group of slaves was an insignificant event to them.

IN THE DESERT

The long march of the Israelites took the better part of a human life; a journey of forty years is either a dream or a tragic mistake, particularly in the physical conditions of Sinai and the Negev. At the very start of the wandering at Mara, or the bitter waters, J says that Moses led Israel from the Sea of Reeds and entered the desert where they walked three days without finding water. They arrived at Mara, yet could not drink there because the water was bitter. The people grumbled about Moses, saying, "What will we drink?" He cried out to Yahweh. Yahweh revealed a tree to him which he threw "into the water, and the water turned sweet. It was there he turned the law concrete, putting them to the test" (152).[25] They expected that Moses, having led them for three days into the desert, would naturally know where he was going. If not, he was either a fool or a lunatic using a dramatic context—but for Yahweh it was just the way he was.

Parts of the "Sinai theophany" have been preserved in the J version in *Exodus* 19 and 24. Ironically, Yahweh is not only almost berserk but keeps warning Moses to tell the people to take care because their God knows that he is about to go out of control. (We should note that warriors like Anglo-Saxons and Vikings often prided themselves on being "berserkers"—possessed like shamans.) Yahweh is furious at the behaviour of the Israelites, shown by J as the actions of a mass of refugees enduring privation in desolate places. The wandering people, accountably, denounce Moses and Yahweh who have led them into their difficulty.[26]

For the first time, J's Yahweh is overwhelmingly self-contradictory when confronted with all the Israelites. J's Sinai theophany marks the moment of the Blessing's transition from the élite Moses family to all the Israelites, and a crisis of representation appears in J for the first time.[27] Yahweh said to Moses: "I will come to you in a thick cloud, that the people may hear that I speak with you and that they may trust you forever afterward." When Moses reported the people's words to Yahweh, Yahweh replied: "Go to the people, warn them to be continent today and tomorrow. They should be prepared, for on the third day Yahweh will descend upon Mount Sinai, in the sight of all the people." Yahweh then set restrictions on the people, saying:

> Beware of climbing the mountain or touching the border of it. Whoever touches the mountain shall be put to death; no hand shall touch him, but either he shall be stoned or shot; whether beast or man, he shall not live. When there is a loud blast of the ram's horn, then they may ascend the mountain.

Moses repeated his message to the people.[28]

Sinai is taboo, but is this only a taboo of touch? What about seeing Yahweh? It is likely that E filled in verses 16, 17 and 19; but in verse 18 we clearly hear J's voice: "Now Mount Sinai was all in smoke, for the Lord had come down upon it in fire; the smoke rose like the smoke of a kiln, and all the people trembled violently."[29] So J continues: "Yahweh came down upon Mount Sinai, on the mountain top," and said to Moses: "Go down, warn the people not to break through to gaze at Yahweh, lest many of them die. And the priests who come near Yahweh must purify themselves, lest Yahweh break forth against them." Moses reminded Yahweh of his previous restrictions so Yahweh said to Moses: "Go down and come back with Aaron, but do not allow the priests or the people to break through to come up to Yahweh, lest Yahweh break out against them." And Moses descended to the people and spoke to them.[30]

This is the first time that Yahweh has been a potential horror, and it occurs in the change from an élite to a whole people. For J, the true Covenant was a dramatic *agon* with Abram, Jacob, Joseph and David, but not with Moses nor with Solomon. With Moses and the mass of the people, J's Yahweh becomes dangerously confused—he both favours and threatens the host of the people.[31]

There is a tradition that the Hebrews went from Mount Sinai (Horeb) in the south of the Sinai peninsula, to the oasis at Kadesh in the north, before occupying Canaan. Was this true? The appearance of Yahweh in the desert is accompanied by smoke and earthquakes, like the old thunder-god of the Aryans, yet neither Mount Sinai nor Kadesh had volcanos in this period. The nearest volcanic field was in the northern Hejaz in the land of Midian. There was a link between Moses and the nomadic tribe of Jethro[32] whose daughter he married[33]—a Kenite clan of nomadic smiths associated with Midian. Did the Kenites, or Midians, leave volcanic Hejaz to go to Kadesh? Did they take their ritual myths of an original mountain sanctuary with them?[34]

As the Israelites leave Sinai, Moses makes a very human request to his reluctant brother-in-law: he needs a guide through the Wilderness, and he feels that he never will overcome his reluctance to lead. In *Numbers* 13 Moses sends spies to Canaan: the spies cut down a huge branch of grapes and also bring back a vision of the Nephilim of *Genesis* 6:4—giants, fruit of the union between Elohim and mortal women—for whom J creates a wonderful metaphor: the spies say that the Israelites looked like grasshoppers to the Nephilim. The Israelites weep in fear, and wish to choose "a captain back for Egypt."

Moses has to cajole Yahweh again for the lives of the people. (J, who is deeply disillusioned with Rehoboam and Jeroboam, contrasts the wanderers in the Wilderness and their descendants, David and his warriors.) J also tells of a Reubenite defiance of Moses, punished by being swallowed up by the earth to go alive down into Sheol, the Hades-like underworld. What Moses calls for, and receives from Yahweh, is a negative creation, and the horrified Israelites run screaming away lest they are also swallowed up by the earth—another fabulous tale, probably from ritual.[35]

Of all the fabulous events in J's story, the most terrifying is Yahweh's attempt to murder his prophet Moses (*Exodus* 4:24–26) without cause or reason. Something was probably cut from J's text here.[36]

The Covenant

In the desert, Yahweh appeared to Moses and the Israelites to make a Covenant with them.[37] Later Moses had a second conversation with God and received the "two tablets of the Testimony, tablets of stone inscribed by the finger of God."[38] The present text cannot date from the time of Moses and, in the parts written by J, the Covenant was affected by a sacred meal on top of the mountain where Moses, Aaron and his two eldest sons, together with seventy elders, "beheld God, and ate and drank."[39] In still another part, probably written by E, all Israel took part in the Covenant ceremony at the foot of the mountain where a sacrifice was made; Moses built an altar at which animals were sacrificed, half the blood being dashed against the altar, and the other half sprinkled upon the people to mark the Covenant.[40] In the J tradition the people were only involved through their representatives (a ritual tradition); but in the E tradition the people took part directly—and both approaches were put together in *Exodus* 24.

After the escape into the desert, the struggle against false gods began when the daughters of the Moabites persuaded the Israelites to sacrifice to their gods.[41] But the Second Commandment did not prohibit the cult of idols; rather, *it prohibited the representation of Yahweh by a cult object*. Yahweh had human qualities and faults; also his "wrath" was at times so irrational that he had a demonic fury like the Indian Kali, the Hittite Telipinu, and the Canaanite Anath. This mix of traditions stems from dramatization—the ritual performance was reinterpreted by several biblical authors at different times.

The Covenant Code shows the agricultural interests of later Israel rather than the nomadic needs of the Hebrews in the desert. Nor were the Commandments very original: from the time of Hammurbai of Babylon (c.1700 B.C.) there had been a known universal moral law, and the rules of

Yahweh were part of this Near Eastern pattern. The novelty was in the *giving*: for the first time moral law was revealed prophetically as an expression of the moral will of one God. Moreover, the Commandments in *Exodus* 34 (J's version) agree only in part with the more familiar versions in *Exodus* 20 and *Deuteronomy* 5. In J morality is absent and the Commandments are related to ritual.

Bloom surmises that in J's original text the Commandments, however phrased, came *after* some fragments of J that we still have in what is now *Exodus* 24. Then Yahweh told Moses to come up to him, "with Aaron, Nadab, and Abihu, and seventy elders of Israel, and bow low but from afar. And only Moses shall come near Yahweh." The seventy-three did not come near (the people did not come up with him at all) but they saw the God of Israel—under his feet there was the likeness of a pavement of sapphire, like the very sky for purity[42] as Martin Buber in *Moses* says:

> They have presumably wandered through clinging, hanging mist before dawn; and at the very moment they reach their goal, the swaying darkness tears asunder (as I myself happened to witness once) and dissolves except for one cloud already transparent with the hue of the still unrisen sun. The sapphire proximity of the heavens overwhelms the aged shepherds of the Delta, who have never before tasted, who have never been given the slightest idea, of what is shown in the play of early light over the summits of the mountains. And this precisely is perceived by the representatives of the liberated tribes as that which lies under the feet of their enthroned *Melek*.

But if J wanted us to believe that the seventy-three elders of Israel saw only a natural radiance, Bloom remarks, he would have said so. Yet J is blunt: "they beheld God." The one visual detail J provides: "Under his feet there was the likeness of a pavement of sapphire, like the very sky for purity" is a great image.[43] As at Mamre, Yahweh sits on the ground, and yet it is as if the sky were beneath his feet—as if the world had been turned upside down. This, says Bloom, is a *dramatic* confusion that J's Yahweh had to show if his Blessing was to reach an entire people.[44]

The early version of the Commandments was probably taken by author J from a dramatic *scenario* and, when separated from its present literary setting, is as follows:

[1]   Thou shalt worship no other god.

[2]   Thou shalt make thee no molten gods.

[3]   The feast of the Passover thou shalt keep.

[4]   The firstling of an ass thou shalt redeem with a lamb; all the firstborn of thy sons thou shalt redeem.

[5]   None shall appear before me empty.

[6]   Six days shalt thou work, but on the seventh thou shalt rest.

[7]   Thou shalt observe the feast of ingathering.

[8]   Thou shalt not offer the blood of my sacrifice with leavened bread, neither shall the sacrifice of the Passover remain until morning.

[9]   The firstlings of thy flocks thou shalt bring unto Yahweh, thy God.

[10] Thou shalt not seethe a kid in his mother's milk.[45]

This, the oldest version of the Ten Commandments, was entirely concerned with practical ritual.

When J's Moses smashes the tablets of the Law, he is petulant and impatient. J's irony here is twofold: [1] everyone—the people, Aaron, Moses, even Yahweh—mistakes the calves, the platform of God, for godlings in their own right (which is unfair on Jeroboam); and [2] the people now carry the Blessing of the Patriarchs, as Moses properly reminds Yahweh, but it makes no pragmatic difference whatsoever. The broken tablets are replaced by Yahweh's fresh order to Moses, who at dawn presents himself on top of Sinai, the new stone tablets in his hands. There Yahweh proclaims himself, with terrifying self-knowledge: "Jealous One is my name, Jealous Yahweh" (164). What Yahweh dictates to Moses, according to J, is rather different from the P and Deuteronomist versions of the Ten Commandments. There are more than ten, and a comparison of the three versions of the Commandments is bewildering. J's emphasis is much more pragmatic than ethical; Yahweh is passionately concerned with what is his, the firstborn, which must be redeemed by sacrifice. The irony is that J has shown us the triumph of the younger sons throughout. In J's Commandments there are not the crucial "shall nots"—swear falsely, murder, commit adultery, etc.—and the elders "beheld God, and ate and drank."[46] In still another part, probably written by E, all Israel took part in the covenant ceremony at the foot of the mountain where a sacrifice was made; Moses built an altar at which animals were sacrificed, half the blood being dashed against the altar, and the other half sprinkled upon the people to mark the covenant.[47] In the J tradition the people were only involved through their representatives (a ritual tradition); but in the E tradition the people took part directly—and both approaches were put together in *Exodus 24*—which may have seemed too obvious to J.[48]

Balaam

J's splendidly controlled irony in the Balaam story (*Numbers* 22–24) is best seen in the great passage of Balaam and his sensible ass. There are also indications that behind it lies a ritual drama. The story, despite its comedy in J, is taken very seriously by subsequent Jewish legend.[49] In J, Balaam is a prophet-for-hire who fears Yahweh and will not curse those whom Yahweh has blessed. Balaam's ass, like the serpent in Eden, is a talking animal. Martin Noth comments: "At the heart of it lies the idea that an unprejudiced animal can see things to which a man in his wilfulness is blind; there is certainly also in this respect the presupposition that Yahweh's messenger was in himself 'visible' in the usual way."[50]

Balaam can only see the actual but Balaam's sensible ass sees Yahweh's angel standing in the way with a drawn sword. The ass swerves into the fields and receives a first beating from Balaam. Confronting the angel in a fenced lane, the ass presses herself against the wall, thus squeezing Balaam's foot against it and provokes a second beating. When the angel stations himself where swerving is impossible, the ass lies down, carrying the furious Balaam with her. As he beats her with his stick—

Now Yahweh opened the ass's mouth. "What did I do to you," she said, "to make you lash out at me on three occasions?" "Because you have been riding me," Balaam said to the ass. "If I had a sword in my hand, it would whip you dead this time."

"No! Aren't I your own ass? I'm the ass you've been riding on as long as you've owned me," said the ass to Balaam. "Have I been trying—to this day—to make an ass of you?" And he: "No." (174).[51]

The humour lies in the terrible context. The Israelites are staggering out of the Wilderness toward Canaan with rebellions and laments. Moses leads them, by now half-mad, calling for earth to swallow up people and similar ghastly punishments. The she-ass is more human and more likeable than anyone else, divine or mortal, in *Numbers*. There is an implicit parallel between her protest at Balaam's violence and the grumblings of the Israelites at their hardships, and their inability to protest against the vengeful violence of Moses and Yahweh.[52]

The narrative and ritual traditions of the ancient Near East, as well as the Israelites, include the repetition of three parallel incidents; and vocal beasts (usually monsters, but not always) are common in ritual-myths (e.g., in the Akîtu).

The Desert Ritual

We do not know when the Commandments in *Exodus* 34 were first written as ritual instructions. It could have been in the desert or, perhaps, in Canaan. Nothing definite is known concerning the performance of the ritual-myth during the forty years the Hebrews spent in the desert. However, we can conjecture a wilderness Festival to honour Yahweh where the ritual drama focuses on the flight from Egypt. The most ancient of Hebrew rituals of which we know was *The Book of the Wars of Yahweh*,[53] a collection of songs telling what happened in the journeys through the desert. From the same period come the song to the well,[54] the sentence about Amalek,[55] and the song of the Ark.[56]

The first thing that happened, after the pharaoh and his army had been destroyed and the Hebrews entered the desert, was that Miriam called for a song of adoration: "Sing to Yahweh, for he has been greatly exalted."[57] Song, music and dance were essential parts of popular religious festivity and it is likely that they were plentiful in the desert rituals.

Shortly, however, the annual Festival of Yahwism was also the celebration of the Exodus. It is probable that at the first encampment of the tribes after their escape, when they felt themselves secure, they celebrated their first holyday in song and dance to Yahweh. They baked *massoth*—a favourite quick dish in these lands to the present—out of the provisions they had brought with them from Egypt. And this became an annual celebration thereafter. From the start the Festival absorbed an older pagan spring rite of sacrifice of firstlings. Firstlings had been sacrificed and their blood smeared on doorposts to ward off evil spirits.[58] Later, in Canaan, this was assimilated to the legend of the rescue of the firstborn in Egypt and became part of the Moses Festival Play.

The Golden Calves

J's voice is heard again in the story of the golden calf (*Exodus* 32:7–14), although Deuteronomic diction masks the original J material, and 32:25–29 is not J's.

There is clear irony in the golden calf incident, which makes reference to Jeroboam and his breakaway kingdom of Israel, the northern rival to Rehoboam's Judah. Resentful that his subjects continued to go south to Solomon's Temple in Jerusalem, Jeroboam made two golden calves and set up rival shrines at Bethel and Dan, opposite ends of his kingdom.

The story (in *1 Kings* 12:26–33) projects a vision of Yahweh looming above the whole kingdom of Israel: the calves were seen as the platform-throne of Yahweh, just as the sphinx-like cherubim in Solomon's Temple enthroned God. J, who may be trying to work out the idea of a stage-platform, is very funny: Jeroboam's attempt to replace Solomon's Temple is equated with the Israelite host's betrayal of Moses while he is up on the mountain with Yahweh.

The formula, "These be your gods, O Israel, that brought you up from the land of Egypt," defiantly sounded by Jeroboam, is ascribed by J to the Israelites as Aaron gives them the golden calf (*Exodus* 32–4).[59]

The Tent and the Ark

In the desert was a sanctuary with (at least) two sacred objects: the Tent of Meeting, or Tabernacle;[60] and the Ark,[61] both cultic objects within ritual dramas and ceremonies. The Ark was the focus of processions, often to or from the Tent. It is likely that the Tent sheltered the Ark. The Tent of Meeting was first mentioned at Sinai; then it appeared when the people were at Kadesh and in the wilderness. It must have been something like the red leather tent-shrines known among ancient Semites.

Before the Israelites' arrival in Canaan, the Ark was allegedly a gold inlaid acacia-wood chest containing a stone phallus from Mount Sinai. There is even a tradition that when Nebuchadrezzar occupied Jerusalem in 597 B.C., the Ark was unveiled to reveal a womb symbol enfolding a red-stone phallus. Considering the people's long sojourn in Egypt, and that Isis hid a model of the dead Osiris' phallus in an ark (annually carried to the river by the priests), this should not surprise us. Whether true or not, by the time Joshua crossed the Jordan the people at least *thought of* the Ark as a portable throne on which Yahweh invisibly sat and was present in the midst of his people. According to Herodotus,[62] the Persians similarly carried their invisible god, Ahuramazda, on a wagon to war, while there were several instances of the empty thrones of deities in the Hellenic area.[63]

In the earliest biblical accounts[64] the Ark was a cherub-decorated seat conveyed on a wagon—likely the representation in the Moses Festival Play. Only the Deuteronomic accounts made it into the "Ark of the Covenant," hence the container of the tablets of the laws. In times of wandering or battle, the invisible Yahweh went before the people as their leader, enthroned on the Ark.

The Tent became the shrine of the southern group, especially the tribe of Judah. The Ark came to be identified at Shiloh with the northern group, particularly the Joseph tribes that Joshua led into Canaan. Later in David's ritual drama, these two objects were reunited, and were the responsibility of priests. Priesthood proper was reserved to the family of Aaron, a tradition that might have begun in Egypt. Aaron was the first to receive Moses' message; he became Moses' "mouth" and "prophet." The element of magic, native to Egypt, may have reached the priesthood through Aaron.

The rituals of the Tent were probably very simple. Since it was portable, it required porters and guardians who were Levites, fellow tribesmen of Moses. There was a rivalry between the Aaron priests and Levites: when Aaron made the golden calf for which Yahweh nearly destroyed him, it was the Levites who rallied to Moses and avenged God.[65] How far back did these traditions go? A public cult must have existed in the desert period, including a daily sacrifice, a lamp (cf. *I Samuel* 3: 3), and shewbread (Ibid. 21: 7); "The ritual of the Day of Atonement, with the scapegoat being sent away into the desert ... may also go back to this period."[66]

The simplicity of these rituals, however, contrasted with the complex performance of the Moses Festival Play that evolved once the Hebrews settled in Canaan.

Death of Moses

Deuteronomy absorbed J in two crucial passages: 31:14–15 and 23 where Moses hands over command to Joshua; and 34:1b–5a, 6, and 10, where Moses and Yahweh have their final confrontation, face to face in the mode of Abram.

Moses stands at the end to see the dimensions of an Israel he himself is not permitted to enter. As Bloom points out, there is the same rhetorical structure in the creation of Adam and the death of Moses—Yahweh makes the first man with his own hands, and then buries his chief prophet with his own hands.[67]

But whereas Israel based its salvation on the Exodus from Egypt, the travels and events in the desert, and the gift of the promised land, these were conveyed to them through the Moses Play as they entered Canaan.

6
THE MOSES PLAY

There was an Israelite New Year Festival from Egyptian times. Probably quite small to begin with, it changed with contemporary events. When the Hebrews had crossed the Sea of Reeds, the initial ritual drama incorporated the flight from Egypt, and subsequent events were added over time.

Once the Hebrews had occupied Canaan and begun to form the nation of Israel, they altered the existing Festival ritual drama to cope with their new context: a series of religious ceremonials about Moses and the Exodus was performed as a ritual drama. As those who had fled from Egypt came into contact with others in Canaan—including the Habiru—religious views expanded and that led to a transformation in ritual action. The style and scale of this performance became larger and more lavish than any of the rituals in the desert.

The Book of J

J wrote for listeners (and some readers) who shared his urban sophistication. Yahweh's great acts in legendary history were more about the remote past than about the world in which J lived.[1] *The Book of J* may be the story of Yahweh, but it is not the history of Yahwism. J tells his tale dramatically, with Yahweh as his protagonist and Yahwism as his content.[2] He links a vision of Creation through the patriarchal story to Moses and the Exodus using the original Yahweh Festival Play into which he inserts the Moses Play.

Whether J believed in the historicity of the whole story cannot be judged, but his ironic handling of Moses may mean that he doubts even his historicity. Thus *The Book of J* is written as "a fiction." Paradoxically, J is not a fervent believer in Yahwism, nor is he a religious writer in the same sense as P and R and most others. He is a comic dramatist, full of paradoxes; his rhetoric relies upon the wordplay of false etymologies and puns. Like Shakespeare, J shows that nothing is quite what it seems to be, not even Yahweh.

It is J who introduces the relation of appearance and reality into Western consciousness. He emphasizes process, dynamism and movement more than the external world as we see it. Nor does he tell us what anyone looks like, particularly Yahweh who is not invisible. *J invented the preference for time over space*—hearing over seeing, the spoken word over the visual image.[3]

J's stories are told or retold in scenes. As with any other dramatist's scenes, they are told as if the author was there when they were happening—in the "here and now" as if J was a witness. Much of the original *Book of J* must have been in direct speech. But it was edited and revised by post-Exilic authors until J's heightened language had been irreparably distorted. As David Rosenberg tells us, the play of word with, and within, word produces a basic poetics of diction and rhyme. It is a diction based on Hebrew phrasing that can only be translated into English if it is recreated.[4]

To prefer the spoken word over the visual image is to imitate reality through *mimesis*—basic inter-*action*. J conveys restless interactions between persons, persons and groups, and individuals and groups with Yahweh. Even covenants are forms of interaction, or drama.[5]

THE CONQUEST

Legendary history tells us that the Hebrews who had travelled through the desert with Moses did not directly invade Palestine. First they moved from Kadash in the Negev to the Transjordan. There they faced several recently formed agricultural kingdoms. In the south lay Edom, traditionally related to the Hebrews through Esau. They travelled around Edom, and also around the kingdom to the north of it, Moab. They then faced the Amorite kingdom of Sihon whose king sent an army to crush them. The Hebrews won decisively, occupied the whole kingdom, and then went north to also defeat the king of Bashan, who was a giant called Og. This group of Hebrews thus controlled a large part of the Transjordan to the east of the River Jordan, near Jericho, and were ready for an attack into Canaan to the west. It is at this point that the biblical narrator inserted the story of Balaam.

The invasion of Canaan is told in *Joshua*. This book is permeated with the later Deuteronomic theme of obedience to Yahweh will be rewarded with victory and prosperity; but disobedience will bring the divine judgment of suffering and failure. Author D also tells us, in *Joshua* 1–12, of the sudden conquest of the promised land. However, the older J tradition (in *Judges* 1 and elsewhere) shows a more gradual infiltration. Scholars indicate[6] that there is truth in both views—the Hebrews both attacked swiftly and infiltrated slowly, mingling with the Habiru.

Joshua 1-12 tells the story in a mythic and glorified way: Joshua led three swift campaigns, in the first of which he achieved a firm foot-hold on the west of the Jordan and camped at Gilgal. The crossing of the River Jordan, however, was made heroic by a tradition that the river was dammed upstream so that the Hebrews could ford the Jordan with the Ark in the lead. This legend may have an historical precedent: a real landslide took place at Adam (the modern ed-Damiyeh), which was not the place where they forded the river. The parallel of this crossing of the River Jordan with the crossing of the Sea of Reeds—one mirrors the other—is obviously a ritual tradition. Repetitions and parallels are a sure sign that a myth covers a ritual practice.

The *Joshua* story goes on to say that, from Gilgal, Joshua laid siege to Jericho and conquered it. This famous tale—the Hebrews going round the city in circles with trumpets blazing and the walls tumbling down—is clearly a description of a ritual.

After Jericho, Joshua then captured Ai (probably confused with Bethel), a hill town a few miles to the north. Finding no resistance, he marched on to Shechem where he built an altar and established the first large-scale ceremonial. Part of this was the Moses Play, the focus of our attention here. At Shechem, Joshua made a Covenant with the people whereby they were organized into a twelve-tribe confederacy. Eventually the centre was moved to Shiloh, to which the dramatic ritual was also transferred.

The nature of monotheism altered with actual events. After the simple beliefs and rituals in the desert, the occupation of the promised land changed human needs and, thus, complicated the beliefs, myths, and rituals.

Historically, after the invasion there may have been a decisive campaign, led by Joshua, that enabled the Hebrews to occupy the southern hill country and deal the Canaanites a great blow. But although the Israelites occupied various city states, they were not so successful against the people of the plains who had Iron Age weapons. The Bible says that the final campaign took place to the north of the Valley of Jezreel (later known as Galilee), where Israel won a decisive battle at Hazor. Most likely, however, the conquest of the rest of Canaan by the Hebrews was facilitated by treaty, intermarriage and absorption. There is no archeological evidence for further battles.

Slowly all the tribes came to accept Yahweh. This was particularly the case (in the biblical version) after brilliant victories: Yahweh directly intervened in battle with remarkable results; and the war was waged as a holy war. The values of the herders began to be loosened; for example, Jael treacherously broke the sacrosanct law of hospitality when she invited the Canaanite chief, Sisera, into her tent and killed him in his sleep.

The Tent, or Tabernacle, was no longer used and worship took place in sanctuaries and sacred sites. And the beliefs of the Hebrews began to mingle with the Canaanites.

These religious changes began while Joshua was alive, but continued over a long period of time. It is most likely that the nature of the ritual drama continually changed right up until the time of the Exile.

THE SCRIPT

Today the original script does not exist. But scholarship has managed to provide a modern translation of what was said and done in The Moses Festival Play.

Textual Matters

The biblical description of the Exodus was taken from ancient sources which were records of a sacred drama, probably *scenarii*. This leads us to examine details of textual matters in the Bible. Modern scholarship, specifically that of J.N.M.Wijngaards, has shown that the Exodus story as written in *The Book of J* is full of references to "you have seen" (in modern terms, "before your own eyes"). And what was seen was a performance of almost theatrical quality—not quite, however, for the first theatrical performance in the West was of Aeschylus in Athens.

Thus when the oracle of *Exodus* says, "You have seen what I did to the Egyptians, and how I bore you on eagle's wings and brought you to Myself (i.e. to the sanctuary at Sinai),"[7] this is one of ten such passages showing that Israel has *witnessed* the performance of an Exodus ceremonial.[8]

Among all known tribal peoples, ancient and modern, *witnessing* is necessary for the act to be real and effective. The presence of a participating audience gives the act communal authority—they can then testify to its validity.

As merely one contemporary example, the purpose of the *potlatch* on the Pacific Northwest Coast of Canada is to validate the high rank given to a chief's son during the performance of a ritual-myth. Any dramatic act exists in the present tense—"the here and now"—so that the performance event brings the past into the present. Those in attendance witness the *potlatch*; they are given gifts to take home so that those not present at the performance are also regarded as having witnessed it. The rank is thereby validated by "all the people." Other examples abound among traditional hunting and fishing peoples.

The Hebrews, by *witnessing* the acts of the dramatic performance, made the Moses Festival Play into a living event where salvation existed in the present tense. As John Gray indicates:

> The tradition of the genesis of Israel, whatever its original historical character, [had] become a Drama of Salvation. This dramatical and theological character of the tradition transforms history, and incidentally renders in vain all attempts to reconstruct the circumstances of the Exodus by the literalistic interpretation of details.[9]

These ten biblical references to the *witnessing* of the Moses Play affect our understanding of other passages. By witnessing public acts, Israel *sees "signs"*—thus phrases like "So that you may know that I am Yahweh" (or equivalents) occur frequently in the battle between Yahweh and the idealized Pharaoh in Egypt, and in the victory at the Sea of Reeds.

In other words, the performance of these events forces the witnessing Israel to acknowledge that they are signs—that Yahweh is the Lord.[10] The ten passages showing the witnessing of a dramatic performance are merely one example, says Wijngaards, of the ritual remnants left by biblical authors. Another instance is when the Exodus theme occurs all by itself; that is, without the theme of the Land-giving.

Then it is usually embedded in *direct speech*—specific words spoken in the ritual; thus "I am Yahweh, who led you out of Egypt" (or equivalents) occurs sixteen times; and "The people which You have led out of Egypt" (or equivalents) occurs eight times.[11] These are liturgical phrases spoken within the dramatic performance of the ritual-myth that proclaimed Yahweh as "God of the Exodus."

A further example occurs when the law is proclaimed. Then two ritual sayings are repeated: [a] "I am Yahweh" when motivating the law on the grounds of God's holiness; and [b] "I am Yahweh your God" when motivating the law with the historical benefits.[12]

Stylistic Matters

These textual matters lead to a major stylistic feature of the Exodus as written by J: the constant repetition of events that are "signs." This also includes the use of parallels: one event mirrors another, as we have seen with the crossing of the Sea of Reeds and the River Jordan. This repetitious style in prose and verse is always a major indicator that, buried deep within it, are the remnants of a ritual performance.

Repetition particularly applies in the battle between Yahweh and the Pharaoh—the poisoned Nile, the frogs, the hornets, the cattle diseases, the hailstones, the locusts, the terrifying darkness, the death of the firstborn and, finally, the climax in the defeat of the Egyptian army at the Sea of Reeds. In each episode there is usually the following sequence:

* Yahweh's word to Moses;
* Moses' demand in Pharaoh's court; the threat of a sign;
* Pharaoh's refusal;
* Moses calling down the sign;
* description of the sign;
* Pharaoh's request to have the sign removed;
* Moses' prayer effecting the removal; and
* Pharaoh's hardening of his heart.[13]

This type of ritual repetition is universally common. All over the ancient Near East, ritual-myths were performed through a simple structure of action which was repeated over and over again. Once we realize this, we can imagine the ancient ritual performer declaiming, "You have seen all I did to Egypt!"[14] or the modern English mummer declaiming, "I am St George!"

Nor is repetition the only stylistic feature that is revelatory of an original dramatic ritual. As we shall see below, the scene structure, the *agon* between *protagonist* and *antagonist*, together with other stylistic matters, indicate a ritual origin.

David Rosenberg tells us that not all the "he says" and "she says" and "God spoke untos" are part of a primitive style but sometimes merely a form of punctuation: quotation marks. or stage directions. Often the pronoun is wilfully indistinct, like the tense. For a moment we are unsure who is speaking. Yet this too allows the author playful ambiguities. To ignore this drama of the Hebrew narrative—as translations sometimes do—removes poetry from the text.[15]

Wijngaards also shows that Yahweh's important speech, "Let my people go that they may serve Me!" dominates the whole play:

The demand is phrased in juridical terminology. It could freely be translated to mean: "Give up your claim on this slave so that he may be in my service!" It is truly the leitmotif of the story: it marks the beginning of many a new episode (*Exodus* 7: 16; 7: 26; 8: 16; 9: 1; 9: 13; 10: 3); it becomes increasingly exacting in the course of the dispute; it is brought to a dramatic and triumphant conclusion in Israel's passage through the Sea of Reeds and the Covenant at Sinai.[16]

The Bible also reveals the beginnings of the Moses Festival Play as the Israelites reached the promised land. At the heart of the Hexateuch lies an archaic ritual:

> The Wandering Aramean was my father; and he went down into Egypt and sojourned there, few in numbers; and there he became a nation, great, mighty, and populous. And the Egyptians treated us harshly, and afflicted us, and laid upon us hard bondage. Then we cried to the Lord, the God of our fathers, and the Lord heard our voice and saw our affliction, our toil, and our oppression; and the Lord brought us out of Egypt with a mighty hand and an outstretched arm, with great terror, with signs and wonders; and He brought us into this place and gave us this land, a land flowing with milk and honey. And behold, now I bring the first half of the fruit of the ground, which Thou O Lord has given me.[17]

This is from a source probably at least as old as Joshua. The themes of this liturgy are elaborated at greater length in the Hexateuch, so that we can think of this passage as "the Hexateuch in Miniature." This archaic ritual came originally from a dramatic ceremonial in the wanderings in the desert.

Then, "In Israel the pagan Festival lost its magical-natural basis and became assimilated to the historical legend of the rescue of Israelite firstborn in Egypt and the Exodus."[18] It was from this old liturgy that the Moses Play developed, and was first fully performed after Joshua had led the Israelites into the promised land. There is little doubt that the coordinating force in the final version, celebrating the Coronation of Yahweh, was that of Joshua.

The design of the Moses Festival Play is highly effective. It ends not with the Conquest of Canaan or with the Judges, Saul, David or Solomon, but with a longing prospect of Yahweh's promise fulfilled. The images of exile in the earliest Israelite history culminate in the Wilderness and in the death of Moses, still outside the land.

THE SITE OF THE FIRST PERFORMANCES

After conquering Canaan, Joshua gathered all the tribes outside Shechem—an important fortress, a religious site, and the first centre of the Israelite confederacy. There the Moses Play took place. With the assembled Israelite tribes and their leaders as witnesses, Joshua rehearsed Israel's "sacred history." In their ears rang the warning that Yahweh is a jealous God, a holy God, who would not tolerate the worship of "strange gods." The people affirmed their decision to serve Yahweh, who brought them out of Egypt and guided them into Canaan. The ceremony concluded with the making of a Covenant, the giving of law, and the erection of the memorial stone beneath the sacred tree.[19]

When the tribes gathered at Shechem, half were arranged on Mount Gerizim and half on Mount Ebal as an antiphonal chorus—both of them facing the priests who acted out the ceremonial. It is likely that the performers were raised on a stone platform hewn out of rock. This ceremony was a reaffirmation of the sacred Covenant that was made at Sinai.

By creating a major ceremonial, Joshua unified his people. Subsequently, as the ceremonial was expanded to include the travels in the desert (the processional) and the Land-giving (the conquest of Canaan), the site of the performance changed. Joshua had formed the dramatic tradition of Jewry that has lasted until the present day—even if it is not through a Festival play.

THE STRUCTURE OF THE PERFORMANCE

The Moses Play was one part of a total ritual Festival structure that demonstrated the symbolic enthronement of Yahweh and the celebration of his mighty acts, probably as follows:

[1] The call to assembly.[20]
[2] The ritual-myth:
    [a] The Moses Play; and
    [b] The Land-giving.[21]

[3] Call to decision for or against Yahweh.[22]
[4] Removal of foreign gods.[23]
[5] The Covenant ceremony.[24]
[6] The reading of the covenant law.[25]
[7] The ceremony of blessings and cursings.[26]
[8] The dismissal of the tribal representatives.[27]

The whole ceremonial may have taken place for seven days in the autumn, the New Year of the Israelites.

From this structure, it is immediately obvious that it bears a great resemblance to the New Year Festival of Babylon, the Akîtu, which over the centuries had influenced the structure of the Canaanite ceremonial performances at their New Year. Joshua, the successful general, was also the master of cultural assimilation. Despite the fact that he used the Babylonian-Canaanite Festival *structure*, he placed within it the *content* of the monotheism of Yahwism.

The Place of the Creation

Yet it is probable that Joshua did not take over the Babylonian structure whole.

The Akîtu Festival had contained two parts: Creation and Coronation. The Moses Play was clearly similar to the Coronation drama, and there is a tradition that the ceremonial contained no Creation. Was this the case? Or was there, perhaps, a Creation Festival Play performed alongside the Moses Festival Play? Or was it performed separately?

In *Genesis* there are two stories of Creation: in Chapter 1–2: 4a there is a version produced by editors writing after the Exile; in Chapter 2: 4b–25 there is a much earlier story possibly first written by J. And other references in the Jewish Bible (Old Testament) and in Hebrew poetry suggest that many forms of the Creation myth may have been current in Israel. The motif of Creation in the later Exile allowed no forces opposed to Yahweh in his act of creation:

all powers are entirely subject to his sovereign will. Nonetheless, in the temple rituals there must have been occasions on which the community employed references to Yahweh's overthrow of the powers of chaos as he established order. These references have been removed or relegated to the position of poetic embellishment of texts used in the cult.[28]

Where there are conflicts, the basis may be ritual. With no conflict there was probably no dramatic action.

As far as we can tell, the ritual dramatist concentrated his attention on Yahweh's treatment of the people on earth. This is explicable because, unlike the pharaohs, Israel's earthly kings were not divine in the sense that they represented incarnations of Yahweh.

Other ancient Near Eastern ritual dramas showed one group of gods confronting a second group. In strict contrast, the Moses Play had one God, Yahweh, confronting a man, the symbolic Pharaoh. Yet: "the creation story comes in connection with the harvest Festival ... It belongs, has its place in the ceremony, but in a different context."[29]

Did the Yahweh Festival, which was performed before the entry into Canaan to celebrate both agriculture and Yahweh, include the stories of the Creation and the Patriarchs? If so, it was probably slowly altered during the desert wanderings and, as Canaan was occupied, it became a second festival. Or did it remain as background to the Moses Festival Play, celebrating Yahweh's victory on behalf of the people, in occupying the promised land?

The Moses Festival Play

The Moses Festival Play focused on the Coronation of Yahweh, and showed his power through the events of the Exodus. The beginning of the nation was traced to this miraculous happening: "God, who brought thee out of the land of Egypt, out of the house of bondage"[30] was a statement of God's control over nature and humanity. It was the Exodus that kept Israel firm in the knowledge of God's love: his purpose was a saving purpose, and his righteousness was concerned with the weak and the dispossessed. The victory of Yahweh over Egypt was, in essence, a Holy War by which Yahweh, once and for all, brought Israel into existence. It was the primordial war of salvation which may be compared to the earlier primordial war by which Yahweh achieved Creation.

The Moses Play had four acts with some of the scenes indicated in *Exodus*:

[1]   The miracles in Egypt.
    [a]   Moses sent from Sinai[31]
    [b]   The first encounter with Pharaoh[32]
    [c]   The Nile turned into blood[33]
    [d]   The frogs[34]
    [e]   The hornets[35]
    [f]   The plague on the cattle[36]
    [g]   The hailstones[37]
    [h]   The locusts[38]
    [I]   The darkness[39]
    [j]   The firstborn[40]
[2]   The miraculous crossing of the Sea of Reeds.[41]
    [k]   The covenantal invitation[42]
    [l]   The conclusion of the covenant[43]
[3]   The journey through the desert.
[4]   And perhaps, the arrival "in this place."[44]

The dramaturgical structure had a natural symmetry. The crossing of the Sea of Reeds [2] was clearly the climax to the miracles in Egypt [1], just as the arrival [4] was the culmination of the desert journey [3].   This sophisticated design may possibly have had more of J than any *scenario*.

PERFORMERS AND WITNESSES

The people of Israel were the cultic community. Within the ritual-myth they had two roles: those on the mountainsides *witnessed* the drama and the ceremonial; those on the acting area (priests and acolytes) *experienced* the drama as groups of actors. Israel's witnessing of Yahweh's deeds made them into public, legal acts.

In the actual dramatic ceremony there were three groups of performers:

* The leading group was led by Yahweh, the protagonist, supported by the characters of Moses and Aaron, as secondary actors.[45]
* Yahweh's antagonist was the Pharaoh,[46] supported by his courtiers, his army, or frequently "the Egyptians."
* The third group was the "witnesses": Israel itself assembled on the mountainsides.

These kinds of performers were common to the performance of all ritual-myths in agricultural societies.

The Israelites witnessed Yahweh saving them. At Shechem the people were an integral part of a ritual drama where consecrated priests symbolized actions and hallowed formulations—the symbolic Yahweh annihilated the symbolic Pharaoh and his court with ritually determined actions and formulae. The liberation of Israel from Egypt was the first major theme. Like all liturgical plays of this type, there was a simple structural action which was repeated over and over again. The signs which Yahweh worked, which forced Egypt to surrender, repeated a similar pattern, and each followed one another in a crescendo performed in ritual stylization.

This stylization did not make the performance "theatrical" in the sense used of theatres in modern industrialized societies of the West. It is true that Western theatre evolved from ritual drama, specifically in the case of Greek tragedy and comedy and, later, with Renaissance plays. The fundamental difference between ritual drama and theatre lies in two factors:

* ritual actors use mimesis (generalized action) while theatrical actions use mime (realistic action).
* in ritual drama, those who are not performing are witnesses; in theatre they provide the audience.

In modern Western theatre, however, there is a clear separation between performers and audience; they do not necessarily share the same religion or value system; the audience, far from being witnesses, are more like voyeurs.

The Performers

The Israelite actors performed in stylized fashion: each had the same characteristic attitudes, made the same symbolic gestures, and repeated their stock phrases. Tension was maintained:

* by introducing slight variations;
* by intensifying the conflict of demand and refusal; and
* by introducing different and increasingly severe "signs."

These signs were carefully arranged to symbolize a gradual climax of devastating punishments. The signs had a specific purpose: Yahweh was showing his power "that you may acknowledge that I am Yahweh!" The reason why Yahweh allowed Pharaoh to harden his heart was "in order that I might be able to work My signs among them, so that you could tell your sons and grandsons what I did to the Egyptians and which signs I wrought among them; that you might acknowledge that I am Yahweh!"[47]

The dramatic contrast of Pharaoh was exploited to the full. The symbolic Pharaoh became a test case of unbelief; the *antagonist* representing all sceptics and religious rebels. Within the drama, Moses' function was as mediator: he acted as Yahweh's messenger with Egypt—he proposed the pact[48] and mediated the sacrificial ratification.[49]

The Vitality of Yahweh

We know virtually nothing about an archaic Yahweh, of whom there are survivals in J. But we know that J's Yahweh was very different from the God of the Bible. He may have been a solitary warrior-god, sometimes surrounded by a wilful group of angels, who were not pleased by the creation of humankind.[50] We may assume that J's model for Yahweh was an actor—the priest (or priests) who acted Yahweh's role in Solomon's time or a little later. As Bloom puts it,[51] by normative standards, Jewish or Christian, J's portrayal of Yahweh is blasphemy; rather like a Shakespearean character who runs off the page into our lives. At the start, J's Yahweh is large and vivid—a being free of inhibitions. Over time, the player recognized that Yahweh changed; he developed anxieties brought on by his fury when he thought any of his creatures showed contempt for him. By the time he chooses Moses, presides over the Exodus, and makes his Covenant at Sinai in the Moses Play, the player of Yahweh is more uncertain. Finally, when Moses is buried, the player is quite a different figure from the Yahweh who shaped Adam.

Much later, from the return from the Babylonian Exile, J was considerably revised by those who regarded writing as a form of sacrifice or worship—strictly "religious writing"—and denied drama. This contrasted with J. The "scandal" of J, as Bloom puts it,[52] is that his Yahweh is, simultaneously and paradoxically, both very human and also non-human—a deliberately comic creation.

Vitality is the prime characteristic of J's Yahweh, since all life whatsoever has been brought into being by him. Yahweh in J is not a gentle being; his deliberate ironies are ferocious and contradictory. His ironies move toward two limits: [1] at our creation, where Yahweh implicitly says to us, "Be like me; breathe with my breath"; and [2] at the Sinai theophany: "Don't you dare to be too like me."[53]

In the Moses Play, J's version of the Commandments has no Sabbath. His Yahweh *is* presence: he is the will to change—his essence is spontaneity and originality. His main quality is not holiness, justice, love, or righteousness, like the later God of the Jews and the Christians; rather it is the sheer energy and force of Becoming—of bursting into fresh being. What the audience encountered in him was not an abstract Becoming or Being but an outrageous personality.[54]

In the play, J's Moses was no worker of miracles, no founder of a religion, and no military leader. He was an inspired shepherd whom Yahweh used to make his will known to men. He is certainly used, and even ill-used, by Yahweh. Reluctant at first, and then doggedly stubborn, Moses loyally plods along in J.

COSTUME

Fascinatingly, we have a description of the possible design for the stage costume of Aaron. Chapter 39 of *Exodus* is from a late source (probably of the pre-Exilic period) and was designed to explain the divine sanction for the ritual dress of the Jewish high priest. Thus: "And of the blue and purple and scarlet stuff they made finely wrought garments, for ministering in the holy place."[55] Although this description of the costume is late, and describes the priestly dress in the ceremonies just before the Exile, there is every indication that its origin was very old, probably dating back to the period of Joshua.

Aaron's costume served distinctive ritual purposes. The tunic-like *ephod*, the origin and nature of which is surrounded in mystery, was woven of gold, blue, purple and scarlet thread. The use of it was a means of divination connected with some sort of oracle. Into the *ephod* were inserted onyx stones engraved with the "names of the sons of Israel," which were "to be stones of remembrance for the sons of Israel."[56] On the *ephod* was a "breastpiece" of similar composition; it was fixed to the ephod by gold rings. In the breastpiece were set four rows of twelve different precious stones, each engraved with the name of an Israelite tribe.

Attached to the blue robe below the *ephod* were pomegranates and bells of pure gold so that they rang "when he goes into the holy place before the Lord (Yahweh), and when he comes out, lest he die."[57] Pomegranates symbolized fertility in Jewish folklore.

There was then a coat, a bonnet and breeches of "fine linen," and a needlework girdle of blue, purple and scarlet. On his head, Aaron wore a mitre or turban of fine linen; attached high on this, upon blue lace, was a golden plate engraved with the words "Holy to the Lord (Yahweh)" indicating his dramatic role as intermediary between Yahweh and the people within the ceremony.

Quite clearly, the costumes of the ritual performers were remarkably spectacular and symbolic.

THE FEAST AND MONOTHEISM

From its beginning in the desert, the ceremony had concluded with a feast. It is virtually certain that this happened at Shechem and continued when the central sanctuary was moved to Shiloh with the Ark. A feast to conclude a ritual drama was universal not only in the ancient Near East but also in all traditional cultures: e.g., Turkey and the Balkans, the Americas and the Pacific, Indonesia and Tibet. The feast symbolizes the "wealth" (goodness or health) of the community, an appropriate way to conclude a ritual drama.

Most importantly, the construction and creation of the Moses Festival Play was the beginning of the history of monotheism, and the beginning of the end for paganism. Although *the practice* of monotheism began in the burning bush and *the idea* of monotheism began in the community at Sinai with the Covenant, *it was the ritual drama which gave monotheism historicity*. It tells a historical saga, but one that originates with the appearance of Moses. The God who appears to Moses is opposed not by other gods, but by a defiant pagan empire, symbolized by Pharaoh and his magicians. This God controls all nature; and no room remains for a battle of gods.[58]

PLAYS OF THE LAND AND THE SEASONS

When the ancient Israelites entered Canaan, the New Year Festival Play was of two parts: the Moses Play and the Land-giving Play. We can now turn to the second part of the ceremony.

Within *The Book of J*, evidence about the Land-giving ritual drama is much harder to find than the Moses Play—it is additionally confused, paradoxically, by having too much data. Land-giving rituals are closely tied to the seasons, but there are other Israelite seasonal rituals which may or may not be connected to the New Year. This Land-giving Festival was the most important of a series of ceremonial performances that grew from a mixture of influences. In this chapter, the Land-giving Festival Play and several other land and seasonal ritual dramas of early Israel will be examined.

When the Israelites arrived, Canaan was full of farming rituals related to the calendar. These became incorporated by the Israelites who were now living in a mixed herding and agricultural society. Ritual performances of the Near Eastern farming cultures were specifically based on the "death and resurrection" theme, and in Canaan many rituals were part of a total social drama that annually restored the cosmos, humanity, and life itself—a concept held more widely than simply by the invading groups.

The Israelites incorporated this concept of annual renewal into the rituals they brought with them, including those of the Festival which celebrated Yahweh's coronation annually. But when the monotheistic and herding Israelites came into contact with the polytheistic farmers of Canaan, the ritual performances were particular and, in some instances, confusing to the modern reader.

FERTILITY NORTH AND SOUTH

By the time of the Judges, there were specific differences in the religious practices of the Israelites as between those in the north and those in the south.

In the north, the ritual of the Covenant was celebrated as a communal meal with God. In the south, although the sacrificial animal was cut up, those who bound themselves to Yahweh did not eat—thus there was no sacramental meal. This was largely because those in the north were more influenced by the Canaanites, while those in the south were better able to resist the religious practices of those already living in the promised land.[1]

The early worship of Yahweh was much nearer to the fertility religion of the rest of the ancient Near East than has sometimes been assumed. The Israelite concept of God was a mixture from various traditions. For example, when Jacob wrestled with the angel-daemon at the Ford of Jabbok he was henceforth known as Israel, the "wrestler with God"; probably related to the river spirit of Jabbok, the daemon yet originated in El, the fertility God. This is indicated in the blessing and the promise—the land of Canaan for his "seed as the sand of the sea"[2] and "seed as the dust of the earth"[3]—exactly the same words as those given to Abram. Yahweh was an odd syncretism of fertility-and-place-daemons, fire-and-volcano-god, Mesopotamian sky god, neolithic rain bull, shaman-husband of the land, and many others besides, "before the fiercely tribal god-protector of the Chosen People became the Hellenistic universal God."[4] The original meat orgy of the Judaic tribes (parallel to that of the Dionysos cult in Greece) was steadily eliminated through priestly opposition over the years. The more modern concept of God slowly emerged after the different Bibles were put together.

The mixing of the religions of the Hebrews and the Canaanites meant that some Canaan sanctuaries dedicated to El became consecrated to Yahweh. There was also some confusion between Yahweh and Baal—it was only later that the cult of Baal was condemned. Much of the Canaanite sacrificial system was taken over, particularly in the north: most sacrifices were seen as food for the divinity but, at this time, the Israelites also began to practise the burnt offering. In addition, they participated in orgiastic rituals which intensified later, particularly under the monarchy.

Some sanctuaries were built in the Canaanite style with altars. There were priests and Levites, seers and diviners. The ecstatic prophecy of Israel, which had a long tradition, was probably based on traits common in Canaan and the Near East.

However, in the north the fusion with Baal and related agricultural cults was more permanent. The Canaanite ritual intercourse (originating in the "Sacred Marriage") sought to increase the fertility of the fields. Such sexual rituals, together with orgies of alcohol and dance, led to promiscuity which, in northern Israel, was used with the sacrificial meal, the singing dance and sacred harlotry. Later advocates of pure Yahwism thundered against this mixture of beliefs, but the continuation of their outcries shows that it did not end. Moreover, the fight was waged by men who came from the south; or they were predominantly not farmers but came from families of stockbreeders —Elijah came from Gilead, Elisha was a peasant, and Amos was a shepherd from Tekoa.[5]

CIRCUMCISION

Joshua saw that it was necessary for the first Israelites to establish themselves as a nation. To this end, he took two existing elements of the Israelite religion—circumcision and the Exodus—and made them the focus of many ritual practices.

Circumcision had not been possible on their long desert trek, so Joshua ordered the operation to take place not only on all male babies but also on boys and men. In other traditional tribes, circumcision was thought to make a man magically equal to his circumcised opponents and, therefore, superior to the uncircumcised; these tribes carried out the operation at puberty as an initiation rite. In contrast Joshua, by circumcising everyone and all new-born male babies thereafter, consecrated it as a national symbol of Yahweh—the Yahwic mark of the Covenant.

Perhaps beginning long before when Yahweh was a phallic cult, circumcision under Joshua became a form of sacrifice[6]—a psychological sacrifice uniting the people with Yahweh in celebration of the Exodus and the arrival in Canaan. Only then could the traditional interpretation of the Passover be that an Israelite in every generation must look upon himself as if he personally had come forth from Egypt, in keeping with the biblical command, "Thou shalt tell thy son in that day, saying, it is because of that which the Lord bid to me and the land while I went forth from Egypt."[7]

The Passover and circumcision became the focus of many Israelite rituals and they remain so today. Yet when the Hebrews first occupied the promised land these two rituals were mingled with fertility and seasonal celebrations, probably under the influence of Canaanites.

THE FESTIVALS OF IN-GATHERING AND BOOTHS

The history of the events in the Israelite calendar is complex. A number of religious Festivals became associated with specific times of the year once the people had settled in Palestine. However, over the years there were a number of changes.

The New Year was originally in the autumn and it corresponded to the Festival of In-gathering (Asif) which celebrated the gathering-in of the wheat.[8] It is likely that this was a seven day Festival from the earliest times.

About the seventh century B.C., under Assyrian influence, the official New Year was changed to spring. However, the Israelite New Year Festival, together with its religious performance, remained autumnal.

Also associated with the New Year was the Festival of Booths (or Tabernacles) which was an autumnal event. The date was at first variable depending upon when the harvest was gathered; later it came to be fixed on an astronomical basis.

The two Festivals of Booths and In-gathering (Asif) were combined to celebrate both the gathering-in and the Wandering in the wilderness when the Hebrews dwelt in booths—a type of leather tent. It was preceded by a solemn Day of Catharsis (Yom Kippur). The principal features of the celebration were: the reaping of crops and fruits; the bringing-in of the vintage; the performance of rituals to induce rainfall; and the custom of dwelling in booths for the entire period of the Festival.

The Moses Festival Play became associated with it and, in addition, it was linked to the tradition of pilgrimage feasts.

DRAMAS OF PILGRIMAGE

Pilgrimages to the central sanctuary at Shechem were held from the time when Israel was organized into twelve tribes.[9] The Covenant stipulated: "Three times in a year shall your males appear before Yahweh—God of Israel,"[10] and three annual pilgrimage feasts resulted: the Feast of Booths , the Feast of Unleavened Bread, or Passover, and the Feast of the Weeks of Pentecost.

The Festival of Unleavened Bread was held in the spring at the beginning of the barley harvest. It became associated with Passover which, as we have seen, was an ancient rite originating among shepherds that had been given new meaning with the Exodus. Then it became a family ritual to protect the home and flock against the demons of the night. It centred upon the power of blood on tent posts to drive them away, and it included a solemn meal offered to God. Because it became associated with the Exodus (seen as a pilgrimage for freedom), the Feast also became a pilgrimage.

The Feast of the Weeks of Pentecost was originally a minor Festival compared with those of Booths and Unleavened Bread. It appears to have been a one day event; only much later was it expanded into seven days.[11] It took place seven weeks after Passover at the time of the wheat harvest. This corresponded with the tradition of the anniversary of the giving of the Ten Commandments: "The Festival thus became the birthday of Israel ... and it is known (today) as the season of the giving of our Law."[12]

RITUAL PROCESSIONS

The Land-Giving

From the moment they entered the promised land, the Israelites celebrated Yahweh's giving of this land in a great ritual procession that re-enacted the event. Initially part of the New Year Festival, it may have became separated from the Moses Play to be an independent ritual drama. Initially the ritual crossing of the Jordan took place at the north end of the Dead Sea. The people gathered at Shittim, on the east bank of the Jordan; they then crossed the river at the fords of Adam and arrived on the other shore at Gilgal. It is likely that this was linked to the Feast of Booths: "During the crossing the ark-bearers remained in the middle of the Jordan near a monument of twelve stones ... There are reasons to believe that Joshua was the cultic hero of this tradition and that the liturgical celebration took place on the feast of Tabernacles."[13] Probably the Covenant was renewed there.

At the centre of the ritual was the direct connection between the Ark and water: the ark-bearers stood in the middle of the river to uphold the water. Water remained a main symbolic connection for the Ark for many years. This repeated Moses' gesture at the Sea of Reeds: one actual event was re-ritualized in another actual event—the Jordan symbolized in action the Sea of Reeds, and vice versa.

It was the later Northern tradition that maintained that the Ark remained in the middle of the Jordan until all the people had crossed. In contrast, the Deuteronomic historian said that the Ark crossed the Jordan ahead of the people.

It was the Northern traditions, also, that held that there was a monument of stones built in the middle of the Jordan. This monument was associated with Joshua who organized the Shechemite procession and it is likely that he became a ritual personage in performances.

Parts of the biblical description of the crossing of the Jordan were of the first ritual procession that repeated the initial crossing. When placed in sequence, they are:

[1]   Moses gives instructions before the crossing;[14]

[2]   the next morning the River Jordan is crossed; this is "witnessed;"[15]

[3]   a song is given;[16]

[4]   there is a dance of women:[17]

[5]   after the crossing, the Covenant is concluded.

This liturgical pattern corresponds to the one given in *Joshua* 3–4.

The site for this initial procession is unknown. It might have been at Gilgal but, more likely, it was held at Shechem. It was certainly performed there after Shechem became the major religious site in Israel. The people gathered at Succoth, just to the east of Shechem across the Jordan; this was named after the Succoth in Egypt from where the Hebrews fled into the desert. Thus the Succoth on the Jordan was dramatized as: Shittim, which re-enacted the first Jordan crossing, and as the Egyptian Succoth, thereby re-enacting the crossing of the Sea of Reeds. The parallel between the two crossings was quite explicit. At Succoth the people dwelt in tents, re-enacting the role of the Hebrews at Shittim about to invade Palestine. This was a liturgical re-play of how the forefathers of Israel had lived in the desert and how they approached the promised land. The fact that the actual historical crossing took place far to the south was largely ignored. In the ritual tradition, the procession crossed the Jordan because a "dam of water" heaped up on one side.[18] The Ark was the focus of the ritual procession.[19]

This dramatization at Succoth went even further. The people, dwelling in tents, dramatized themselves as imaginatively sited at Mount Sinai (Horeb).[20] Thus in the ritual drama Succoth was thought of in three ways—as Shittim, as the Succoth in Egypt, and as Horeb. Dramatization had brought about a series of parallel symbolic meanings. Once Succoth was dramatized as the symbolic Horeb, the Moses Play was performed and Yahweh was reaffirmed as king.

On the surface this variety of roles for one concept, idea, or thing bears some resemblance to the "double" of Egypt and the gods' use of a variety of roles. What was new in the Shechemite practice was that Yahweh had taken the people to a new land. Horeb (*in casu*, Succoth) is only the beginning of Yahweh's care for his people.

In the cultic procession from Succoth to Shechem they still re-enacted a two-fold reality: [a] Yahweh's journey from Sinai to his sanctuary in the promised land, and [b] the consequent occupation of the land by his people. The ritual of the procession was distinct from the Exodus celebrations; it had become more complex and through it may have been seen as their logical extension.[21] In other words, the dramatic procession from Succoth to Shechem was an attempt to unify the two traditions of the Exodus and the Land-giving.

It is the opinion of J.N.M.Wijngaards that it was E who left the clearest traces of the ritual Land-giving performance[22] in the Bible. Wijngaards shows that an ancient oracle has been preserved in the *Psalms*:

> God has spoken in His sanctuary:
>   "I will exult!
>   I will divide, O Shechem!
>   I will portion out, O Vale of Succoth!
>   Mine is Gilead, Mine is Manasseh.
>   Ephraim the helmet is on My head, Judah
>   My sceptre.
>   Moab is the basin in which I wash.
>   Upon Edom I cast My sandal.
>   I shout victory against Philistia!"[23]

Set in the context of war, the oracle promises the acquisition of new land in Moab, Edom and Philistia. It is a ritual speech where Shechem and Succoth are spoken of as linked sanctuaries where the land is to be given once more—in other words, the Land-giving is to be re-enacted in a ritual drama. In addition, *Psalm* 68 belongs to a celebration where the Ark was brought in procession into a sanctuary. The version of the biblical writer was for later use as a song at Jerusalem but, as Wijngaards shows,[24] it derived from an ancient ritual practice. Specifically the procession mentions localities on the route between Succoth and Shechem—Bashan and Mount Zalmon.

Although linked to the Feast of Booths, this dramatic procession occurred only every seven years: it included the reaffirmation of the Covenant held during "The Year of Release"—once every seven years the whole land was revitalized through a sacred fallow. In Israel this fallow may have been accompanied by the fresh allocation of plots of land by lot.[25]

The dramatic procession from Succoth to Shechem re-enacted the original occupation of the land. The ceremonies foreseen at Shechem certainly belong to the Covenant, because they involve the erection of the sacrificial altar, the inscription of the law and the ceremony of the blessing and the curse (*Deuteronomy* 11: 27). But these ceremonies were considered an extension of the Covenant celebrated in Succoth for the newly acquired land (*Deuteronomy* 11: 29; 27: 2). We might characterize this conception as the early Shechemitic tradition.[26]

Processing

Apostasy was the ritual processions behind the ark—they were acts of following Yahweh, of "walking after Him." "Walking after strange gods" was a general Near-Eastern tradition: imitating a god was originally not a spiritual matter but an actual following—a ritual of actually walking behind the god.[27]

Yet, as Wijngaards concludes, the dramatic procession had an additional purpose: to bring about a liturgical renewal of an original divine deed. In Israel the historical events of the past, the Exodus and the Land-giving, were in some way "renewed." They were turned from "fiction" into a kind of "fictional reality"—they were "actualized," "rendered present" through the procession that re-enacted them. As in today's theatre, those who participated in or witnessed the performance were in a "double state"—they inherently *knew* they were "fictions," but they accepted them as "fact" while they took place. Thus in all descriptions (*Joshua* 3–4, *Exodus* 14, *Deuteronomy* 5–11) events are narrated as if the participants witness the original events when Moses or Joshua were meditating.[28] Although the visible action may be symbolic, the mystery transcends the sphere of "play": it becomes reality— "Through the dramatic, symbolic presentation, realization and reanimation of the particular event, this event is actually and really repeated." When the actors are processing, they bring the ancient event forward into "the here and now," like all ritual performers.

The Ritual of Jericho

At least one other major ritual drama was performed in the time of Joshua —the ritualized circumambulation of Jericho.

The Bible tells us that Joshua besieged Jericho and, after marching round the walls seven times, on the seventh day seven priests preceding the Ark blew seven times on their trumpets. The people then uttered a loud shout and the walls came tumbling down.[29] Despite extensive excavation at the site, archeology can say nothing definite about Joshua's attack upon the city. If there was such an attack, however, it is likely that it did not take place in the period of Joshua but centuries before, in the time of the patriarchs when the city may possibly have been captured by the pre-Israelite Hebrews (the Habiru). By identifying it with Joshua, the Israelites collapsed time. It is likely that the Bible describes a ritual performance rather than the facts of history.

T.H.Gaster has carefully related the description in *Joshua* to traditional ritual traits the world over.[30] The remnants of this custom are to be found in the "beating of the bounds" in modern English parishes. Seven was an ancient magical and ritualistic number. The purpose of circumambulation was to form a closed circle of power ("the magic ring") which, magically, would prevent the entry of demons and evil spirits. Such religious circuits were often made round an altar during worship, a bridal couple at a wedding, and a bier at a funeral. Stories of magic horns which break down walls are not uncommon among folklore in all parts of the world. Everywhere noise is regarded as a method of expelling demons and evil spirits.

It is likely that the Bible describes a ritual performed in the time of Joshua, many years before it was written, which was itself based on an extant Canaanite ritual drama. This is given some credence by a later passage in *Joshua*[31] where, after the destruction of Jericho, Joshua imposed on the people an oath never to rebuild the city: anyone who did so would lose his eldest son in order to lay the foundations, and his youngest son to set up the gates—a prediction fulfilled by Hiel of Bethel during the reign of Ahab. This oath was based on the ancient tradition of foundation-sacrifice.[32] When a new building was constructed, a sacrifice (human or animal) was slain and buried under the threshold to prevent demons, evil spirits, or dead ancestors from bringing misfortune. This tradition was well-known in ancient Mesopotamia where, sometimes, figurines replaced real human beings. It was also practised among the ancient Celtic and Germanic peoples, and in Syria, Palestine, Greece, Rome, and elsewhere.

Hints and suggestions in *The Book of J* indicate many other Land-giving and seasonal rituals.

PART 3:

ROYAL RITUAL DRAMA

Part 3 of this book deals with what happened to the Festival ritual drama

after Joshua. Like all ritual dramas, it altered as society changed. Not all

the transformations are clear: the story is confused in places and there are

huge gaps. But the major alterations are two: first, the Royal Drama of

David and, second, the differences between the two kingdoms after

Solomon's death. Only when the Babylonian Exile is over does the Festival

and the ritual drama become suppressed.

Stage 1	Stage 2	Stage 3	Stage 4	Stage 5
Moses Covenant	Ark (Samuel)	Saul Saul's house	David Jerusalem Temple	Dynasty David's house Solomon
beginnings	non-order			order
pastoral nomadic tribalism	pre-monarchic			centralized dynastic office

Figure 6: Stages and Transitions in the Yahwist Ritual Drama

Stage 1	Stage 2–3	Stage 4	Stage 5	Stage 6
Moses	Samuel–Saul	David	Solomon	Josiah
Ark Wilderness/ Land	Ark Land	Jerusalem Dynasty Temple plan United Land	Jerusalem Dynasty Temple United Land	Jerusalem Dynasty Temple Reunited Land

Figure 7: The Deuteronomists' Perspective

8

FROM JOSHUA TO DAVID

When we see what happened as the Israelites and the Canaanites mingled, we realize that in the Israelite ritual drama there were more changes of content than of form. The performance of the Moses Play remained monotheistic: the figures of Moses, Aaron, and others recited and acted as if there was only one God.

In contrast, Canaanite and all other ritual dramas in the Near East were polytheistic in content and the stories of their many gods were different from those of the Israelites. Despite this contrast in content, all the evidence indicates that the Israelites took most of the *form* of their ritual drama from other cultures in the area; e.g., the shape of the Moses Festival Play was similar to New Year Festival Plays in Canaan and Babylonia.

This principle of change was continuous over a long period of time. The early Yahwists in Cisjordan remembered, in the Amarna Letters, their emergence in Canaan as the Habiru. They took over the name and identity of the Canaanite El-worshippers and associated El with Yahweh.

"Isra-el" was a verb compounded with "El"[1] applied to a tribal league which was already in existence in Palestine before the Exodus or the emergence of Mosaic Yahwism.[2] "The Song of Deborah"[3] shows that the non-Yahwist Israel was a ten-tribe confederation,[4] a non-national and retribalized league.[5] The northern (central Cisjordan) coalition known as "Isra-el" merged with a Yahwist Benjaminite group pictured in the accounts of Saul.[6]

This Isra-el was probably the Israel mentioned in the Merneptah Stele (c.1208 B.C.) which refers to the Cisjordan highlands east of Shechem.[7]

THREE NARRATIVE-DRAMATIC TRADITIONS

Once the Moses Play was performed, Israel changed as it adjusted to the new environment of Canaan. The transitions from Joshua's ritual drama to that of David and Solomon is treated in three different ways in the Bible: [1] by the Deuteronomists (including *Samuel*); [2] by the Chroniclers; and [3] by the Psalmists, particularly *Psalms* 89 and 132. Each tells roughly the same story about a time long gone, but with highly significant differences.

These three accounts were written at different periods and each reveals a changing ritual drama. Moses is the focus of the Deuteronomic corpus which leads to Davidic ritual; it mostly tells an earlier story and reveals earlier ritual than the Chroniclers. Dramatic ritual is most obvious in the *Psalms*, many of which were created for or about the ritual drama of David. Step by step, the figures of Moses and David were recalled and set in new surroundings when the Yahwists were transformed, or when they struggled against foes. The purpose of the performance was to stabilize the community during change: Moses, David, and other dramatic figures seemed real because the people were confident that their ritual actions would solve differences in reality.

This belief in the "truth" of ritual specifically applied to the future. Thus, if a ritual was correctly performed it was believed to affect future events. This belief is not as ancient as is sometimes believed. For example, Charles I and the English cavaliers believed that the performance of the Stuart masques would prevent the chaotic threat of Cromwell and his Roundheads. They were proved mistaken. Today, most tribal peoples also believe in the efficacy of ritual.

After the Moses ritual drama began, it went through a series of transitions described by *Psalms* 132 and 89, *2 Samuel* 6–7 (see *Figures 6* and *7*). These changes were at two levels: the narrative level of myth, and the action level of ritual. For example, in the narrative of *2 Samuel* 6[8] when the Ark is ritually taken to Jerusalem, David announces the end of Saul's house (stage 3) and thereupon affirms his divine election (stage 4). The restoration of the Ark and rejection of Saul's leadership (stages 3 and 4) mix as one episode that leads to the reaffirmation of David's ascendancy (stage 4) and his dynasty is announced (stage 5).

The mixture of Canaanite-Israelite and El-Yahweh traits appeared at the beginning of *Samuel*.

In *1 Samuel* 1, the David story starts as if in mythical time by recalling the birth of Samuel (= "His-name-is-El").[9]

Poems in the El–Yahweh tradition even continued to be celebrated on major occasions by Yahwists during Iron Age IC and later.

The tradition had other complications that represented the merging of several early myths and rituals, and confusion often resulted. The route of Elkanah and Hannah is an example. "Elkanah (= "El has produced"), Samuel's father, left his home in Ramathaim,[10] east of Tel Aviv to go to Shiloh in the eastern hills, north of Jerusalem."[11] He did so repeatedly to worship Yahweh Sabaoth. Shiloh was where Samuel lived as a child, it was the residence of Eli's priesthood, and it was the resting place for the Ark before the Philistines captured it. Then Elkanah went home to Ramah (not Ramathaim) where Samuel was conceived and born.[12] "Ramah became important later as a place of refuge and prophecy during David's escape from Saul's persecution.[13] Elkanah finally returned to Shiloh to dedicate his son to Yahweh."[14]

The link between El and Yahwist themes was maintained in the failures in Eli's house and Samuel's call in the temple at Shiloh.[15] The link between El and Yahwist also happened when Saul, a Benjaminite, met Samuel in Zuph, near Ramathaim, and was then sent back to Benjamin, Gilgal and Gibeah.[16]

The authors who wrote down these incidents were well aware of the story's ambiguities. They include many allegories ,[17] as when Samuel, serving the Ark of Elohim, ministered to Yahweh at the temple in Shiloh, and was called by Yahweh to displace Eli's family. The deity called "His-name-is-El" three times. Finally Eli and Samuel recognized the source and responded.

No attempt was made to impose logic on the stories because that would have drained them of their richness and meaning. As a result, dramatic and ritual sources are confused.

Drama of the Judges

At the time of the Judges (c.1220–1020 B.C.) Israel had settled down to a new farming life in the promised land. The main problems were the mixture of different peoples, oppression by various foreign invaders, together with low moral and religious standards.

The Judges were spontaneous leaders who grew out of each situation to deal with crises: Ehud, Shamgar, Deborah, Gideon, Jeptha and Samson. Each had to solve different issues. The danger from the Philistines and others were greatest in the time of Samuel's leadership (c.1040–1020 B.C.) and the need grew to unify the country. This happened with three kings: Saul (c.1020–1000), David (c.1000–961), and Solomon (c.961–922). Religious rituals grew, leading to the great ceremonies in Solomon's Temple. In the time of the Judges, Israel had a sacrificial cult, first with an altar and later with a sanctuary.

Although there was an ancient prohibition against human sacrifices, the practice continued with the Judges, and outcropped later from time to time—it was even reported of the kings Ahaz and Manasseh. But even from the time of Samuel there was a tendency towards a higher form of worship, as when he said: "Behold, to obey is better than to sacrifice, and to hearken than the fat of rams."[18]

So, too, there were prohibitions against self-castigation and self-mutilation in moments of ecstasy,[19] as later happened with the priests of Baal on Mount Carmel.

The New Year Festival

At this time, the New Year Festival of the Israelites coordinated a variety of dramatic traditions. These included the ancient New Year dramas common to the Near East, the Festival of Ingathering, the Festival of Booths or Tabernacles, the Land-giving, and the Moses Play. Every seventh year (a magical number) all were combined to commemorate "The Year of Release." This occurred in a gigantic ritual Festival that started at Succoth and slowly processed to Shechem. It represented a climax to the cyclic series of ritual ceremonies.

At Succoth, the people celebrated the Festival of Booths while Yahweh was confirmed as king in the Moses Play. This was the "three days' journey into the wilderness,"[20] dramatized as a feast celebrated at the foot of Mount Sinai. At Succoth, too, the Covenant was renewed "after three days."[21] The pilgrimage from Succoth to Shechem, with the crossing of the Jordan, was increasingly dramatized as a re-enactment of the crossing of the Sea of Reeds, and various "holy places" grew up along the route. These included Adam, Galed, Jacob's Houses in Succoth, Shechem and, perhaps, the footprints of the Ark bearers.[22]

The ceremonial of the Land-giving became used as a conscious piece of propaganda. In order to make the settlement easier among an illiterate and ritually-conscious people, the Land-giving became a liturgical procession that was religiously highly persuasive. By dramatizing Yahweh's journey from Egypt to Sinai and simultaneously from Shittim to Gilgal, Yahweh was confirmed as king and he occupied the land on behalf of the people. This enabled the Israelites to re-integrate into their covenantal relationship with Yahweh.

The total Festival also included the Day of Purgation, or Atonement (Kippurim), or Yom Kippur. This was originally the culmination of a ten day lenten period which included a purgation of the sanctuary, its vessels and personnel; a ritual purification of the people; and the scapegoat sacrifice as a means of removing impurity. It was accompanied by the community observing a public fast and suspension of activity.

The total community was invigorated through a series of rituals at New Year's Day and the Feast of Booths. It is possible that there was a mimetic combat between Yahweh and a Dragon, or some similar adversary, together with magical rites to stimulate rainfall and fertility.

The Bible still contains remnants of these events, some of which make the appearance of the Dragon very like that in Babylon:

> In certain of the *Psalms* of the Old Testament (47; 93; 95–100, to mention the most important) we have survivals of the Old Israelite New Year's Feast and its ritual: Jehovah's ascension of the throne with preceding entry and procession after the victory over the demons and "the determination of destiny" (i.e., the annual creation, in later times: doom)—a ritual which was probably enacted dramatically.[23]

Thus the Israelite New Year Festival came to resemble, even further, the fertility New Year Festivals of Mesopotamia and Canaan. At some point in time, the whole Festival may have been transferred to Shiloh. However we are unsure of the facts.

Fertility Rituals

The confusion between Yahweh and other local gods continued in the time of the Judges. Indeed, until post-Exilic times Yahweh was worshipped without any scruples alongside other gods in one and the same sanctuary or temple. This syncretism also enabled the Israelites to incorporate the ancient fertility Goddess into their rituals. This information was suppressed by the post-Exilic authors.

Not long after Joshua conquered the Canaanite hill country, the people "served the Baals and the Asherahs." Ancient Israelite shrines had two main objects which celebrated the Canaanite religion: the *massebah*, a stone phallic pillar, and the *asherah*, a wooden pole carved like a female figure. The worship of Asherah, the chief goddess of Canaan, continued throughout the period of the Judges and the Kings. (Later in his Temple, Solomon worshipped her.) There is little doubt that "the Sacred Marriage" of the god and goddess (inherited from Sumer) was dramatically imitated by Israelite priests and priestesses and, even, by the people themselves at a communal feast during the New Year Festival.

Also popular was the Canaanite goddess, Astarte, the warrior and lover, whom the Bible mentions early in the Israelite history in Canaan. Purged by Samuel, she was also worshipped by the Philistines who deposited the armour of the defeated Saul in her temple. We can only conjecture the rituals that accompanied the various goddesses.

The legend of Jeptha's daughter[24] would seem to indicate the existence of annual wailing rites for the death of an ancient female vegetation deity. This paralleled rituals in Mesopotamia, Egypt and Greece, as well as modern Europe.[25] Among the many other remnants of fertility rituals in the Bible were two: the hair as the source of Samson's strength may have derived from hair-cutting as part of shamanic initiation rituals; and the rape of the women of Shiloh is a legend based on the fertility ritual of communal intercourse at seasonal Festivals.

The figure of Samson, while probably based on a historical figure, appears linked with fertility rituals. The cycle of Samson stories is a hero-legend associated with the origins of several places. Samson is in his prime in summer but ends his days in darkness (winter). Many scholars have noted the resemblance of the Samson cycle to that of Herakles: killing a lion with his bare hands, betrayal by a woman, and deciding his own death with a descent into darkness—Samson to blindness and prison while Herakles goes to the Netherworld.

Nearby Mycenaean settlements in the period of the Judges indicate that the Samson cycle may have been derived from both Greek and Mesopotamian fertility traditions.

The Deuteronomists

A Deuteronomic history extends from *Deuteronomy* to the end of *2 Kings*. The Deuteronomic historians saw Saul's era as a period of national disaster and personal uncertainty. They incorporated the Samuel rituals into their own, and extended the narrative from *1 Samuel* 1 through *2 Samuel* 24.

The function of the Deuteronomic narrative units explains two sets of differences: [1] between *Samuel* and other portions of the narrative, and [2] between the *Samuel* image of David and that in *Chronicles*. Like genealogies, these narrative units were strung together serially in a pseudo-chronological sequence—a characteristic of Deuteronomic writing.

Samuel is the largest literary unit to be lifted more or less intact by the Deuteronomists. Their account reflects an interest not simply in the outcome of early Israel's activities, but in explaining to contemporaries how and why various fortunes rise and fall.

The David story comes at the pinnacle of the account. There it fulfills the promises to Moses, and it sorts the permanent from the transitory. Although *Samuel* is also part of the Deuteronomic corpus, it has been re-worked and the effect is to describe a complex social drama. Saul's eldest son, Jonathan, rebelled with David against his dynasty. Saul put David under house arrest[26] and tried to kill him, pursuing him relentlessly in the Judean wilderness.[27] David's portrait in *Samuel* is particular with regards to Saul. David killed the giant who threatened Saul's soldiers,[28] he laboured for the hand of Saul's daughter, Michal,[29] he spared Saul's life,[30] he mourned Saul's death,[31] he cared for Meribaal, Saul's grandson, and saved him from death at the hand of the Gibeonites.[32]

Michal has a vital place in the *Samuel* social drama: she is married to David, and she devises plans to save him from Saul.[33] But she is taken from David and given to Palti as wife,[34] to weaken David's claim within the northern house.[35] Her return is a condition for David's negotiations with Abner for Ishbaal's crown.[36] But she falls into David's disfavour and is confined to a childless life in the Jerusalem harem,[37] which leaves her weak when bartering for dynastic power with other wives and concubines.

By the end of *The Book of Samuel*, every known male in direct and indirect lines of descent from Saul is dead, except two or three ineligible successors. Only Saul's grandson, Meribaal, and his great-grandson, Mica, survived. The slaughter of the last seven sons by the Gibeonites is the end of the Saulide line.[38]

The Social Drama

From the time of the Judges, the Israelites were coming to see their society through the dramatic metaphor (life is drama/drama is life). Anciently this had begun in shamanic rituals, but it was not put into words until much later. It began with the Israelites but was only fully explicit with Pythagoras, Heraclitus, and the Emperor Augustus who repeated the metaphor on his death bed.[39]

In this social drama, David's role as leader in Judah did not rely on his affinity to Saul but rather on his marriage into Saul's family.[40] For social drama to focus on the descent line of marriage is common the world over. Various events curtail succession among the Saulides. The survival of Mica keeps the hope alive but unfulfilled.[41] David took advantage of a practice that enabled the husband to take the role of (to stand in for) his wife and to inherit from and succeed her father.[42] Whether the line would continue from David or return to Saul's house, was raised by Michal's childlessness and was resolved only by the Dynastic Oracle.

Like other pastoralists expanding their network of relationships to gain power, David married outside his kin group, taking wives among both Yahwists and non-Yahwists.[43] Saul's conviction that Jonathan should protect his succession rights against David[44] shows that David's temporary loss of paramount status led him to flee to an outlying district where he created his own power base outside Saul's domain.

In *Samuel*, the story moves in two directions at once: [a] it traces religio-political change from the birth of Samuel to the mature years of David's reign; and [b] it portrays reversals, encounters, and cycles—individuals, events, and attitudes move around, on and off the acting-area during narrative time. Many concerns introduced at the beginning return, albeit transformed, at the end of the narrative. Jerusalem is the focus of both movements. It divides the plot into two parts.

In Part One of the plot, the city's capture and legitimation mark the end of Saul's leadership, extra-Jerusalemite rule, and the Philistine military threat to Israel. The Ark is lost: it crosses the frontier into Philistine territory where it fails to find a home. It returns to the borders of Judah and Israel, but not to prominence until David reclaims it. The Philistines' prominence begins in *Judges* and continues in *Samuel*, where it is linked to the Ark, land, conquest, and Jerusalem themes. The Philistines' role is as *a collective antagonist*: they have a variety of social roles—enemies of Israel, allies of David, enemies of David, and so on. Their fate and the Yahwists' are not diametrically opposed, but the associations are ambivalent. David both needs and rejects the Philistines. In the Bible, the Philistines have a position that is both contradictory and paradoxical.

David flips roles. He goes from Saul to the Philistines. In *Samuel*, he becomes their warrior and uneasy client. His relations with Saul and the

Philistines are at times congenial but never completely so. David, like the Ark, moves from camp to camp within a world of constantly shifting allegiances. Both are abandoned by Saul, taken into custody by the Philistines, and united in Jerusalem. The portrayal of David is full of paradoxes, contradictions, reversals, and unexpected ritualized events. David uses fluctuating roles: complex and ambivalent at one time, neither/nor or both/and roles at another, as he migrates between friend and foe.

Repetition is a sure sign of ritual and the David story is full of it. In his lifetime, he is evicted twice from centres of power, first from Saul and then from Jerusalem. On both occasions, he seeks refuge in the wilderness that is figuratively beyond Israel's borders. His first protection comes from the Philistines in the social drama; yet in the ritual drama, with its anointing scene, the witnesses know that he has been chosen to lead Israel. His "refuge" among the Philistines balances with that in Transjordan during Absalom's coup. He finally subjugates the Philistines and displaces the Ark as the sign of Yahweh's presence. However, once it is clear that Yahweh prefers David to Saul,[45] the scene shifts. But there are still tensions because of the rebellions led by Absalom and Sheba. In the books of *Samuel* the only genealogical units that refer to David's family are the remarks about his "sister" Zeruiah who is the daughter of Nahash of the Ammonites,[46] the lineage of Bathsheba and Solomon,[47] and lists of sons born at Hebron and Jerusalem.[48] Genealogical lists indicate the compilers' judgment of shifting statuses, roles, and relationships within the story. In *1* and *2 Samuel* the stages in David's rise are parallel to those in the genealogical lists.

These stages hint at the main segments of a ritual drama of David's rise: Samuel, Saul, David at Hebron, David at Jerusalem before his exile, and David upon his return to Jerusalem. Conceptually, David and Jerusalem are on one pole opposite to the Saulides and Philistines.

Part Two of the plot begins with relocating in Jerusalem. David's survival rather than succession is the key issue in *Samuel*. His difficulties are not resolved until the end of *2 Samuel* when the opening scenes and problems of

1 Samuel are reversed. The unifying links are the tension between David and Saul and his house, the changing fortunes of the Ark, and the voice of Yahweh during David's exile. The focus is Israel's lack of enthusiasm for the Jerusalemite leadership.[49]

There are competing northern and southern actors' rituals to the Deuteronomists. It is an all Israelite group that accompanies the Ark in its initial entry into the land of Canaan; but in *Samuel* it is the Judahites.[50] The centres of power and legitimacy were shifting from north to south, from Israel to Judah and Jerusalem.

Absalom's and Sheba's rebellions show that the old allegiances struggled to survive against the new. Resistance to David enabled Sheba to organize a Benjaminite rebellion. Absalom's power base was northern despite his decision to start his revolt at Hebron. This ancient southern Yahwistic centre had been settled by an independent and very early Yahwist group that did not share the conquest traditions of the Deuteronomists.[51] Absalom's and Sheba's rebellions were religiously motivated.[52] Both attempts failed and, in the ritual drama, this was to re-play Yahweh's triumph.

The stories set in Jerusalem, showing how David overcame threats from the Philistines and the house of Saul, have reversals, ambiguities and contradictions—characteristic of ritual. David had to:

* withstand an attempted coup to return to his house;
* suppress a second rebellion;[53]
* allow the slaying of Saul's survivors;
* do final battle with the Philistines;[54]
* offer a song of thanksgiving;[55] and
* utter his final words.[56]

To consolidate his power, David finally ordered a census for which he had to do penance.[57] The penance is puzzling because Yahweh had initially encouraged David to take it. Perhaps enrolling in a census required ritual purity:[58] Violations would lead to a plague, betraying a hidden condition that had to be removed if David's leadership was to survive. His sovereignty and its relationship to Yahweh were not resolved until he repented, bought a site as a final resting place for the Ark, and made offerings.

The major theme in *1* and *2 Samuel* was the tension of Saul versus David, not succession. The question is, which group legitimately represented Yahweh? That is not explicitly addressed until *Kings* 1–2.

The Deuteronomic Ritual Drama

In Deuteronomic history the major themes in the ritual drama are Moses, land, covenant, ark/temple, kingship/David, Jerusalem. Each reveals aspects of ritual.

Moses is the key. The writers wish for kings to return the nation to its Mosaic foundations: wisdom from experience. The story opens with a proclamation of the second law, a divine promise of land to Moses, and the people about to enter Canaan.[59]

It ends with a reform based on the discovery of a law book[60] and an effort to reunite the territory under Josiah's leadership.[61]

The structure of the book of *Deuteronomy* has a covenant form and imagery.[62] The legitimation of Zion (*2 Samuel* 7) divides the Deuteronomic history into two main parts:

[1]   The early stories tell of Yahweh's promise of land, the journey to its south and east borders, a unified capture-settlement, and life in Canaan.[63] The Philistine threat and Israel's response are extensions of the land theme.[64]

[2a]   Davidic and Solomonic times are eras of expansion and consolidation. Judah and Israel focus a federation based on Jerusalem.[65]

[2b]   The post-Solomonic period has a fragile unity which dissolves in bickering over legitimacy and succession rights, and exterior forces. Reform movements under Hezekiah and Josiah try to regain Yahweh's rightful land by restoring the deity in Jerusalem.[66]

The Deuteronomic history ties the pre- and post-Davidic stories together. It stresses the religious legitimacy of Judahite kings, and links the land and conquest themes in one territorial conquest. Thus it demonstrates the completion and its fulfillment in the Davidic era. David is held up as a model for post-Davidic leaders.

Ark/Temple and Other Themes

Like the other major themes, ark/temple focuses attention on David and Jerusalem. By connecting Ark to house, the transitions from Saul-and-ark to David-Jerusalem-temple and David-dynasty are fused in a single continuous theme. The stages are presented serially: the period of Moses and the Judges; the time of Saul; the reign of David; and the reign of Solomon. Solomon appears as part of the dynastic issue, not as part of the founding phase preceding the Schism as in parts of *Chronicles*. Competition for succession begins earlier in the Deuteronomic view.

Between Moses and David other Festival rituals develop. Moses builds the Ark and entrusts it to the tribe of Levi;[67] he places the law within it, and prepares for his successor, Joshua, to escort it into the promised land.[68] Joshua and all Israel cross the Jordan and continue onward;[69] each stage in the ark's progress toward its destination on Mount Ebal is marked by an elaborate ritual.

The River Jordan plays a unique role: it is a dialogic boundary and centre while, ritually, it is the focus of a processional drama. When the Ark enters Canaan, the entire procession from Transjordan to highland Cisjordan is a rite of passage that celebrates the entry and founding of a new homeland.

As we read the Bible today the ritual indicated contains some fundamental symbols:

* The river becomes liminal. It represents a threshold and boundary. It is "betwixt and between," to be crossed when the wilderness is left behind and the community reassembles in Canaan.
* Moses represents the old order, the wilderness, and more exactly, the unsettled, homeless, landless life.
* Joshua at Ebal and later David in Jerusalem symbolize the new order—a continuation of the Mosaic ideal and the end of the Wandering.

For the Deuteronomists, the ark's first home in Canaan is the centre of the northern kingdom. From there it travels circuitously over time to Jerusalem.

As in *Chronicles*, at least two symbolic geographies coexist: [1] the early settlement of the Yahwists and David's conquests extend east of the Jordan, north to Hamath and south to the Negev and Edom; and [2] Moses, Joshua, and David are away from home and outside their land when in Transjordan (the dominant Deuteronomic image). The two images partially overlap. But the writers consider that for the actors the centre is the land of Canaan and eventually Jerusalem—paradoxically a zone within the confines of no other state. Another paradox exists when Saul's successor, Ishbaal, continues to lead Israel but is portrayed as so weak that he must rule from outside, i.e., beyond the borders in Transjordan.

The tension between wilderness and settled communities is resolved by Deuteronomic movements towards legitimation. Land, conquest, covenant, Ark, and house themes coalesce to explain the passing of Yahweh's favour from one style of thought to another:[70] wilderness, wandering, and Transjordan are depicted as former life;[71] and settlement, Cisjordan, and Jerusalem result from the divine plan. There are two levels of movement: [1] evolutionary progress from wilderness to settled life; and [2] a cyclic and oscillating movement so that relationships between the two sides of the Jordan are reciprocal and revolving. Thus, the wilderness beyond the Jordan is both a place of exile and refuge, and also a place of nostalgia and recuperation where leaders seek Yahweh's protection, the support of loyal allies, and the time to recover from life's rejections. On both levels, its edge is marked by the Jordan, a liminal space.

The Temple

Saul occasionally, and David often, prayed directly to God. National sanctuaries like Bethel, Shiloh and Gibeon had daily services where the whole assembly would burst out in devotional outcry. At Gibeon, long before David, there were professional Levitical singers, some of whom David transferred to the new sanctuary at Jerusalem.[72]

Solomon's Temple was an innovation because of the ancient Yahwist tradition that opposed temples. Before this, the sanctuaries were only high places, tents and tabernacles. With the Temple, however, it was no longer imagined that God dwelt on earth which made a deep impression on the people and helped to spread the idea of one God. Yet Solomon also permitted the worship of other deities in Jerusalem.[73] The service in the first Temple began with the priests offering sacrifices. One would raise his hands and bless the people (apparently the benediction) followed by the confession of sins while further sacrifices were burned and the Levites sang psalms.[74]

The *Kapparot* ceremony is still today a widespread custom after the morning service of Yom Kippur. The celebrant waves a fowl around his head, while reciting a verse three times: "This is my substitute, this is my exchange, this is my atonement: this fowl will go to its death, and I shall enter a good and long life and peace." A substitute is a dramatic symbol: it takes something else's place. The chicken is then "redeemed" by money, given to the poor, and then slaughtered to be eaten for the meal preceding the fast.[75] Such ancient dramatic practices, including sacrifice, continue today.

The Limping Dance
The story of Agag,[76] the king of the Amalekites, reveals certain dramatic actions: a known performance mode among the Israelites.

Agag having been defeated by Saul, was led into the presence of the prophet Samuel. He walked "delicately" and exclaimed, "Bitter indeed is death." As the Hebrew word "delicately" really means "with limping gait," Agag was in fact observing a custom of Semitic funerals whereby mourners shuffle round the bier with a peculiar limping or hopping step even today.[77]

Originally this dramatic dance may have been associated with the land: centuries before the Hebrews crossed the Jordan, the Egyptian pharaoh performed such a land dance in a special kilt - and he danced it twice on behalf of Upper and Lower Egypt.

But among the Israelites in Canaan, it had become a mourning dance. Female relations and friends of the deceased met together by his house on the first three days after the funeral, and there performed a lamentation and a strange kind of dance of which Gaster says:

> They daub their faces and bosoms and parts of their dress with mud; and tie a rope girdle ... round the waist. Each flourishes in her hand a palm-stick or a neb-root (a long staff), or a drawn sword (so as to forfend demons), and dances with a slow movement, and in an irregular manner; generally pacing about and raising and depressing the body.

Gaster also says: "The point of our Scriptural narrative is, then, that Agag, like an arch-hypocrite, approaches the prophet in the manner of a mourner, intoning a typical dirge!"[78] The performance was the dramatic act proper, an act of impersonation. But we should note that Agag was a "hypocrite": a particular kind of actor—one who is false, as the English puritans accused all actors of being, or as Shakespeare created Richard III and Malvolio.

Samuel ordered Agag to be hewn to pieces "before Yahweh at Gilgal"—an indication that he was both "false" and the victim of a ritual ceremony. Was he then hewn into pieces and his flesh served as a feast (*omophagia*) in a tradition that went back to Paleolithic times and continued in the worship of Dionysos in Greece?

In Athenian dramatic dance, a hopping limp may have been used by the chorus in dances of "lamentation." This gait for mourning was also known by the ancient as well as modern Mesopotamians. In Israel, the dirges composed for the dance were in a limping (scazontic) metre.

Magic

Elsewhere we have seen that shamanic actions were part of ancient Israelite practices, particularly among Moses and his family. Samuel was also called *ro'eh* or "seer," an oracle of the shamanistic type. Samuel "turned into another man" when he prophesied[79] as, later, did Elisha. King Saul "stripped off his clothes and prophesied and lay down naked all that day and all that night,"[80] characteristic of the shamanic temperament. The prophets also often fell into such ecstasies.[81] Indeed, the Hebrew word for "prophecy" means to "utter in a low voice," "to bubble over with speech."[82] Saul sought the help of the Witch of Endor—a female shaman who spoke with the voice of the spirits. She called up the spirit of the dead Samuel who pronounced Saul's doom—a scene of necromancy that reminds us of *Macbeth*. Deborah, too, was an ecstatic sorceress.

The sin of necromancy is denounced continually in the Bible, yet instances abound, and the very reiteration of the ban indicates that the sin was everywhere practised.

When Solomon dedicated the Temple in Jerusalem at the onset of the rainy season,[83] he chose the date when the ancient god of fertility and rainfall (among Canaanites, Hittites, etc.) had overcome the Dragon who controlled the waters. The god was then brought in triumph and enthroned.

Throughout the ages, Solomon has been renowned as a great magician. *Solomon's Key* is a very old book of ceremonial magic and, whether written by Solomon or not, it had a great influence over a long period of time. Even in the first century A.D., Flavius Josephus, a Jew, tells us there was such a book. Of Solomon he says:

God also enabled him to learn the art which expels demons, which is useful and works cures for men. He composed charms also by which diseases are alleviated. And he left behind him forms of exorcisms, by which people drove away demons so that they never return; and this method of cure is of very great value unto this day: for I have seen a certain man of my own country, whose name was Eleazar, curing people possessed by demons in the presence of Vespasian and his sons and captains and the whole of his soldiers. The manner of the cure was as follows: he put a ring that had under its seal one of those sorts of roots mentioned by Solomon, to the nostrils of the demoniac, and then drew the demon out through his nostrils as he smelt it: and when the man fell down immediately, he adjured the demon to return into him no more, still making mention of Solomon, and reciting the incantations which he had composed. And Eleazar, wishing to persuade and show to the spectators that he had such a power, used to set a little way off a cup or basin full of water, and commanded the demon, as he went out of the man, to overturn it, and so let the spectators know that he had left the man.[84]

As we have already seen, the shamanic belief in magic and possession is founded on a dramatic way of comprehending existence. The acts performed are dramatic *per se* because the belief in power over spirits, and other people, is based on the view that by "putting oneself in another person's place" one gains control over events.

Under the influence of the Levites, however, belief in shamanic magic steadily declined. This was not the case in Babylonia, for example, where the gods brought good but demons brought evil. Yet for the Levite priests (and specifically for the prophet Amos) this was not possible: Yahweh was responsible for evil too. This exerted an all-pervasive influence upon the religious development of Israel,[85] although it took many centuries before magic practices were not prevalent.

CHRONICLES

The Ark

The Deuteronomists and the Chroniclers have different attitudes to history and ritual. The Deuteronomists mention the Ark only once in *Judges*,[86] when the Israelites battle the Benjaminites. It is not mentioned again until the Philistines capture it, move it to Ashdod, and later return it to Yahwist control.[87] In the Massoretic Text Saul is accompanied by the Ark when he fights the Philistines at Michmash,[88] but versions refer to an *ephod* (ritual tunic) instead. In *2 Samuel* 6 there is a portion of the Ark narrative[89] where the Ark goes from the north to Jerusalem in another rite of passage.[90]

Shifts in *Chronicles*

The writers of the *Chronicles* re-wrote narratives from the Deuteronomic history after the return from the Exile; they summarized the pre-monarchic period in an extended genealogy, more distanced from the events than other accounts, that reached from Adam to Jerusalem.[91] The Chroniclers record no ritual crossing of the Jordan, yet it is echoed in the processions to and from Transjordan.[92]

The Chroniclers rearranged materials to fit their world-view: a synchronic image of Yahwist life and its dependency on David; a story comprising units that were previously independent or were parts of different structures. Although this was a post-Exilic history and some records of the ritual drama were suppressed, the performances had yet to die out. The re-structuring of the story level (myth) indicates the way in which the individual rituals made up the overall shape of the ritual drama:

[1] *Early Israel.*

Israel was named consistently in *Chronicles* (other sources refer to "Jacob") which shows that the earliest stories climaxed in the twelve sons of Israel.[93]

[2] *[Moses and the covenant.]*

True to their anti-ritual bias, they passed over The Moses Play.

[3] *Saul.*

Saul was transitional: the world he personified ended with the rise of David; and David's marital ties to Saul's house were not important —his status rested on other grounds.

[4] *David replaces Saul.*

Saul's death was the termination of former history: "Therefore the Lord slew him, and transferred his kingdom to David, the son of Jesse."[94] Yahweh killed the leader, transferred power to David, and a new age began.

[5] *David takes the Ark to Jerusalem.*

David's decision to move the Ark to Jerusalem and prepare for the construction of the temple[95] was seen as a turning point that set Yahwism on a new course. David's procession was directly parallel to Joshua's procession over the Jordan.

This procession was a precedent for later leaders to follow: like David who brought the Northern worship home to Zion, his

successors had to restore a united post-Exilic people who would
worship in Jerusalem and rebuild the Temple.

[6]   *Yahweh confirms David's house, Jerusalem and Zion.*
In performance, David was a Judahite. His rise was exceptional, he
succeeded Saul, and he had heirs and potential successors.

[7]   *Solomon takes the Ark to Jerusalem.*
The Davidic ritual drama had the Ark in a northern cultic centre,
preferring "Elohim" as the divine name, before Solomon brought it in
procession to Jerusalem.

This had not been completely suppressed in post-Exilic times for the
Chroniclers presented a scene where Solomon repeated David's
procession to Zion. Solomon received a blessing in Gibeon and
carried it to Jerusalem; he legitimated both the city and his
enthronement in a rite of passage. The lineage continued through
Solomon and was joined to another genealogy of Judah.

The repetitions indicate that some rituals treated David and Solomon as
two parts of a single episode in Israel's history.[96] Certainly the Temple
dominated the narrative and the ritual: David and Solomon shared
responsibility for instituting temple worship; their reigns were seen as "a
Golden Age" when true Yahwists re-assembled in Jerusalem.

In the *Chronicles* and the ritual drama, Solomon was a pious, just and
faithful Yahwist who revived the religious rites of his father (as well as many
others). In post-Exilic ritual drama, the fidelity of Solomon became the
dramatic symbol of the future.

The symbolic geography in the Chroniclers' minds show how they ordered
concepts that strengthened Judahite claims on Davidic legitimacy, and the
transitions from a tribal society to a dynastic nation. The Chroniclers had at
least two primary meanings of "all Israel": a religio-geopolitical expanse, and
a group of Yahwists in both the north and south.[97] Saul leads Israel[98] but no
reference is made to "all Israel" during his reign. That is reserved for the time
of David and Solomon when the term means the Yahwist territories under their
control.[99] While a few glimpses of a separate Israel and Judah survive, as in

the report of the census,[100] the Chroniclers do not think of a "United Monarchy." Instead, David and Solomon lead a single unified people known as "all Israel," and this was a basic assumption in the David Play.

THE JUDEAN ROYAL DRAMA

Whereas in the Moses Festival Play we have few surviving fragments of dialogue, there is even less direct speech left of David's Festival Play. This is largely because there is little of the Davidic plot in *The Book of J* except as a subtext. Yet David's Festival Play was built on that of Moses.

The Book of J

In coming at last to David and Solomon, paradoxically we arrive at the centre of *The Book of J*, which never mentions either of them. This paradox has been closely examined by many major scholars, to whom I am deeply indebted.

The work of J and the Court Historian of *2 Samuel* have together been called "The Judaean Royal Theology," a monarchist idea of order with David and Solomon at the centre, not Yahweh. *The Book of J* finishes as the Israelites cross the Jordan, but while J tells us this story of the remote past, he also transforms it. J sees it as the necessary prelude to David—pre-Conquest events are ironic parallels to other events in the reigns of David, Solomon, Rehoboam and Jeroboam. Thus J's approach to David is by innuendo, often through his surrogate, Joseph. In other words, *J metaphorizes Moses in terms of the kings, and vice versa.*

This is a highly complex technique meant for a sophisticated audience, but royal decorum would have prevented J from including David (or Solomon).[1] The unconditional pledge concerning Solomon and his descendants[2] influences all J's versions of the patriarchal covenants. They suggest the huge size of David's military state from the Nile to the Euphrates, the transition to Solomon's commercial empire, and the weakness of Rehoboam and, eventually, the division of the kingdom into Israel and Judah.[3]

The era of David and Solomon was a great literary period: the *Psalms*, the Song of Songs, *2 Samuel* and *The Book of J* are the heights of Hebrew imagination, and it is doubtful if they have ever been surpassed: "it cannot be said that Israel regarded God anthropomorphically, but the reverse ... that [he] considered man as theomorphic."[4]

J writes differently of Moses and the Exodus than of the virtual destruction of Israel's national life with the transition from Solomon to Rehoboam.[5] J did not share in the "nomadic ideal" of the Prophets and Moses: Cain is punished by nomadism; Ishmael's geographical destiny is not presented as a blessing; and the wanderings in the Wilderness are dramatized by J almost as a nightmare.

David as a Dramatic Character

Just as we know the pre-Conquest events primarily through J, we do not know the *historical* David.

But we do know the David of *1 and 2 Samuel, 1 Kings, 1 Chronicles* and the *Psalms*. Like Yahweh, he is a dramatic character who has become a religious force due to Yahweh's peculiar favour. Yet David appears to transcend his representations; he is not the son of God, even though Yahweh proclaims that he will be a father to David's children. David, simply, is the object of Yahweh's election-love.

There is something magical in David's charisma; he is refreshing as a character. Between the primitive kingdom of Saul and the advanced empire of Solomon, David carries his people from an obscure hill clan to a high culture dominant in its part of the world. David is a new kind of man: a new image of human existence, with all human potentialities fulfilled in him. He is "a hero," in the same sense that Sophocles creates heroes. This happens in the change of perspective from Saul to David with its permanent emblem in Jerusalem.[6]

David has a complex personality based on various roles—the fugitive chief of outcasts; the dancer before the Ark; the unscrupulous man who liquidates Uriah the Hittite when he stands in the way of his monarch's lust; and the mourner of his first child by Bathsheba who, when the child dies, returns pragmatically to full vitality.

J's David is to be distinguished from J's Moses: to no one in J does Yahweh speak as he speaks to David, through the prophet Nathan, in *2 Samuel* 7:12–16.[7]

Before David, there is almost no Hebrew literature but, after him, great writers appear. Contemporary written records are lacking for Iron Age IC and, were it not for the Bible, history would not know of David at all. We have only religious testimonies about him, and we lack independent, non-Yahwist witnesses of his existence and conduct. Thus the events of his life are difficult to confirm or deny.

The Bible tells us that he lived in Israel, but what does that mean? The biblical "all Israel" references change according to who is using them. The first Israel was not Yahwist. The second was an "all Israel" federation of the old Israel and Benjamin. Next was an "all Israel" that included the old federation, Benjamin, and Judah. For Deuteronomists, Benjamin stayed with Judah and was separate from "all Israel." Finally, in the *Chronicles*, the name "all Israel" was used for Judah and Jerusalem.

Not only does David's role and character alter but also his place in his society changes. The various biblical materials about him were written when his times were already remote history.[8] The biblical David is nearer to myth than to history; that is, the historical David is of less interest to the writers than his religious significance.

THE DAVID PLAY

The Plot

The Deuteronomic plot, unlike that of the *Chronicles*, retained the *Samuel* writers' views of David's faults as well as his virtues. This gave a depth to his personality. Of poor and humble origin, from a shepherd's pasture, he eventually became a king of great power. He served Saul, married his daughter, befriended his son, but was not acceptable in his court. He worked with Israel's main enemy, the Philistines, and was their vassal at Ashdod, Ziklag and Hebron. He led his house in war against the house of Saul and benefitted from the treason of Abner, Saul's uncle, and the murder of Saul's son. He committed adultery with Bathsheba and arranged the death of her husband. In his middle age, David captured Jerusalem and aggrandized it, pacifying the entire eastern end of the Mediterranean, and uniting it under his sole authority. Few ever have achieved what David accomplished in such a short time, or without help from an outside military power, but the limits and nature of his paramountcy in the first half of the tenth century may never be known. The Bible says that David subdued most of the states around Canaan, and made alliances with Phoenician and Aramean (Syrian) leaders who agreed to live peaceably with him. Older biblical historians, who accepted the Bible as accurate history, assumed that David's control stretched from Anatolia to Egypt, from the Mediterranean to the Euphrates. Modern historians are increasingly skeptical of so expansive a description.

His sons committed incestuous rape, fratricide, and revolted against his authority. He was slow to quell unrest in Benjamin, and he allowed his sons to struggle for premature succession before he finally allowed Bathsheba to dictate his successor.

The Deuteronomists

The Bible presents David in a panorama of scenes from his youth to his old age. Together they make a coherent ritual play.

Many of the scenes are self-contained and have the quality of great art, whether as narrative or as drama. The books of *Samuel* are at the centre of the Deuteronomic view: the transfer of the Ark and Yahweh's covenant with David are the core of the stories and rituals; and possession of Jerusalem and Yahwist legitimacy for its ruler are the foundation of religious and political thought.

It is the Deuteronomists who provide us with the clear and rounded picture of the David found in ritual drama. He is nearer the surface in *Samuel* and the Deuteronomists than in other books. This is largely because, in contrast to the idealism of the *Chronicles*, the Deuteronomists are down-to-earth. These writers are biased towards Jerusalem and centralization, and they mythologize the early periods of Moses and Joshua. They see events as if they are participants in them. Like all good dramatists; as we read them they feel like witnesses to the action. This is particularly so in the *Samuel* material, but also with Solomon in the book of *Kings*. Among the Deuteronomists this feeling is much stronger than in their impressions of Moses and Joshua, Rehoboam and Jeroboam.

The David Ritual-myth

The David story is a unified ritual-myth (or "myth-history").[9] Even its early forms would be compatible with a number of historical settings and circumstances.

The events of David's life were so influential that they have become a pivotal epoch in world history—as evidenced by the prominence and tenacity of the Davidic tradition within Israelite, Jewish, and Christian religions. The early Iron Age in the Near East was a transitional period: serious social traumas and political turmoils were caused when international forces withdrew and left Syrio-Palestine in a power vacuum. The inhabitants were swept up in a swirl of competing religious, military, political, and economic currents which the legendary David exploited for his own and his deity's gain. This was ideal soil in which a rich social drama could grow.

Paradoxes and enigmas about David abound. The roles of the biblical David and his reincarnations create ironies and ambiguities that stretch human imagination. In fact, the story is a metaphor carried by dramatic tradition to be used and reused.

Stages in The Ritual-myth

The Davidic ritual-myth was an enacted and self-validating story that confirmed people's beliefs when performed in both social and ritual dramas.

We should not be deceived by evolutionary biases to assume the stages were entirely sequential. Nine broad spatio-temporal divisions may be indicated as described by James W. Flanagan.[10]

Figure 8 distinguishes northern and southern Yahwistic traditions, the latter in *Numbers* 13–14, *Judges* 1, and *Joshua* 14.[11] The complexity is shown by the mixing of El and Yahweh rituals, Samu-el stories as Yahwist accounts, and the variety of "all Israel" meanings; i.e., transformed with Benjamin, Judah, and so on.

PERIOD	CHARACTERISTICS	REFERENCES
Pre-Yahwist	deity El; pre-Yahwist Israel	*Judges* 5, Samuel, Ark of Elohim
Early Yahwism (c.12th c.)	refers only to Yahweh; does not mention Israel	*Exodus* 15
Symbiotic Yahwism (c.11th c.)	uses "Yahweh" and "El"; "all Israel" = Israel + Benjamin	Ark of Yahweh, Ark of Elohim, stories of Saul
Syncretistic Yahwism (c. early 10th c.)	some variety in divine epithets; "all Israel" = Israel + Benjamin and Judah	David stories, *Samuel*; lists - David's family at Hebron
Later Syncretistic Yahwism (c.Mid-10th c.)	many divine epithets; "all Israel" = Israel + Benjamin and Judah	2 *Sam.* 21-24, lists - of David's family in Jer'm, of court officers (2 *Sam.*8, 20; *Pss.*89, 132)
Eclectic Yahwism (c. late 10th c.)	many epithets; knows of Sol's succession; "all Israel" = Israel + Benjamin and Judah	succession stories, Sol's list of court officers; reposition Dyn. Oracle (2 *Sam.* 7)
Divided Yahwism (Schism)	"all Israel" = Israel minus Benjamin and Judah	post-Schism stories in the Deut. History; El Psalter
Theologically United Yahwism (Deuteronomic)	aspires to a united Israel; sees a united past to support it	Deuteronomy stories of conquest in *Joshua*
Priestly Yahwism (Chronicles)	knows Judah alone as "all Israel"	genealogies, lists and "all Israel" references in *Chronicles*

Figure 8: Stages in The Davidic Ritual Myth

The changes move narrative and ritual units toward Yahwism and centralization. In *Samuel*, David's legitimacy and succession were separated. The Deuteronomists telescoped Davidic and dynastic legitimacy, linking them to Solomonic succession and Joshua's legitimacy. The *Chronicles*, however, mixed Davidic, dynastic and Solomonic legitimation in a single epoch.

THE NATURE OF THE SOCIAL DRAMA

The trauma of the times and the rapidly changing culture were ripe for the creation of a major social drama. The biblical literature portrays what happened. David's social drama, like others, was an aharmonic processual unit "which, seen retrospectively by an observer, can be shown to have structure,"[12] the structure of a rite of passage:

* the breach was the loss of the Ark,
* the crisis was the Philistines,
* the ineffective redressive action was the paramountcy of Saul and his son, and
* David's paramountcy became the effective redressive action which in terms of the social drama:
    - reintegrated the Yahwist community that had been sundered by the blunderings of Saul and Ishbaal, and
    - affirmed the loss of hope in effective leadership from Saul or his house.

But when the central rite of passage in *2 Samuel* 6 is viewed in this way, there is a question about the drama's ending.

The Oracle Problem

Does David's social drama end immediately in *2 Samuel* 7 or does it not? In the text, the contents of *2 Samuel* 6 and 7 are obviously a unity. This leads us to see that the process of fusing David's and Solomon's images has already begun.

Chapter 7 is usually seen as an anti-temple, pro-David, Dynastic Oracle that ends Saul's legitimacy and opens the way for Davidic successors.[13] Yet neither a successor nor monarchy is implied. *Samuel* refers solely to David and his leadership, not to Solomon. David's dialogue with Michal stresses that Yahweh has chosen him over Saul and Saul's house, without a reference to David's house.[14] The exception is the Oracle. If the story ends there, that would confirm the course many older commentators have taken. But this answer does not account for the rest of the story about David's house (Stage 4 in *Figure 8*).

James W. Flanagan shows that *2 Samuel* 7 (the Oracle) is out of order.[15] It belongs after the cosmic duel, the purchase of the threshing floor, and David's submission to Yahweh portrayed in *2 Samuel* 24 when the census has been thwarted. The issue of a ruling house was not resolved in the story at the time of the relocation of the Ark. Indeed, most critics believe that the Dynastic Oracle in *2 Samuel* 7 was amended several times—like genealogies—in order to keep it up to date. Mythically *2 Samuel* 7 summarizes and completes themes that extend through *Samuel* down to *2 Samuel* 24. The redressive action of raising David over Saul's house, ritually enacted in *2 Samuel* 6, reaches Stage 4 in *Figure 8* in the social drama at the end of *2 Samuel*.

The Oracle scene, with its ritual inferences, completes the rite of passage begun at Shiloh and Ramah and advances by the relocation of the Ark in Jerusalem. The world that was centred around the Ark is fulfilled and displaced by another world centering on David and his house now firmly established under Yahweh in Jerusalem.

This was a shift in root paradigms. The Dynastic Oracle forbids the centralization implied by temples. David's house is affirmed but without full centralization.

David As Liminal

In *Samuel*, dynasty and succession are positioned between tribalism and monarchy. In the J ritual-myth there is a sequence: tribalism ⇒ dynasty ⇒ succession ⇒ monarchy. David is a mediator always remembered as liminal

—for being betwixt and between. He lives in a cultic life portrayed as standing between:

north	south
the Judahites	"all Israel"
the Benjaminites	Judahites
Saul's dynasty	David's dynasty
egalitarianism	monopolized force
the human	the divine
semi-agrarian, agrarian	pastoral, semi-pastoral
political devolution	political evolution
kings	chiefs
David the ally of Saul	David the refugee
Philistine opposition	Philistine alliance
House of Saul	House of David
Ark	temple
Yahweh	earthly and cosmic foes

In the plot, David is between each of these. Successors must measure their legitimacy against David as a model.

Structure

In accordance with the stages of the ritual-myth (see *Figure 8*), the social drama of David has a particular structure:

[1] The pre- or non-Yahwist Isra-el, in which Samu-el plays a role, merges with Yahwists of Benjamin to form "all Israel" under Saul.

[2] After a while, David rises to lead the Philistines. Eventually the council of elders accepts him as leader of both Judah and the Philistines.

[3] Later he assumes leadership over the northern group and also leads the two moieties, Judah and Israel. Then he turns against the Philistines.

[4] His own legitimacy is continually threatened until, in the myth, first he, and then his house, is legitimated. This is not the succession theme associated with Solomon, but a Davidic theme whereby he displaces first Saul, then Saul's

house, then the Philistines, and finally the Ark of the Covenant.

[5] Only afterward, in a final combat with Yahweh where census-taking and plagues are the weapons, does David finally submit himself and his model of leadership to the deity. Chieftaincy over the two large moieties, Israel and Judah, and other sociopolitical units is legitimated. The process is a dramatic one, and continues under Solomon.[16]

In the ritual drama, David's relationships are paradigmatic and foundational; they contain implicit order that becomes explicit later. The dynasty unfolds in tumultuous and unexpected ways. Each repetition creates its own sequence, but the underlying transitions remain, nested like levels in a segmented genealogy. Four examples illustrate this: the Deuteronomists changed the position of the Dynastic Oracle; the Chroniclers ignored the role of Samuel in the story of David's rise; Solomon's legitimation was portrayed as another level in the transition from Saul; and Josiah's reform was presented as a re-play of David's legitimating role.[17]

But was the David–Solomon Play one unity, or (as is more likely) was the David Play first performed in Solomon's time, and the David–Solomon Play first performed after Solomon's death? This is still a puzzle.

We will now discuss two major ritual dramas: the Ark processional below, and the coronation drama in Chapter 10.

THE ARK PROCESSIONAL

As the Israelites entered Canaan, Joshua had created a processional ritual drama about the crossing of the Jordan which paralleled the crossing of the Sea of Reeds. Later the journey from Ramathaim in Zuph, to Shiloh and Ramah, and back to Shiloh, entwined stories about Samuel with those of the Ark and Saul. The story-line moves progressively toward centralization.

During Absalom's rebellion, Zadok and the Levites carried the Ark from the city in procession, only to be sent back by David. The ritual of the procession was growing and slowly approached ritual drama. That it was ritualistic is seen in a repetitive pattern: if we compare it with David's return we see that he met many of the same individuals and groups that he had encountered during his visits.

The people had to choose between the Ark and David. After the move to Jerusalem, the Ark was less frequently mentioned: its significance diminished as the importance of the houses of the deity and the monarch increased.

In the dialogue between David and Uriah, where the soldier exhibits a lingering attachment to the Ark, "house" is used seven times;[18] it was stressed again when Nathan rebuked and David repented.[19] In David's time, those who were not engaged in temple-building kept their allegiance to the Ark; but those who built the temple stressed the dynastic claims of David. The importance of the Ark was made explicit by David's words, "If I find favour with the Lord, he will bring me back and permit me to see it and its lodging. But if he should say, 'I am not pleased with you,' I am ready; let him do to me as he sees fit."[20]

Rebellion and exile were placed in the larger context of divine control over David's destiny.[21] The competing views supported and opposed David's legitimacy, and were acted out in the social drama.

The leader was dethroned, chaos reigned, and although he was custodian of the Ark, David was driven beyond the border in a ritualized retreat to the wilderness. The procession was more than a retreat before an aggressor. It was also the undoing of the first entry into Canaan.

By leaving the Ark behind but returning to the house, David performed another rite of passage and a new entry parallel to the ark's first entry. This one involved:

* The river Jordan was crossed twice: from Jerusalem to the wilderness to Jerusalem—from aggregation to liminality to reaggregation.
* Like the ark's journey from Transjordan to Gilgal and eventually to Jerusalem, David returned across the river, first to Gilgal and then to Jerusalem. He left the land without the Ark in order to test Yahweh. He re-entered, regained Jerusalem, and replaced the Ark and the allegiance to it.

*   The Ark and the view it stood for were displaced. The cycle from Moses
     to David was complete.

David became the symbol of Yahweh's presence in Jerusalem. He was the
new Moses, the new Joshua, and the new Ark, the permanent representative
of Yahweh among the people. The processional drama of David echoed that
of Joshua but ritualized the new events of David's time.

10
THE DAVID PLAY

Nowhere does the Bible say that there was a monarchic ritual drama about David—the post-Exilic authors have expurgated it well—nor are there any archeological findings to show that it existed. Yet there is internal evidence from which we can strongly *infer* that the David Play was the key to the social drama. It is likely that performances had the same *form* as the Moses Festival Play, although it had many differences in *content*.

The play occurred over some days; the king and priests took the main roles at some times but acted as themselves at others; and there were many small dramas incorporated into the whole and linked by processionals. This was the general pattern of ritual dramas in the ancient Near East in the Iron Age and there is no reason to think that David's was any different.

Yahweh's covenants in the wilderness and in Jerusalem, the temple, and dynasty at the mythic level—all are clear signs of the divine plan guiding life. David maintained and fulfilled the Mosaic covenantal tradition with Yahwists in Jerusalem. He ensured its continuance when he established a dynasty and constructed a permanent resting place for the Ark in the house of Yahweh in Jerusalem.

Dynasty and David

Dynasty was introduced in *2 Samuel* 7 after David relocated his capital in Jerusalem. The transition is made quickly in *2 Samuel* 6 and 7 when David displaces Saul and dynasty is promised—which takes much longer. By putting *2 Samuel* 6 and 7 ahead of the problems David faced, the Deuteronomists shifted the focus from past to future—from Saul's fate to Solomon's succession—and they laid the groundwork for questions about succession and individual successors. Dynasty becomes the issue immediately—after the childlessness of Michal, the Davidic dynasty is at once proclaimed. David mediates the transition between themes while Solomon is the outcome of the dynastic promise rather than a founder of Jerusalem. Thus there is a double focus to the Oracle: [1] dynasty is not yet established—events must unfold during the rest of David's reign; and, [2] dynasty is declared by *2 Samuel* 7.

James W. Flanagan[1] shows that *2 Samuel* 9–20 through *1 Kings* 1–2 was not a single composition but two. *2 Samuel* 9–10, 13–20 was a "Court History" showing how David maintained paramountcy; and this was revised to include Solomon and became a "Succession Narrative."

Jerusalem signals the start of a new phase in Yahwist life. David's divinely authorized leadership moves from the northern Israelites to the south and Judah—the focus is Zion, so changing the central questions in the story.

In *Chronicles*, David formulated the plans and arrangements for the Temple; and he designated his successor who had to execute his plans. *Chronicles* links the dynasty to the Schism, but the Deuteronomists link David's dynasty and personal legitimacy with Solomon's succession. The David and Solomon stories unfold in unison as the threats by the elder sons are eliminated one by one. Solomon's role is part of David's legacy in *Chronicles*, but he is the dynastic successor for the Deuteronomists. He plays neither role in *Samuel*: David and Davidic dynasty are chosen, but no successor is named.

The Hero

A major alteration from the Moses Play to the David Play is a change in emphasis. Originally Yahweh was the *protagonist*, with his helpers Moses and Aaron. The *antagonist* was the Pharaoh while Moses was a sort of hero, but he was very much the helper of God. The new hero described by the Deuteronomists was David,[2] and interest shifted from the *protagonist* to the hero. David was the model for Solomon, Asa, Amaziah, Ahaz, Hezekiah, and Josiah;[3] repeatedly they were condemned by failing to meet his standards,[4] and he was given credit and lauded for his plans to build the temple,[5] even though Yahweh opposed the scheme.[6]

The Deuteronomists linked the David–Solomon–Temple theme but the Chroniclers treated their reigns as a single epoch: the two kings shared temple worship as a sign of their religious importance. Yet behind the structural change of the Moses Play to the David Play stood a common value system, one that Moses represented and that David and all leaders obeyed. Unlike his figure in *Chronicles*, the Deuteronomic David appeared as the new Moses who combined loyalty to the Covenant, unity of the land, and a need for centralized leadership in Jerusalem. Solomon, on the other hand, excelled when he completed his father's plans, as in *Chronicles*, by building the temple. But he failed by submitting to self-contradictory pagan (decentralizing) worship.

Patterns within The Succession Narrative suggest that its writing was "not far from an oral stage of transmission, though its precise relation to oral story-telling is impossible to determine."[7] This brings the Succession Narrative close to ritual drama.

THE CORONATION RITUAL DRAMA

In the David–Solomon period, the Israelite ritual drama had at its core the Davidic and Jerusalemite legitimacy—at least as represented at the action level in *Psalm* 132. Contained within the Coronation performance were the rituals and myths of the previous stages. The performers recalled earlier transitions in both myth and ritual. They then presented these transitions as both cause and effect.

As in Babylonia and Egypt, the leading performer in the Coronation ritual drama was the king, either in actuality or by a priest representing him. This accounts for why the titles of nearly seventy hymns in the Psalter claim David as author, although he is explicitly named within only five.[8] To the Psalter's editors, David was central to the Yahwist performance tradition.

The actor-psalmist and his assistant performers re-presented two creative acts as discrete parts of a single moment in the ritual-myth. Thus:

* He moved the ark—he represented a breaking away from the chaotic uncertainty caused by the absence of a sacred place.
* He established a new ruling house—he made a guarantee against future uncertainty caused either by weak or non-existent leadership.

Sanctifying a place (Jerusalem) and blessing a lineage (the dynasty) were inextricably linked to the royal ritual drama.

The performances were the focus of the New Year Festival: they occurred seasonally or at threatening times of change (e.g., inaugurations of leaders, confrontations with enemies) when the Davidic transitions were recalled and re-enacted. There may have been other important transformations (e.g., the Philistines displacing Yahwist dominance) but we cannot trace them as ritual. Yet we can infer that the actor-psalmist: [a] personified the David character, [b] symbolized Yahweh's choosing Jerusalem and dynasty, and [c] included most, if not all, of the previous transitions within Yahwism.

Ritual Battles

David's rise is the main thread of the Coronation ritual drama; it dominates *1 Samuel* and *2 Samuel* 1–5. The principal rite of passage is set in *2 Samuel* 6, and a series of threats to David's sovereignty are described in *2 Samuel* 8–20. Omitting the David and Bathsheba materials in *2 Samuel* 11–12,[9] the plot ends at *2 Samuel* 24 before the Solomonic succession scene in *1 Kings* 1–2.

Yahweh is still the *protagonist*—as was the case in The Moses Festival Play—but David dominates the new ritual drama. Compared with Moses, David is a highly complex figure, and he becomes an *activator*, a spirit-mediator. The energy moves from the Ark to David; then David is positioned between Yahweh and the people, rather than between Yahweh and the Ark.[10] And ritual combat becomes a central focus.

One ritual combat happened in the rivalry between Saul's and David's houses during Ishbaal's reign; the attempt to contain violence begins with a ritual duel between the representatives of David and Ishbaal.[11] This trial-by-ordeal is unsuccessful and the conflict widens to include David's followers and the men of Israel. A negotiated settlement is attempted but, when this fails, war engulfs the two houses.[12] The context and dialogue, told from David's perspective, shows Ishbaal's ineptitude to restrict the conflict. The structure of the ritual shows that both David and Ishbaal are absent.

The conflict begins at once after reports of their respective accessions in Judah and Israel; the initial struggle is for the allegiance of Benjamin.[13] This ritual battle has many subtleties: David waits as he seeks to expand his network of allegiances; when Abner approaches and offers the allegiance of "all Israel," David still waits as he attaches conditions to protect himself.[14] To stress his legitimacy as Saul's successor, he demands the prior return of his wife, Michal. The re-marriage is a sign of the current peace treaty: it assuages the insult Saul gave David by giving Michal to Palti without compensation to David;[15] and it gives David a role in determining the destiny of Saul's family.[16] In dramatic style, this calculated slow pace contrasts with David's immediate action against Ishbaal's assassins.[17] The well-planned structure reaches a climax when David accepts the treaty of Israel's elders.[18] Genuine drama is beginning to emerge from the ritual battle.

The second ritual battle reminds us of the dramatic elements of the Greek *agon*. David rejects illegitimate opportunities given by opportunists, and is ready to answer the call of his deity. Far from the simple psychology of the Babylonian and Egyptian ritual battles, it is also a cosmic duel by using a census and a plague as the instruments. The battle is full of the imagery of ritual; it is the ultimate contest that makes David a vassal and mediator in his own right rather than just a custodian of the Ark. In ordering the census, David acts like a tyrannical monarch: he asserts a secular political power that violates religious values. Yahweh's response is a plague. This attacks the population base that David's plans depend on; it reduces David's economic surpluses and increases resistance to taxation and conscription. Yahweh's sovereignty is demonstrated in socioeconomic realities; chieftaincy is maintained, monarchy is forestalled, and the limits of legitimate centralization are set.

A natural balance is maintained *in the myth* by the cosmic struggle. But *in the ritual* it is transformed into and maintained by a battle. At the story level, the deity has a cosmic struggle against the forces of chaos.[19] This is reinterpreted as the enactment of a human combat against enemies, where the struggle in the social world parallels that in the divine realm.[20] Finally God and king are linked in both praise and guarantees of continued kindness.[21] So David's attempt to monopolize force is thwarted. A threshing floor is purchased, an altar erected, and offerings made.[22] The legitimacy rooted in the Ark (Samuel–Saul), and handed down with the Ark, comes to rest in David's offerings on Aruanah's threshing floor in Jerusalem—foreshadowed by the threshing floor at Ramah, the place of Samuel's birth.[23] Other scenes also reverse or balance earlier ones: an examples is the slaughter of the house of Saul[24] and the symbolic suppression of the Philistines.[25] The message is that just as Samuel, Saul, and Saul's house lived under Yahweh's judgment, so David must also accept and express his dependency. As so often, ritual exemplifies proper order.

DRAMAS HIDDEN IN VERSE

The creators and performers of the poems were not necessarily a single Yahwist group. Despite their differences, they make a fundamental assertion —*stability on earth depends on divine intervention*. The focus in the ritual drama of the Yahwist cult was order. Yahweh, David and Jerusalem were the basic symbols of Davidic theology which, in the ritual context of the hymns, were direct actions as well as representations.

Psalm 132

Psalm 132 reveals a ritual performance. It commemorates Yahweh's election of Jerusalem and the Davidic dynasty:

* David wants a permanent dwelling place for Yahweh (vv. 1–5);
* the Ark of the covenant is transferred to Jerusalem (vv. 6–10);
* Yahweh has promised to establish a dynasty (vv. 11–13); and
* to dwell permanently in Zion (vv. 14-18).

The *Psalm* reflects the *structure* of the performance.

It is also an excellent example of the Jerusalem hymnic and ritual traditions, for it mythologizes events alleged to have happened in David's time. It incorporates them into the liturgy, and it recalls them in ritual dramas at crucial moments in time. These performance acts renewed the mythic order maintained by kingship. Their power helped to resist the threatening chaos, and gave meaning and order in the performers' world. By re-enactment, the *Psalm* preserved the transitions that secured Jerusalem for Yahweh and leadership for David's house. Re-enacting the myth in the ritual perpetuated the divinely sanctioned order.

Unlike the same tale in *Samuel*, in the *Psalm* all is symbolized in a single quasi-exchange of gifts: the hero, David, is already in charge and plays the mediator role; he is the actor-agent who gives Yahweh and Israel a permanent place of worship while receiving in return a promise that his house will rule forever. David is ritualized. He stands eternally in sacred Jerusalem, in a sacred time where Ark and dynasty meet briefly within him while history moves on.

The psalmists make the ritual drama relevant to their own day. They combine episodes, making them two scenes in the same ritual act. Transferring power to Jerusalem and perpetuating Zion become a single divine choice. Only the significant transitions accomplished by David are celebrated in the *Psalm* because they remain relevant for later ages. The narrative version emphasizes David, the *Psalm* focuses on Jerusalem.

The emphasis in *Psalm* 132 on the Ark and its transfer to Jerusalem is replaced by a rejection of a warrior (Saul) and the anointing of youth (David). As in *2 Samuel* 6, to displace David's predecessor is an epoch-making event: it marks the beginning of confidence in Yahweh's control. But the central performer (possibly in the role of David or his surrogates, an individual or a group) fears a reversal—a cancellation of Yahweh's election of David. The performer experiences a rejection that, combined with sterility and old age, threatens the promised dynasty. This emotional content is a forerunner of the Greek *agon*.

Psalm 89

Psalm 89 encapsulates a two-act ritual drama, mixing memories of the promised Davidic dynasty with mythical elements common in ancient Canaanite dramatic poems. The sequence of real and potential catastrophes suggested by the *Psalm* is similar to episodes described in the Deuteronomic history.[26] The *Psalm*'s theme is announced in a prelude (vv. 2-5), followed by a hymn to the creator (vv. 6-19), a dynastic oracle (vv. 20-38), a description of a king's humiliation (vv. 39-46), and a plea by the king begging Yahweh to remember earlier divine promises (vv. 47–52). *Psalm* 89 hides ritual action in two parts:

* *The deity.* Israel's true king (v. 19) controls all creation while the adopted son, the earthly leader (v. 27), controls the land stretching from the sea to the river (v. 26).

* *Disaster strikes.* Yahweh will not withdraw his dynastic promise (vv. 37-38), but the actor-speaker[27] is determined (v. 45), although he is taunted by neighbours (v. 42), stripped of youthfulness, and robbed of manhood by sterility (v. 45).[28] Humiliated but confident, he pleads for Yahweh to be faithful to promises made to David (v. 50).

The crux lies in verses 20-21 which refer[29] to a major transition in Israel's political life: "I made a lad ruler in preference to a warrior, I exalted a youth above a hero," and "I found David my servant, with my holy oil I anointed him."

Within a ritual performance, *Psalm* 89 shows the Yahwists' delicate political and religious situation. For David to displace Saul, Yahweh's favour had to be withdrawn from one and bestowed on other. Such a change in divine plans was exceptional. It was also dangerous—it could easily be undone later.

The *Psalm* in performance generated the metaphorization of the rites of passage contained within the ritual. The hero, David, was in a mythological liminal state. He was situated precariously between two acts of divine favour. But in the event, as the ritual is performed, Yahweh decides to discontinue Saul's house, and promises dynastic succession—at the very moment when one ritual action was completed and the other anticipated. *Psalm* 89, in other words, captures the transformational process of ritual drama.

The Reversible World

In the Deuteronomic narrative, David's legitimacy as successor of Saul had depended on: [a] his marriage to Michal, Saul's daughter, and [b] on David's potency. From David, offspring were refused to Michal and not possible for Abishag. Bathsheba, however, was a non-Saulide and non-concubine wife-mother to David. Yet questions about Saulide legitimacy persisted in the narrative. The issue of whose house would inherit, Michal's or David's, was not squarely faced until the time when David's successor was chosen. Then, a son by Bathsheba was selected, and the final transition from the house of Saul to the house of David was achieved.

We have seen that ritual is repetitive and works with parallelisms. The David rituals, however, have additional characteristics. Ritual is ambiguous and paradoxical, presenting two or more meanings at once, and even inverting them. The David stories include reversals and displacement of actions within the content and structure of the plot. The episodes are serial, but scenes can be inverted in two ways: [1] one scene, inverting a second, can "nest" within the other as the plot unfolds; and [2] reversals can occur from several smaller but similarly structured episodes.

This reversible world is integral to the David story. Metamorphoses of the story include structural reverses like David succeeds Saul, Jerusalem replaces holy places like Shiloh and Hebron, and Philistine dominance is overcome by David and Jerusalem. Also the principal storylines are repeated on smaller scales in many units: e.g., David's elegy for Saul and Jonathan,[30] Meribaal's house arrest,[31] the parable of the wise woman from Tekoa,[32] and others. Each encapsulates the relations that are inherent in the whole ritual world.

We have already seen that a major characteristic of ritual is that it "stops time." This is most obvious in *Samuel* when progression and reversal occur simultaneously. Thus, after the relocation in Jerusalem, the plot moves forward and ends in a second "capture" of Jerusalem. But the story also reaches back constantly to the past, to undo and re-do things said and done before. Thus fulfillment themes—now metamorphoses—reappear constantly. The inter-actions of the present–past processes are like contrasting but spiralling forces that try to push the story forward while constantly refocusing it on a single vortex. In the Bible, these are literary versions of the horizontal and vertical axes found in rituals that are canonical and indexical. In the story, a central message endures but its telling and acting are reshaped repeatedly from scene to scene. The fundamental transformations are mapped and recalled as the story unfolds; thus *2 Samuel* 21–24 should be read in light of the reversal, displacement and fulfillment themes, and the David story presents two or more meanings at once, and can even invert them.

Order and Balance

Many other biblical poems related to David reveal aspects of an underlying monarchic ritual drama.

Order and the appropriate balance of natural and supernatural worlds are basic to all ritual drama. In the Song of Hannah, "a god who balances his actions" guards the king.[33] In David's lament for Saul and Jonathan, the dominance of the Israelites over the Philistines is thrown into imbalance by the deaths.[34] Also David's Last Words[35] credit the eternal Covenant for ensuring the dynasty; it has solar imagery that expresses confidence in perpetual order and stability; it promises that the loyal will flourish and the opposition wither;[36] and it pairs Yahweh–El and Israel–Jacob to make their contrasting relationships important factors in maintaining the balance.

Psalm 68

The Davidic ritual drama included segments that celebrated God's earlier actions. This is shown in *Psalm* 68 where Elohim is mentioned twenty-four times.

The *Psalm* was likely sung as the Ark was ritually carried into battle—and then repeated in the ritual of the battle. The Exodus and Conquest, the choice of Zion (vv. 16–19), Israel's victories, and the ark's procession (vv. 25–28) were all re-enacted. The performances evoked memories of past events, but also provided a solid basis for belief.

Jerusalem

We can infer from *Psalm* 78 in the Elohistic Psalter that, in places in the David Play, God was portrayed as choosing to dwell permanently in Judah and Zion, and to elect David, the shepherd of Jacob.

The transitions are parallel to the recollections in *Psalm* 132 where the nomadic way of life gives way to the settled urban environment.[37] *Psalm* 72, also in the Elohistic Psalter, was probably celebrated at the Coronation for one of David's successors: just rule, glorious reign, universal dominion, protection of the poor, and the prosperity of the kingdom were commemorated as the religious goals. Jerusalem was the mythic centre to which the tribes of Yahweh processed and where the house of David rested.[38] But Zion ritually stood in a liminal state as the holy place where Yahweh dwelt.

Psalm 144

The final explicit reference to David in the texts of the *Psalms* is the supplication beseeching Yahweh's blessing, with its confidence based on David's survival, in the composite *Psalm* 144. It is, of course, not known for certain whether the mythological or ritual levels of the *Psalms* were based on real historical events. But the *Psalms* do provide information in the realms of public ideas, held by worshipping Yahwists over many generations, and represented in story and action.

STEPS IN THE DAVID PLAY

It is obvious that we know less about the David Play than the Moses Play. David continued the amalgamation of dramatic Festivals which had begun before his reign. He first took two disparate elements—the Ark and the Tent —and brought them together as cultic objects for the first time since Moses.[39]

Although he wished to replace the old Tent with a splendid royal Temple patterned after the temples of other nations, conservative religious traditions voiced by the prophet Nathan prevented him.[40] He had to be content with other types of reorganization and one of these was in the use of religious music—David was a reputed musician[41] and he used this skill to reorganize the temple musicians into guilds.[42] He reinterpreted the Moses Play into a celebration of the founding of Zion as the place chosen by Yahweh for the true worship, supported by establishing the sanctuary of the Ark in Jerusalem. Thus he made Judah as the centre of the belief in a God without image as the only correct one; and the house of David as divinely appointed to rule from the holy city.

David's royal dramatic performance took the old New Year Festival and modified it still further according to the fertility religion—probably under the priesthood of Zadok. Despite the biblical writers' later attacks upon what they saw as pagan worship, in this performance fertility imagery was prominent. Although there were ritual curses, these were not spoken in the same way as in Babylon (by the god, Marduk). Rather, they were chanted by the community itself. Further, like all Israelite New Year Festivals, the David Play began in the middle: those centred on non-Israelite deities began with the Creation, but the early Israelite ceremonies all began with Moses.

Adonijah, a pretender to the throne of David in his old age, staged a ceremony of installment and anointment at a specific stone near the Fuller's Spring, not far from Jerusalem. David retaliated by having his son, Solomon, formally anointed beside another spring, called Gihon. From this we know that the Hebrew ritual of anointment was related to the fertility traditions of water: as the source of all primal virtues and wisdom, as propitiation to water spirits (gods, goddesses), and as baptism to provide "intelligence" (power).[43] Israelite kings, like many others in the ancient world, were crowned near stones, or stone pillars, or wood pillars[44]—the *massebah* or *asherah*, which united the Hebrew concept of Coronation with the shamanic tree of life.

SOLOMON

It is likely that in the Festival events in the time of Solomon the David Play took its final form. Centred on David, it was particularly splendid and ornately spectacular.

There are two references to the Ark in the Solomonic succession scene.[45] In the second, after offering sacrifice at Gibeon, Solomon returns to Jerusalem to stand before the Ark and offer sacrifices. Thus in spite of the Deuteronomic demand for centralized worship, the king circulates as the Ark had done before.

The final appearances of the Ark in the Deuteronomic history are during the construction and dedication of the Temple.[46] Again the theme is permeated with references to houses. "House" is used frequently to refer to both the Temple, the house of Yahweh,[47] and the palace—the house of the king.[48] The Ark is placed in the Temple and a dedication prayer is offered linking the temple to the promise made to David. The Ark, now displaced by the Temple and house of David, is not mentioned again in *Deuteronomy*. If the post-Davidic succession is not addressed, the passages may have been written before questions of dynasty were decided. Not until *2 Samuel 7*[49] is Yahweh's plan for the future revealed.

A paradox emerges. In one sense, the Temple stands as a continuation and extension of the hopes symbolized by the Ark. The building is a "house" for Yahweh, primarily because it shelters the Ark. But in another sense, the Temple displaces the Ark by making Jerusalem Yahweh's permanent home and David the permanent representative. The change is so great that the Deuteronomists make no mention of the sacred chest after it is situated in the temple sanctuary.

We should note in passing the remarkable coincidence that *the concept* (not the word) "house" was also used in the medieval Mystery plays to indicate a stage locality. Was it also so used in ancient Israel?

But once Solomon died, and the state was divided, there were other vast changes in ritual.

11

DRAMA IN THE TWO KINGDOMS

After Solomon's death, the country split into two parts (the Schism): Israel under Jeroboam in the north, and Judah under Solomon's son, Rehoboam, in the south. Religious observances and dramatic ceremonials developed differently in each country. We can follow some ritual changes mainly from *Chronicles*.

Building the Temple gave legitimacy to David's successors. But the personal and military goals of other monarchs were dwarfed by the accounts of David's campaigns: he dominated the Philistines, Moabites, Edomites, Ammonites, and Aram and, with alliances, Tyre and Hamath.[1] His successors did not aim so high. In the *Chronicles*, strong foreign armies combined with internal lack of harmony among the Yahwists to restrict Jerusalem's leaders after Solomon.

Rival ways to represent the true Israel emerged in the post-Solomonic era. At first, Rehoboam went to Shechem to be made king of the whole country ("all Israel"),[2] but Jeroboam and Northern Israel (ten tribes) eventually broke away and left him with the "children of Israel"—those who lived in the cities of Judah.[3]

Rehoboam fled to Jerusalem and "Israel has been in rebellion against the house of David to this day."[4] He gathered the houses of Judah and Benjamin to fight against the north, but the prophet Shemaiah ordered Rehoboam and "all Israel in Judah and Benjamin" not to fight against their brethren.[5] Judah and Benjamin remained with Rehoboam,[6] and priests and Levites fled from "all Israel" in the north to join him.[7] He dealt prudently with the people in Judah and Benjamin,[8] but eventually he and all Israel, it was said, abandoned the law.[9]

The distinction between "all Israel" as one religious group and the geopolitical regions (Israel, Judah and Benjamin) that the writers introduce at the time of the Schism, continued during the remainder of their account. Finally, during Josiah's Passover, the Levites were identified as responsible for instructing all Israel.[10] The reforms of Hezekiah and Josiah retained David as the norm against whom subsequent monarchs were judged—as with the popularity of Solomon. The Chroniclers showed concern for cultic matters, priests and Levites, and law;[11] and by addressing issues about the Temple, the Passover, and the proclamation sent throughout all Israel from Beersheba to Dan,[12] they showed an admiration for Solomon that slowly made him the model instead of David. Some contemporary scholars even think that the Chroniclers perceived Hezekiah as a second Solomon.[13]

Shechem, site of Jeroboam's coronation as king of Israel, is the setting of a doubtful passage, revised from J, in *Genesis* 34:21, where Hamor and Shechem speak to their townspeople, saying of the sons of Jacob, "Look: the land is broad enough to embrace them" (75). J's irony is double: [a] Hamor, Shechem, and those they address will soon lie slaughtered on the land, and [b] those who live under Rehoboam have seen the revenge of Shechem under the leadership of Jeroboam, who has taken away Israel. In *Exodus*, this ironic refrain continues, first in 3:8, when Yahweh says to Moses, "I beheld the burden my people held—in Egypt. I come down to lift them out of Egypt's hand, to carry them to a broad, open land" (115). The allusion is to Rehoboam: it contrasts the return to the promised land with the unfortunate king's destruction of the work of Yahweh.

The declaration of the Commandments in *Exodus* 34, where Yahweh chants, "So be it: I will disperse a nation in your path, broaden your road and borders; so no one dreams he can embrace your land on your way to Yahweh; as you go up to face your God three times a year" (165), is ominous for Rehoboam because it echoes his name's root—Rehoboam has been attacked through ironic allusion. The ironies are of the Patriarchs and of Moses, but it is the imperial theme of David and Solomon that implicitly provides the sense of glory that Rehoboam does not meet.

DEVELOPMENTS IN THE NORTHERN KINGDOM
(922-722 B.C.)

The later biblical scribes in Judah remained faithful to the Davidic line and the Jerusalem Temple. As a result, Jeroboam was pictured as a political renegade about whom they said nothing good. In reality, he must have been a man of outstanding personality to have been unanimously chosen as head of the breakaway kingdom, and also to maintain it as a strong state.

His first capital was Shechem but, after a brief interval, he established a new capital at Tirzah, seven miles north-east of Shechem. He understood that his people's religious thought had to be turned away from the Temple at Jerusalem[14] so he developed two ancient sanctuaries: Bethel to the south, and Dan to the north-east. In both he built the image of a calf and destroyed the power of the Levites as priests. He also fostered worship at local shrines of "high places." The annual feast of Succoth he fixed in the ninth month of the Jewish calendar, instead of in the eighth month as in Judah. All these changes were devised to break religious ties with Jerusalem, but the scribes in Judah regarded them as evidence of a drift towards paganism.

Changes in The Coronation Drama

Jeroboam altered the Coronation Drama. He began to dismantle the Davidic traditions to change the custom of making pilgrimages to the Jerusalem Temple. He tried to return to the ancient Festival of Joshua during the Feast of Booths held in the autumn of the year. Some of the psalms are part of this ritual drama in the Northern Kingdom.[15] For example, *Psalm* 81 has close affinities with Joshua's covenant renewal at Shechem.[16] The initial verses (vv. 1–5) give a summons to worship "the God of Jacob" and the sanctuary "on our feast day." The next section (vv. 6–10) recites the deeds of benevolence performed by Yahweh, including the announcement, "I am Yahweh." The climax is reached with an appeal to the community to hear Yahweh's voice and receive his blessings (vv. 11–16).

Northern traditions deliberately dramatized the crossing of the Jordan as the re-enactment of the miracle of the Sea of Reeds. For the earlier Shechemites, the crossing of the Jordan had symbolized the taking possession of the land as well as the Exodus. But after the Schism the procession from Succoth to Shechem was almost entirely understood to re-enact the crossing of the Sea of Reeds by the cultic crossing of the Jordan[17]—as in *Psalm* 114. The two crossings also symbolized God's decision to initiate the conquest of Canaan.

The Land-giving followed the Covenant and was vital; in contrast, at Gilgal in the south the Land-giving was the result of the conquest. Further developments came in the organization of the liturgy. The processional route continued to boast many famous shrines but the north developed the sanctuary at Shechem as the centre of all ritualized events. Steadily, therefore, this Shechem sanctuary became the cultic Sinai of the Covenant—it was dramatized *as if it was Sinai.*

Elijah and Elisha

As Moses had been acknowledged as God's representative because of the miraculous crossing which he planned, so Joshua had won acknowledgement of the same title for a similar reason.

The Bible also made Elijah and Elisha the officers of God. Elijah was purposely presented as a new Moses, and Elisha as a faithful imitation of Elijah. Like Moses on Sinai, so Elijah on Carmel mediated a Covenant between Yahweh and the people.[18] As Moses destroyed his adversaries with a curse, so Elijah destroyed the King's soldiers by calling down fire on them.[19] Like Moses, Elijah received the privilege of seeing God pass.[20] As Moses handed over his task to Joshua, so Elijah anointed Elisha to be prophet in his place.[21] As Moses was taken up by God in the Transjordan and his body was not found, so Elijah was taken up and his body too was never found.[22] As Moses divided the Sea of Reeds, so Elijah first divided the water with his mantle[23] and, afterwards, Elisha performed the same miracle with the mantle Elijah left behind.[24]

These repetitive actions are typical descriptions of early rituals, and it is likely that the historic figures of Elijah and Elisha were incorporated into the New Year Festival and its ritual drama. This provided new incidents of a contemporary kind that paralleled those of Moses and Joshua.

This kind of expansion of ritual drama has always been common among traditional peoples. For example, the ritual-myth of the Wolf was created on the Northwest Pacific Coast of Canada quickly after Captain Cook's arrival (1778) and, shortly thereafter, dozens of different spirits had similar ritual-myths in a gigantic mystery play ("The Winter Ceremonial") lasting months. Also once this mystery play form had been created, a second such play ("Those Who Descended from the Heavens") was created inverting much of the first.[25]

The dramatic competition on Mount Carmel between Elijah and the priests of Baal is a parallel to the competition of Moses and the Egyptian priests. Both have the structure of ritual plays or scenes.

What was involved on Mount Carmel was a competition in rain-making through five rituals during a period of drought. Rain-making is a prime shamanic skill and Baal was specifically a god of rainfall. The priests of Baal tried to light their fire by gashing themselves with knives and dancing in the same way as Agag—a limping and jumping dance that was a funeral ritual for Baal, the dying and reviving god of fertility. When these priests failed in their ritual dance, Elijah mocked them. He called upon them to cry aloud, it being a standard practice to imitate the noise of thunder-storms to bring about rain. He also satirically invited them to cry "Awake!" to their god, a ritual cry that was part of the ceremony of waking the fertility god in many places in the ancient world—like Osiris in Egypt, Dionysos in Greece, and Bacchus in Rome.

Elijah took twelve stones to build an altar to Yahweh. Digging a ditch around it, he ordered twelve barrelsful of water to be poured over it and to fill the ditch. Although the biblical writer suggests this was the renovation of an old Yahweh altar, and that the twelve stones represented the twelve tribes of Israel, an older explanation is more likely. All over the world, certain stones are thought to have the power to bring rain—derived from the *batons* of ancient shamans who had marked them over generations with calendrical signs that told the future. The repetition of the number twelve indicates that Elijah's actions were part of a ritual—twelve was often used for magical properties as a round number. When Elijah filled the trench with water, he may have been engaged in sympathetic magic. Yet he was also reviving an old Near Eastern belief that drought was caused when the waters of the subterranean ocean (which supposedly welled up in the form of springs) disappeared down a crevice; by pouring more water down a crevice, they could be made to rise and overflow. In the same way, on the last day of the Eleusian Mysteries in Greece water was poured into a "chasm of the earth."[26]

Elijah, like Moses, used the procedures of ancient magicians to demonstrate the power of Yahweh. Yet the appeal to the people was that Yahweh's power was of a different quality from that demonstrated by the magicians of other gods. What might seem ironic to a modern reader, however, would not have appeared so to a Hebrew of the period who likely saw the events performed in a ritual play.

The Goddess and Fertility

The Northern Israelites turned further to the gods of the land. Under the influence of Jezebel of Sidon, King Ahab (c. 869-850 B.C.) built an altar to Baal in the capital, Samaria, and "made" an Asherah. Four hundred and fifty prophets of Baal and four hundred prophets of Asherah ate at the table of Jezebel, and it was these who met with Elijah at Mount Carmel.

The prophets of Baal were destroyed. But no mention was made of the prophets of Asherah, and her statue which Ahab had "made" was not harmed. In the same way, when Jehu (c.842–815 B.C.) murdered Ahab and Jezebel to take over the Northern Kingdom, it was the prophets of Baal he slaughtered while also destroying Baal's sacred pillar, razing their temple to the ground, and building a latrine on the site. Still no mention was made of the statue of Asherah.

It was certainly still standing in the period of Joahash. It may have been in existence at the end of the Northern Kingdom when the people were still engaged in dramatic imitations of "the Sacred Marriage" of a god and goddess.

The Hebrew prophets were speakers not writers. As a result, they were always looking for an audience. The biblical evidence shows that they often found listeners at the public performance of rituals. For example, if the people were performing the traditional rite of pouring water as a rain charm, the Hebrew prophet might hurl at them the taunt that Yahweh would shortly pour upon them the vials of his wrath (*Hosea* 5: 10), or if they paraded around the town in a torch-light procession (a familiar feature of popular

Festivals), he might warn them that Yahweh too was carrying his torch—to search out sin in every nook and cranny (*Zephaniah* 1: 12). Other standard elements of the pagan Festivals which also lent themselves to satirical castigation were the nocturnal vigil (*Joel* 1: 13), the ululation for the vanished god of fertility (*Joel* 2: 17; *Zephaniah* 1: 11; *Zechariah* 12: 11–14), the search for him (*Hosea* 5: 6, 15; 6: 3; *Zephaniah* 2: 3), and the divine banquet (*Zephaniah* 1: 7).[27]

But the two religions were basically incompatible. The Yahwist saw Canaanite practices as elevating sex to the realm of the divine: the gods were sexual in nature and were worshipped in sexual ways. These rituals were hidden within the cycle of death and renewal of fertility—the annual death-and-resurrection of Baal. But faith in the south was based on the wonder of the Exodus.

In 722 B.C., the Assyrians took Samaria, the capital of Israel, and carried off nearly 30,000 people as prisoners of Nineveh; these "ten lost tribes of Israel" were transferred to locations west of the Tigris river. The conqueror, Sargon II, brought new settlers in from Syria and Babylonia who mingled with the local population to become Samaritans.

THE SOUTHERN KINGDOM (922-587 B.C.)

In the three centuries before Nebuchadrezzar destroyed Jerusalem, the Deutcronomic historians lived in Judah. To begin with, Gilgal was the key sanctuary for the ritual drama. There the David Play and ceremonial traditions were moulded in the century following upon Solomon (c. 922–800 B.C.).

The priests who worshipped at Gilgal took elements from the cultic practices of Shechem from the north, and combined them with their own Davidic–Zionist theology.

Under King Josiah (c.640-609 B.C.) the Deuteronomic reforms were carried out and Jerusalem took over as the cultic centre of Judah. It was at this time that the Mosaic Covenant tradition was "rediscovered"—reducing the Davidic theology to a secondary place within the liturgical tradition.

The Coronation Drama at Gilgal

At Gilgal, Judah's first religious centre, the history of salvation was seen to be one continuous series of liberations. Added to the Moses Play were Yahweh's other victories in a unified sequence:

[1]   the Covenant was celebrated in Transjordan;[28]

[2]   three days of intense preparation at Shittim preceded the crossing;[29]

[3]   the crossing of the Jordan symbolized the miracle at the Sea of Reeds;[30]

[4]   there was circumcision for those reconverted to Yahwism;[31]

[5]   the feast of the Passover (linked to the Exodus) followed on the fourth day after the crossing;

[6]   there were various rituals to signify the taking possession of the land: the eating of the first produce, the performance of the Jericho Play, and the ceremony of the blessing and the curse. Judah added newer historical events to the original incidents around which the myth had been created.

The Exodus symbolized the exemplary deliverance; each subsequent deliverance was an extension of it. The Gilgal priests assumed that:

[a] when Jeroboam introduced the cult of the golden calves at Shechem in the Northern Kingdom, he belittled the historical position of Shechem;[32]

[b] when the Hebrews crossed the Jordan, a monument was erected and Israel was circumcised;

[c] the first Passover in the promised land was celebrated in Gilgal;

[d] Joshua had his military headquarters for the conquest in Gilgal; and

[e] both Joshua and Samuel delivered their last addresses from Gilgal.

Elijah and Elisha founded prophetic schools at Gilgal where Elijah was presented as a new Moses, and Elisha as a new Elijah. In the New Year Festival at Gilgal it is likely that the deliverance brought by Moses was ritually repeated by Joshua, and then by Elijah, and then by Elisha.

In Joshua's time, the Ark may have been physically part of the dramatization at Shechem; but it is unlikely that the Ark was physically present in the ceremonies at Gilgal. The Bible indicates that at Gilgal stress was laid on priests carrying the Ark, and there are detailed rubrics for the seven-fold process around Jericho as the siege was symbolically re-enacted.

It is possible that other victories of Yahweh were added to the drama, but we know little of the Gilgalite "history of salvation" re-enactments. But the formula, "You have seen ...," which in other traditions is exclusively used when referring to the Exodus Drama, is extended to other miracles by the Gilgalites: the exultation of Joshua during the crossing of the Jordan (*Joshua* 4: 14); the sun miracle (*Joshua* 10: 12); the defeat of the Canaanites (*Joshua* 23: 3); the miraculous storm (*1 Samuel* 12: 16) and the miraculous taking fire of Elijah's sacrifice (*1 Kings* 18: 39).[33]

Fertility and the Goddess

In Judah there was a great enmity between the Yahwists and Asherah—they built "high places and pillars and Asherim ... and there were also sodomites in the land." [34] In Jerusalem, the statue of Asherah was restored by Rehoboam, son of Solomon. This was destroyed and other fertility rites were outlawed by Asa in 893 B.C. But he was not successful because his son, Jehoshaphat, had to continue the suppression. We know, further, that Joash (837–800 B.C.) restored the image of Asherah in the Temple.

Despite subsequent suppressions, immediately prior to the destruction of Jerusalem by the Babylonians, Jeremiah could preach against the "altars and the Asherahs by leafy trees and upon high hills." The worship of Asherah's statue in Solomon's Temple, "was a part of the legitimate religion approved and led by the king, the court and the priesthood and opposed by only a few prophetic voices crying out against it at relatively long intervals." [35]

When Judah's king Ahaz (735–715 B.C.) was threatened by Syria and Israel, Isaiah reassured him that God would protect the people because a young woman would conceive and bear a son, and name him Immanuel ("God is with us"); from his earliest infancy he would feed on curds and honey.[36] This was derived from the ancient Near Eastern ritual-myth which told of the birth of a Wondrous Child who would bring about the Age of Bliss; this Child was the result of "the Sacred Marriage"—the fertility ritual that pervaded the Near East—and thus was regarded as The Spirit of the New Year. This Child was divine and was identified with the rising sun, an idea later adopted by Christianity.

Isaiah has many allusions showing that fertility rituals were common in Judah. The "gardens of Adonis"[37] refer to the ancient and popular ritual custom of planting little seedboxes and watering them—their germination seen as symbolic of the resurrection of the dead god of fertility.

For Isaiah, God will punish the rebel host of heaven and earthly kings by imprisoning them deep in the earth;[38] this was "witnessed" in the Babylonian Akîtu Festival and other Near Eastern ritual-myths. Also in the Akîtu Festival, Marduk conquered the Dragon of chaos; for Isaiah this was the Leviathan.[39] And Isaiah's famous "suffering servant"[40] is a classic ancient scapegoat.

Manasseh (c. 687–642 B.C) was king when Judah was a docile vassal of Assyria. Then fertility images and altars increased even in the precincts of the Temple. Child sacrifice reappeared later in the valley of Hinnom—even the king himself may have sacrificed one of his sons. It was said that the king "worshipped all the host of heaven ... and practised soothsaying and augury, and dealt with mediums and with wizards."[41] The sacrifice of children through fire may refer to old fertility initiation rites which included the passing of children and adults through fire to render them immortal.

Nahum's prophecy took place at the same time that Assyria was overcome (612 B.C). He saw the fall of Nineveh resulting from the wrath of Yahweh whom he pictured as a figure similar to storm-god of the Mesopotamians. Like Marduk or Baal, Yahweh (in Nahum's view) rode the storm as "the Rider in the Clouds" who vanquished the sea, shook mountains, and laid waste the land.[42]

Other fertility themes appear in the book of *Habakkuk*: the theophany of Yahweh is given in typical terms of the Mesopotamian sun-god;[43] men are to be silent before the Lord in his temple because words have magic power;[44] and Yahweh is attended by two escorts, just like the gods in the Mesopotamian *Gilgamesh*.[45] Jeremiah, the tragic figure who foretold the Exile and finished his life in Egypt, wrote in a culture full of fertility rituals. When he discusses rites of mourning,[46] Jeremiah shows that Judah practised rituals of cutting the hair and mutilating the body, and it was a common practice to share funeral meals with the dead, and make laments that repeated those within the Akîtu Festival of Babylon.

The Coronation Drama at Jerusalem

In Josiah's reign while the Temple was being restored, a "book of law" was discovered that may have been an early version of *Deuteronomy*. It allowed Josiah to bring about a series of reforms for the worship of Yahweh. He centralized worship at Jerusalem and undertook a massive destruction of pagan idols, including the statue of the Assyrian sun god set in front of the Temple. As a result of his ritual reforms, the autumn Festival at Jerusalem took on a character of its own.

From various psalms, we can catch glimpses of the changes. There was an "entrance liturgy"[47] and festal processions into the sanctuary, led by singers and musicians,[48] together with dancing and music for Yahweh.[49] There was a blowing of trumpets and the raising of "the festal shout."[50] A major part of the performance was the ark's procession into the Temple where Yahweh was proclaimed king of the universe and he affirmed his Covenant with the house of David.

Psalm 78 indicates how the Exodus–Sinai and the Davidic–Zion traditions were combined. Most summarized Yahweh's historical acts from the Exodus (vv. 1–66); it shows how the people (particularly of the Northern Kingdom) do not keep the Covenant. Then it shifts to the Davidic Covenant tradition (vv. 67–72) showing Yahweh choosing the tribe of Judah, Jerusalem and David and, thus, ended the old sacred history and made a new start with David.

Psalm 132[51] narrates specific historic events incorporated into the performance: David brings the Ark to Zion, and Nathan's oracle to David. In

Part 1 there is a passage that may actually have been said, sung or chanted:

> Arise, O Yahweh, and go to thy resting place,
>> thou and the ark of thy might.
> Let thy priests be clothed with righteousness,
>> and let thy saints shout for joy. (vv. 8-9)

Psalm 89 is similar. It is a hymn to Yahweh who manifested his love by electing the house of David (vv. 1–37); and a lament that his promise has been violated by the defeat of the king, together with an appeal to Yahweh to reaffirm the love he once swore to David (vv. 38–51).

Two other groups of psalms relate this Jerusalem performance to the Davidic–Zion tradition. The so-called Zion psalms[52] confirm that Zion is the place of Yahweh's presence in the midst of his people. This includes *Psalm* 46 which elaborates this theme with the mythological motif of the river of God that flows down the sacred mountain to water the earth. The second group are often called "the royal psalms"[53]—prayers on behalf of the king who is viewed as the anointed of Yahweh. While other contemporary nations deified their kings, these psalms demonstrate that Judah affirmed that the reigning king was the elected agent of Yahweh. *Psalm* 110 has been interpreted by Theodor H. Gaster, with a new translation, as "a book of words" for the ritual enthronement of the King:

> *The king is enthroned*
>> The pronouncement of Yahweh to my lord:
>>> "Sit thou at my right hand,
>> while that I make thy foemen
>>> a footstool at thy feet!"
> *The footstool is placed in position; the sceptre is given to the king*
>> "Yahweh extend the rod of thy might;
>>> from Zion subdue thy foes!"
> *The attendant crowd signify their allegiance*
>> "Thy people shall offer ready service

whensoever thou musterest thy host!"
The king is invested and anointed.

A further group of hymns are known as "enthronement psalms."[54] These are hymns of praise that declare, "Yahweh is king" or "Yahweh reigns," whereby the Hebrews in the Temple celebrated Yahweh's victory over hostile powers and his ascension to his throne. In particular, *Psalm* 24 (which may go back to David's time) provided a singing chorus to accompany the dramatic procession, with Yahweh invisibly enthroned on the Ark, as it reached the gates of Zion:

Lift up your heads, O gates!
    and be lifted up, O ancient doors!
    that the King of glory may come in!
        Who is this King of glory?
        Yahweh of hosts,
        he is the King of glory![55] (vv. 9–10)

12

THE EXILE AND AFTER

Israel was conquered in 722 B.C. by the Assyrians who in 612 B.C. were crushed by the Medes and Persians. Neo-Babylonia expanded to fill the power gap. Under Nebuchadrezzar, it defeated Judah and carried the king, Jehoiachin, into captivity.

In his place Nebuchadrezzar put his uncle, Zedekiah (598-587 B.C.), who conspired to break with Babylon. The prophet Jeremiah thought this foolish and condemned it. He made thongs and yoke bars and put them on his neck, thus dramatizing his prophecy that it was Yahweh's will for Judah to submit to Babylonia. The prophet Hananiah challenged Jeremiah: he broke the yoke bars and prophesized that within two years Yahweh would break the yoke of Babylon from the neck of the nation. Not to be dramatically outdone, Jeremiah made a yoke of iron because, as he said, Yahweh had forged "an iron yoke of servitude to Nebuchadrezzar." He was right. In 587 B.C., the Babylonians besieged Jerusalem, broke through the walls, destroyed the Temple, burnt the city, and carried most of the population into Exile.

DURING THE EXILE

The Exile in Babylon lasted from 587 to 539 B.C., a period of 48 years. Some of the people had been left behind to harvest the crops; and when the Hebrew patriot Ishmael assassinated Gedaliah, the Babylonian governor of Judah, several of the senior Judean soldiers fled to Egypt. They took the unwilling Jeremiah with them. We last hear of him in Egypt denouncing the Hebrew colony for reverting to the worship of the goddess. He attempted to convince them that the national catastrophe had come about as a punishment from Yahweh.

The ordinary people, however, felt the reason was that they had forsaken Astarte-Anath, the "Queen of Heaven." Before the fall of Jerusalem, they said, they had worshipped the Mother Goddess and all had gone well.[1] In Tahpanhes on the edge of the Nile delta, and in Judah, the people conducted a ritual to the "Queen of Heaven":

[1] the children gathered wood; fathers lit a fire;

[2] the women made cakes shaped like Astarte and baked them;

[3] everyone poured out libations and burned incense to the goddess; and

[4] they enacted the proper ritual actions and chanted the correct words.

The cakes were eaten by the celebrants (possibly as a precursor to the Holy Communion). Even today in small, traditional bakers' shops all over Europe and the Near East, similar cakes can be bought in the shape of the bare-breasted goddess. The Hebrews thought that this simple ritual ensured that the goddess provided them with food and secured their welfare. The goddess cult continued in Judah, as well as among the Hebrew exiles in Egypt until at least 400 B.C. In the temple in the Egyptian colony, they worshipped Yahweh and the goddess side by side.

But Jeremiah was right. The future lay not with the Jews in Egypt but with those in Babylon. The prophet Ezekiel carried out his twenty year ministry before the fall of Jerusalem and during the Exile. He had decidedly shamanic characteristics: his oracles often came to him in ecstasy or trance; when seized by "the hand of God" he could be struck dumb, go into a cataleptic stupor, and be gifted with second sight. In fact, his behaviour paralleled that of modern shamans from Siberia to the Americas. Ezekiel's word was accompanied by signs which he enacted with dramatic power:

[a] He lay for 390 days on his left side, then for 40 days on the right side, to indicate the number of years that Israel and Judah respectively would be punished.[2]

[b] He cut off his hair with a sword and separated it into three parts to dramatize the three kinds of fate that would befall the people of Jerusalem.[3]

[c] He foresaw the fate of Judah through the fertility rituals practised there:

*   the setting up of ritual seats for various fertility deities at a seasonal banquet;

* the cult of the dying god in an underground cavern with
  frescoed pictures and statuary of "every form of creeping
  things and abominable beasts,"
* professional actresses who wept for the dying god;
* a ritual where men prostrated themselves to the rising sun, and also
* carried branches at harvest Festivals;
* trumpeters that made noise to scare demons and raise the dead
  fertility gods; and
* a procession of statues of the fertility gods.

All were common rituals for fertility in the ancient Near East.[4] Ezekiel's message was fundamentally one of doom against Judah and Jerusalem; only after Jerusalem fell did he give any messages of hope to his people. Interestingly both he and Jeremiah said that Yahweh could be found *internally* without recourse to theatrical ceremonies: Jeremiah said it was through prayer;[5] while Ezekiel said:

> And Yahweh will scatter you among the peoples, and you will be left few in
> number among the nations where Yahweh shall drive you ... But from there
> you will seek Yahweh your God, and you shall find him, if you search after him
> with all your heart and all your soul.[6]

Away from their homeland, from their sanctuaries and the Temple of Jerusalem, the Hebrews in Babylon were in deep anguish:

> By the waters of Babylon,
> there we sat down and wept,
> when we remembered Zion.[7]

A number of the *Psalms* were written by people who cried privately to Yahweh "out of the depths." [8] They had to worship without a Temple, so they gathered in small groups and worshipped informally. It was from this tradition that the later synagogue developed (synagogue meaning "gathering together").

The prophecies of Malachai were probably composed just after the Persians had captured Babylon and before the Jews returned to their homeland. They were influenced by Zoroastrian lore, adopting an extensive tradition of angels, archangels, spirits, and demons. The complex eschatology of the Iranians affected Jewish thought: there was to be a final ordeal by fire when wickedness would be purged; a saviour's appearance would regenerate the world and bring in a golden age of prosperity. These apocalyptic ideas were developed in the Dead Sea Scrolls.

Deuteronomy

It was probably during the Exile that the Deuteronomic history was completed. The Hexateuch was written as a body of instruction for people who worshipped internally, or gathered in small groups. It was specifically not put together at a time when people participated in ritual dramas. Yet the materials included much that had been performed ritually in earlier ages. These theatrical materials were specifically re-written for a very different theological purpose.

The new biblical authors had a Divine model that changed the later history of Jewry. The key was the supreme revelation in the Mosaic period—God's special revelation was given specifically to Israel. Thus no ethical or ritual impurity must defile the people. Now the orthodox view was not that revelation is an event that happens *between* God and man—not a dialogue between "I and thou," as Martin Buber might have it. Rather, it is something *given to man* in the form of laws and institutions. This way, revelation was more easily controlled by the priests while ritual drama (as J realized) was *a process*—revelation that happened *in time*.

When revelation is not dialogic, faith is not gained by performance in or witnessing a ritual drama. Rather, it tends to become assent to what is written in an inspired book—as it is to many people today who in this respect are more "priestly" than "prophetic" in their religious understanding.[9]

This theological attitude was very different from that within the Moses Festival Play.

THE POST-EXILIC DRAMA

Cyrus the Great of Persia captured Babylon in 539 B.C., and he abandoned the "scorched earth" policy of the Assyrians and Babylonians. His edict of 538 allowed the Jews to return home and Judah became the district of Yahud in the Fifth Satrapy (province) of the Persian Empire.

Only a minority of the exiles responded. Most of them had taken root in Babylonia, and some of them were prosperous traders working under a tolerant Persian government. However, about 40,000 Jews set out to walk the 800 desert miles to Jerusalem. Their leader was Sheshbazzar, son of Jehoiachin the exiled king of Judah, to whom the Persians returned the gold and silver vessels of the destroyed Temple of Jerusalem.

The returning exiles, organized in family clans, went back to their towns and localities. At the site of the Jerusalem Temple, an altar was constructed, and regular prayers and sacrifices began. There were two men with authority: Zerubbabel as secular leader, and Jeshua the high priest. Zerubbabel was also a member of the Davidic royal family of Judah.[10] Since there is no further mention of Sheshbazzar, it is possible that this may have been another name for Zerubbabel.

From the completion of the Second Temple (515 B.C.) to the appearance of Nehemiah in Jerusalem (445 B.C.) was three generations—the period when the Persian culture was at its height. The Jerusalem Temple was the only temple in the land, although synagogues were increasing. Even in the Temple (according to Malachai), the people were simply going through the motions of the rituals. The morale of Judah was low, so Nehemiah introduced reforms: he enforced a stiff policy of exclusivism, strictly dividing Jew from Gentile and Samaritan—built on birth, loyalty to the Torah, and faithful support of the Temple. Somewhere about this time appeared Ezra, the priest.

Ezra, the Father of Judaism

"Ezra the priest, the scribe of the law of God of heaven"[11] was "skilled in the law of Moses, which Yahweh, the God of Israel, had given."[12] He had permission from the Persians to lead a new caravan of exiles from Babylon to

Judah. He brought with him a copy of "the book of the law of Moses"[13] with which he revived the New Year Festival. Whereas in pre-Exilic times this had been the occasion of the massive Moses–David Play and processional ritual dramas, Ezra gave it a totally different tone, one that was to be very influential in subsequent history.

The people gathered "as one man" in a public square in Jerusalem to *hear* (not participate in) what was in Ezra's book of the Law.[14] Ezra stood on a platform and read to them from early morning until noon. At his side stood the Levite priests who interpreted Law when it was necessary. While it might be attractive to think that the priests acted out certain important passages, it is unlikely. There was little, if any, acting of ritual drama.

Yet the following day the people revived the Feast of Booths, making tents ("tabernacles") out of branches to live in during the seven-day Festival. Readings from the Law continued[15] after which the Covenant was renewed and Ezra offered a prayer on the people's behalf. The people then took an oath to keep the Law.[16]

Ezra probably stopped the Festival Play. He brought back to Jerusalem the teaching of the Second Isaiah (or Deutero–Isaiah) contained in the latter part of the *Book of Isaiah* (40–60). Isaiah did not write this section. It was written more than 150 years after the first Isaiah during the Exile and afterwards. The Second Isaiah gave a new theological emphasis—pardon, deliverance, restoration and grace—all in a rhapsodical language. He proclaimed good news: out of the day of darkness, a new day is dawning. Yahweh's imminent coming is to inaugurate his kingdom in a new Creation, much as the Akîtu Festival brought forth the creation of the New Year. The Second Isaiah showed Israel's future liberation from the Exile with dramatic imagery drawn from the Exodus and the Mesopotamian ritual battle with the dragon:

> Awake, awake, put on strength
> O arm of Yahweh!

Awake as in ancient days,
as in olden times!
Was it not thou that hewed Rahab,
transfixed the Dragon (Tannin)?
Was it not thou that dried up the Sea,
the waters of the great deep?[17]

Thou didst break up the Sea by thy strength,
shattered the heads of the Dragon (Tannin).
Thou didst crush the heads of Leviathan,
didst give him as food to the sharks of the sea.[18]

The Dragon was also likened to the Pharaoh, remembering that the Pharaoh caused the annual inundation of the Nile:

Lo, I am against thee, O Pharaoh,
king of Egypt,
That art as the great Dragon (Tannin)
crouching in the midst of his river,
Who said, "The river is mine,
and I it was who made it."
I will put hooks in thy jaws ...
and haul thee up from the midst of thy river;
And all the fish of thy river
shall stick to thy scales.[19]

Thus the new themes of Jewish belief were still *tacitly* dramatic, but only a few were *explicitly* so. In reading the Torah to the people rather than performing the Moses or David Plays, Ezra turned from dramatic action to literature. He established the later non-theatrical tradition of Jewish worship.

Yet at the Feast of Booths the people still lived in the booths for seven days in memory of Sinai. However, it was more than that. By living in the booths, they were acting *as if* they were the original Israelites in the desert while Ezra had Moses' role, reading the Law to them. What was being performed, in fact, was a *mental act of communal impersonation*. It was this tradition of mental dramatic acts that was transmitted to later Jewry.

Post-exilic Worship

Both the worship within the official liturgy of the Temple, and the popular form offered to the fertility goddess, changed. The books of the Bible written in the Babylonian Exile emphasized prayer and supplication rather than performance. The *Psalms* written in Babylon and later are strikingly like Babylonian hymns in content and style. These influences changed the religious rituals performed by the returning Israelites.[20]

Later, another type of sacred building arose—the synagogue—which was destined to replace the Temple. The synagogue was unique in that it was dedicated to *the study* of the Holy Scriptures and to prayer. There were no sacrificial rites nor theatrical-style ceremonies.

The ancient fertility worship also changed in this period. Despite the Yahwist prohibition of "graven images," early Israel had continued the practice. Later, sexual Cherubim were represented in the desert Tabernacle and in Solomon's Temple. During the period of the Northern Kingdom, ivory plaques of Cherubim had existed in the "ivory house"[21] built in Samaria by King Ahab (869-850 B.C.), and were clearly female.

The sexual content became even more overt. In the Second Temple there was a statue of two golden Cherubim, locked together in a marital embrace. It was probably shown to the people at the end of the New Year Festival whereas, in previous times, there had been a live performance of the ritual of "the Sacred Marriage."

In early times, the New Year Festival concluded with a feast and ritual sexual license, a trait which Israelites shared with others in the area.[22] But this behaviour became intolerable later: in the last century of the existence of the Second Temple, the sages decided to put an end to this Festival "lightheadedness." Originally the women gathered in the Great Courtyard of the Temple (the so-called Women's Court) while the men stood without, but this did not prevent licentiousness. The sexes were ordered to change places to prevent a repetition of the orgy. The following year, however, the measure was shown to be futile. As a result, special galleries were built on three sides of the courtyard with only one side (facing the Sanctuary) left open, and the women were confined to these. We can understand "the stubborn popular resistance to it if we assume that the exhibition of the Cherubim in embrace was continued at the three annual feasts of pilgrimage, while at the same time the populace was prevented by the reform from indulging in its traditional practice of *imitatio dei* called for by the momentary glimpse of divine mystery."[23] In the retrospect of Talmudic times, the Jerusalem Temple was recognized as the very centre of idolatrous fertility enactments.

New Year Festivals

Although Ezra altered the old New Year Festival with its ritual drama into a ceremony based upon dramatic readings, the Hebrews were still exposed to other performances of New Year Festivals.

The Book of Esther is a work of fiction which contains detailed information about the Feast of Purim, or the Feast of Lots. Gaster shows that Purim had a particular fertility structure:

[1]   The celebration of a seasonal queen by a public holiday derived from "the Sacred Marriage."

[2]   The parade of a commoner acting as the king (social roles reversed).

[3]   A fast celebrating the end of the Old Year (in many cultures).

[4]   The execution of a felon (a human scapegoat) at the start of the New Year.

[5]   A ritual battle: the victory of Fertility over Drought, Summer over Winter, the New Year over the Old, Life over Death.

[6]   The distribution of gifts.

[7]   The Festival celebration took place around the vernal equinox, common throughout the ancient Near East and Europe.[24]

Purim became the Jewish counterpart of Carnival and Twelfth Night with many masquerades, mummings and role-playings.

The biblical prophecies of Joel, dating from the fifth or fourth century B.C., provide an excellent non-ritual picture of the ancient seasonal pattern. Joel introduces a sustained series of allusions to the New Year Festival pattern common throughout the ancient Near East and ancient Europe, together with hints of contemporary folklore:

* mortification and ululation;
* an all-night vigil for the lost god of fertility;
* even the gods are starving;
* fasting, lent, and sacred convocation;
* annual blight is rationalized as punishment for sin;
* moral purgation—a means of securing the new lease of life;
* banishing of the Power of Death and Aridity (historicized);
* reinvigoration;
* restoration of rainfall;
* eschatological interpretation of annual determination of destinies;
* ritual combat; and
* an ultimate era of reinvigoration.[25]

Thus post-Exilic times were strongly influenced by ancient fertility rituals. However, their own ritual plays had been denuded of external acts of impersonation; under the influence of Ezra these acts had become internal. In addition to the dying fertility dramas, there was now a drama of the mind.

It is little wonder, therefore, that the modern Jewish religion is highly dramatic.

Conclusion
THE PLAY OF THE JEWS

The Israelites dominated Canaan only from about the twelfth century B.C. when the land teemed with people of many cultures: Canaanites, Amorites, Hittites, Philistines, and others. It was probably Moses who created monotheism and the medium in which it was brought before the Hebrews was a ritual drama. In the first act of known history, Joshua took the structure of the New Year Festival as practised throughout the ancient Near East and placed within it the monotheistic ritual-myth of Yahweh. The performance of this Festival play, both the story of God's victory over the enemy, the idealized Pharaoh, as well as the Covenant and the Land-giving, became the way in which monotheism was transmitted to generations of Jews.

The Jews

These remarkable series of events can be seen as universal on the one hand, and unique on the other. In one sense, the dramatic developments of Israel reflect the growth in human religious belief. In the initial hunting cultures, the world was full of spirits; human beings acted as if they were such spirits (of the bear, of the wolf, of the bull, and so on) in order to obtain their spirit powers. To this end, they became possessed: they drove their way into the spirits in order to "become" them—become one *with* them and so lose their own human identity.

With the great agricultural civilizations, the world changed. Based on the Tigris, Euphrates, Nile, Indus, and Yangtse, the world was full of gods. The world of the gods and the human world were exact mirrors of each other; the human world dramatized the world of gods. In Sumer and Akkad there was a king and his nobles just as, in the upper world, there was a chief god and lesser gods; each had their duties, their own rank, and their job was to act appropriately. However, people were the slaves of gods and, as time went on, the Babylonians and the Assyrians came to see their gods as callous and uncaring.

It was the Hebrews who broke this image of the relationship between the human and the Divine. Monotheism created a fundamental paradox. On the one hand, people became aware of a fundamental duality, of a vast gulf which can be crossed by nothing but the *voice*—the voice of God, directing and law-giving in his revelation, and the voice of people in prayer. On the other hand, monotheism demonstrated a fundamental unity of life—of God, Nature, and Man. The great monotheistic religions live and unfold in the ever-present consciousness of a bipolarity—of the existence of an abyss which can never be bridged, and of life itself which is whole. J stressed unity conceived as continuous time, but to Ezra the scene of religion was no longer Nature, but the human moral and religious actions whose interplay brought about history as, in a sense, the stage on which the drama of humanity's relation to God unfolds.[1]

The Israelites consciously incorporated human dramatization in their rituals and their lives. Yahwism was a national religion in that the Hebrews were "the chosen people," much as the Mesopotamian, Egyptian, Hittite and Canaan religions were national. But there was one God only and he had a Covenant—a binding law—between himself and the people which operated through dramatization, external as with J, or internal as with Ezra. How did it happen that monotheism was created by the Hebrews and not one of the many other advanced peoples in the Near East at that time?

What made the Jews unique?

The answer lies in two factors: *the idea and the event.* The idea probably began with Moses: the miracle of the burning bush was the first human statement of monotheism. But the first event that brought monotheism into practical existence was the placing together of the flight from Egypt and the Passover. Two ancient rituals were unified and then commemorated as a historical event—*in action.* The moment the ritual was re-played as if it was a real event in history, the beginning of Hebrew monotheism was firmly fixed. *Dramatic action re-created the fact in the Moses Play.*

Thereafter it changed according to its context. With Joshua the Moses Play, the Land-giving, and the processional drama became the main vehicles for transmission. Mixed with the fertility religions of Canaan and Babylon in various ways, the performances changed in time and place: as at Shechem,

Shiloh, Gilgal, Jerusalem and other places. And while religious performances were similar all over Israel, there were discrete differences according to locality.

The heroic David throughout his career was surrounded by non-Israelite mercenaries, and the cosmopolitan Solomon opened his empire to commercial and social relations with all neighbouring peoples, some of them quite remote. Though evidently a monarchist, J's disdain for Rehoboam and Jeroboam seems about equal. *What J tells us is that the Israelites dramatized existence through the Moses performance which was echoed in the Schism hundreds of years later*—and we may follow its influence for centuries.

Because external acts of ritualized impersonation were restricted during the Exile, and afterwards by the priests and Ezra, the drama of Hebrew monotheism became internal. After the Exile, the performances of dramatic rituals were suppressed. Yet dramatic action had become integral to Jewish thought; so much so, indeed, that the mental drama of the Essenes at Qumran became a dramatic apocalyptic vision that was only stamped out by the ruthless Roman soldiers. They destroyed Jerusalem and Qumran, and then dispersed the Jews all over the known world. But the mental drama of the Jews sustained and preserved itself: it overcame the destruction of Jerusalem and Qumran; and it continued into history through the horrors of the Diaspora and the Holocaust Even to the present day, the drama of Moses is the drama of the Jews—it has valourized history.

Various authorities have judged J's greatest originality to be the scope of *The Book of J*. From the Creation to Moses, and from *Joshua* to *Kings*, J's work underpins the literature, ritual and drama of the Western world. It has an extraordinary variety, the binding figure of which is Yahweh, a unique God who remains the precursor of what is called God by Jews, Christians and Moslems, and even by secularists of the Western world. J's principal character is God, but his Yahweh remains too original a representation for tradition to assimilate. From the standpoint of normative Jews, Christians and Moslems, J is the most outrageous writer that ever lived. Yahweh is always getting out of hand.

Christians and Others

The Book of J is foundational to the Old Testament and, thus, to Christian life. The ritual drama it reflects becomes the core of Christian behaviour. To understand other people from their point of view, to put oneself in another person's place, to act "as if" we are someone else, lies at the core of Christ's teaching. From it derives the *in imitatio Christi* of Thomas à Kempis which parallels the medieval Mass of Amalarius as well as some modern Christian practices.

And this applies not merely to Christians. While this dramatic behaviour is best exemplified in the gigantic medieval Mystery cycles, there are equally powerful non-Christian mystery cycles today among the American Indians of the Pacific Northwest Coast of Canada and the Southwest deserts of the United States. While the medieval Coventry Cycle has the mutual dialogue and interrelationship of father and son as its basis, so do the Wolf Cycle of the West Coast (Nootka) Indians and the seasonal Festival of the Hopi.

THE DRAMATIC LIFE

It is commonly accepted that monotheism is the great originality of the Jews. But there is also a case for acknowledging their originality in our understanding that life itself is dramatic.

From its beginnings, Israel was focused on enormous events which could only be understood if they were dramatic—if things were seen from more than one perspective. This happened through their social drama, of which the key events were ritual dramas.

The Book of J's description of the Moses Play was, as far as we know, the first statement to make dramatic action *conscious*. How far drama was conscious among the Neanderthals and early *Homo sapiens*, the Sumerians and the Egyptians, we do not know. But when J parallels the dramatic life of Moses with that of David, or the events of the Sea of Reeds with the crossing of the Jordan, he is obviously fully aware of the psychological and social effects of drama. He clearly understands that fact and fiction are different perspectives, and that the issue of reality and illusion is key to human life. This theme, begun by J at the time of Solomon and the Schism, spread throughout Western thought with an importance critics do not always realize. It is central to medieval and Renaissance moralities where actors constantly address one another *as actors*. It is the way Shakespeare metaphorizes the world, followed by Ben Jonson, Wilde and Shaw, Pirandello and Sartre, John Osborne and Tennessee Williams. Ultimately this tradition derives from the multi-dimensional character and personality that begins with J's Yahweh. He is the fore-runner of Sophocles' Oedipus, Shakespeare's Hamlet, and Ibsen's Nora.

NOTES

PART ONE: BACKGROUND

Chapter 1 DRAMA IN THE ANCIENT WORLD

1   For Neanderthals see Solecki (1972).
2   For the Bear Cult see Sarmela (Fall 1982).
3   For Paleolithic period see Marshack (1972).
4   For Mesopotamia see Frankfort (1978), Gaster (1961), Jacobsen (1976), and Pallis (1926).
5   For Egypt see Frankfort (1978), and Gaster (1961).
6   For *The Triumph of Horus* see Fairman (1974) and Courtney (1987).
7   For Aryans see Bowle (1977) 13–16.
8   For Hittites see Gaster (1961), and Gurney (1981).
9   For Canaan see Gaster (1961), and Gray (1964).

Chapter 2 PERSPECTIVES ON BIBLICAL RITUALS

1   Bloom (1990) 49–50.
2   Mendenhall (1970a), (1970b), (1970c).
3   Ibid.
4   Moran (1975) 146–166.
5   Ibid, 155–156.
6   Goody (1977).
7   Halpern (1983) 65–80.
8   Lovejoy (1983) 10 18, 269–273.
9   Goody (1976) 59.
10   Wright (1983a) 69.
11   Albright (1969) 232; (1945) 16–22.
12   Wright (1983b) 80–83.
13   Flanagan (1988).
14   Dever (1977) 91.
15   Gonen (1984) 70.
16   Albright (1932) 53–58, 74; (1938); (1943) 38.
17   Redford (1985) 195–197.
18   Marfoe (1979).
19   Flanagan, *op.cit.*

20   Ibid.
21   Leach (1969) 34.
22   Leach (1983a) 8–12, 23.
23   Leach (ibid, 21) says myth, Gaster (1961, 1950) says ritual, Smith (1889) says both, and Joseph Campbell (1959) says it varies in each case.
24   Eliade (1979).
25   Leach (1969) 32; (1983b) 96.
26   Leach (1983a) 23.
27   Frankfort (1978).
28   Albright (1964) 74–75, 179.
29   Albright (1957) 3.
30   Wilson (1975); (1977).
31   Gottwald (1979).
32   Harris (1979) 32.
33   Turner (1957) xvii–xviii, 91–94; (1974) 32–45; (1977); (1985a) [1969]; (1985b).
34   Turner (1980) 152.
35   Leach (1982) 130.
36   Leach, ibid, 24; (1983b) 97–109.
37   Rappaport (1979) 41.
38   Ibid, 174, 178–179.
39   van Gennep (1960).
40   Turner (1977) 66–67.
41   Ibid, 63.
42   Augé (1982) 65.
43   Turner and Turner (1978) 252.
44   Turner (1957) xvii.
45   Turner (1974) 38–42.
46   Marshack (1972).
47   Gaster (1961).
48   Drennan (1976) 350.
49   McNutt (1983).
50   *Exodus* 12.
51   Ibid, 13: 8.
52   Gaster (1978) 43.

PART TWO: RITUAL DRAMA OF MOSES

Chapter 3 WRITING THE TEXT

1   *Exodus* 24: 7; 34: 27.

2   *Judges* 5.

3   *Genesis* 49.

4   *Exodus* 15.

5   *Numbers* 22–24.

6   *Genesis* 1: 1–2; 4a.

7   Ibid, 4: 17.

8   Vawter (1977) 15–24.

9   The translation of David Rosenberg and the interpretation by Harold Bloom are now basic for understanding *The Book of J*. Direct quotations from David Rosenberg's translation in this book are indicated by page numbers in round brackets.

10   Jahweh in the German spelling; Jehovah is a misspelling.

11   J, however, always used "Elohim" as a name for divine beings in general, and never as the name of God.

12   Bloom (1990) 22.

13   Ibid, 47.

14   Vawter, *op.cit.*, 24.

15   Bloom, *op.cit.,* 317–318.

16   Bloom assumes that J was a woman, *op.cit.*, 9; 19–20.

17   Ibid, 32–33.

18   Ibid, 32.

19   Ibid, 26.

20   There are obvious exceptions, such as Acts I–III of *Pericles*.

21   Bloom, *op.cit.,* 316.

22   Ibid, 320.

23   Ibid, 25.

Chapter 4 WHERE DOES THE MOSES PLAY BEGIN?

1   Bloom (1990) 27.

2   Ibid, 317.

3   Ibid, 27–28.

4   Ibid, 28.

5   This identification flowered in Kabbalistic stories where Leviathan was feasted upon in the days of the Messiah.

6   Adapted from Bloom, *op.cit.,* 30–31.

7   Ibid, 179.

8   Weber (1967) 226.

9   Ibid, 149–50. For the Sabbath, see Schauss (1977).

10   Bloom, *op.cit.,* 176.

11   The serpent become Satan through Jewish heretical writings of the first century B.C.

12   Traditional in each culture.

13   Hooke (1963) 124.

14   See the obscure talk of Cain and Yahweh in *Genesis* 4: 6–7.

15   A point made clearly in *Genesis* 3: 22–23.

16   *Psalm* 90: 10.

17   *Hosea* 4: 14.

18   *Genesis* 9: 6.

19   Bloom, *op.cit.,*188.

20   Ibid, 190.

21   Abraham Malamat cited in Bloom, *op.cit.,*194–195.

22   Bloom, *op.cit.,* 209–210.

23   Abraham: *Genesis* 12: 6–8; 13: 4, 15, 18. Jacob: *Genesis* 33: 18, 20; 28: 11, 18, 13; 35: 7, 12, 8, 27.

24   *Genesis* 15: 7–11, 17–21.

25   Vawter, *op.cit.,* 209–210.

26   *Genesis* 17: 3–8.

27   Ibid, 22: 1–14.

28   Bloom, *op.cit.,* 3–5.

29   Ibid, 309–310.

30   Ibid, 199–200.

31   Ibid, 296–297.

32   Ibid, 299.

33   Ibid, 300.

34   Buber (1939).

35   *Exodus* 26: 23–33.

36   Bloom, *op.cit.*, 39–40.

37   Ibid, 211.

38   *Exodus* 32: 23–33.

39   Ibid, 25: 19–34.

40   Ibid, 35: 1–20.

41   Bloom, *op.cit.*, 210.

42   Ibid, 214.

43   Ibid, 214–215.

44   Parallel with Jessica's theft from her father in Shakespeare's *The Merchant of Venice*.

45   Most scholars assume that the author is E but we hear the voice of J, according to Harold Bloom.

46   Bloom, *op.cit.*, 216. The male awe of a woman's periods placed her in ritual seclusion in most tribal societies.

47   Ibid, 215.

48   Ibid, 225–226.

49   Ibid, 226.

50   Ibid, 229.

51   Ibid, 229–230.

52   The argument is of universal human decency unwilling to break a trust: Adam was given dominion over all that was, with the one exception. Ibid, 230–231.

53   Bloom, *op.cit.*, 231–232.

54   Ibid, 232.

55   Ibid, 228.

Chapter 5 THE EXODUS

1   Wijngaards (1969) 36.

2   Preliterate tribesmen can have a "stage director" who, from markings on magic sticks (*batons*), stones, tree bark, etc., may carry forward the most ancient performance traditions and "rehearse" them (i.e., teach them to others). The classic example is among the Nootka (West Coast) Indians on Vancouver Island.

3   Eliade (1979) 117.

4   Gray (1969) 105.

5   Bloom, *op.cit.*, 242–243.

6   Ibid, 57ff.

7   Martin Buber, *Moses*, cited in Bloom, *op.cit.*, 247.

8   Bloom, *op.cit.*, 248.

9   Ibid, 241–242.

10   Eliade, *op.cit.*, 178.

11   Bloom, *op.cit.*, 243–244.

12   *Acts* 7: 22.

13   Weber (1967) 221.

14   Bloom, *op.cit.*, 244.

15   *Numbers* 21: 5–6.

16   Ibid, 21: 7–9.

17   *2 Kings* 18: 4.

18   As demonstrated in the plagues.

19   The performing Hopi snake priests terrify audiences today.

20   Bloom, *op.cit.*, 314–315.

21   Ibid, 249.

22   Ibid.

23   *Exodus* 12: 37–38.

24   Ibid, 15: 18.

25   Bloom, *op.cit.*, 250.

26   Ibid, 249–251.

27   Ibid, 252.

28   *Exodus* 19: 9–15.

29   Bloom's translation (1990) 253.

30   *Exodus* 19: 20–25.

31   Bloom, *op.cit.*, 254–255.

32   *Exodus* 18.

33   Ibid, 2: 16 ff.

34   Gray (1969) 108.

35   Bloom, *op.cit.*, 263–265.

36   Zipporah performs the circumcision on their son. Ibid, 245.

37   *Exodus* 20: 24–26.

38   Ibid, 31: 18; 34: 1–28.

39   Ibid, 24: 1–2, 9–11.

40   Ibid, 24: 3–8.

41   Ibid, 25: 2 ff.

42   Ibid, 24: 1–2, 9–11.

43   Bloom, *op.cit.*, 257–258.

44   Ibid, 258.

45   Barton (1961): 66.

46   Bloom, *op.cit.*, 259–261.

47   In Jewish legend, Balaam is a Gentile prophet equal to Moses in magical power but malign – the wicked philosopher.

48   Cited in Bloom, *op.cit.*, 265.

49   Ibid, 266.

50   Ibid, 265–268.

51   *Numbers* 21: 14 ff.

52   Ibid, 21: 17–18.

53   *Exodus* 17: 16.

54   *Numbers* 10: 35.

55   *Exodus* 15: 21.

56   Kaufman (1972) 235.

57   Bloom, *op.cit.*, 259.

58   *Exodus* 26; 27; 33: 7–11. *Numbers* 11: 16–17, 24–26; 12: 4.

59   *Exodus* 25: 10–22; 37: 1–9.

60   Herodotus, Book 7: 40.

61   Weber (1967) 158.

62   *Numbers* 10: 35–36. *1 Samuel* 1: 9; 4: 4.

63   *Exodus* 32.

64   Kaufman *op.cit*, 239.

65   Bloom, *op.cit.*, 268–269.

Chapter 6 THE MOSES PLAY

1   Bloom (1990) 280.

2   Ibid, 284.

3   Ibid, 286–287.

4   Ibid, 326–328.

5   Ibid, 287.

6   Wright (1946) 105–114.

7   *Exodus* 19: 4.

8   Ibid, 19: 4; 14: 30 ff. *Joshua* 24: 5–7; 24: 17. *Deuteronomy* 10: 21; 11:
      2–7; 29: 1–2; 6: 21–22; 1: 30–31; 4: 34.

9   Gray (1969) 105.

10   Wijngaards (1969) 48.

11   Ibid.: 40.

12   Ibid.

13   Ibid.: 55.

14   *Exodus* 19: 4.

15   Bloom, *op.cit.*, 329–330.

16   Wijngaards, *op.cit.,* 54.

17   *Deuteronomy* 26: 5–10.

18   Kaufman (1972) 236.

19   Anderson (1966) 92.

20   *Joshua* 24: 1.

21   Ibid, 2–13.

22   Ibid, 24: 14–22.

23   Ibid, 24: 23–24. See *Jeremiah* 35: 1–4.

24   Ibid, 24: 25. See *Exodus* 24: 4–8.

25   Ibid, 24: 25–26.

26   *Deuteronomy* 27; 11: 26–32. *Joshua* 8: 30–35.

27   *Joshua* 24: 28.

28   Harrelson (1969) 53.

29   Ibid, 85.

30   *Exodus* 20: 2.

31   Ibid, 3: 11–14; 18–20.

32   Ibid, 5: 1–23.

33   Ibid, 7: 14–18, 23–24.

34   Ibid, 7: 25–29; 8: 4–10.

35   Ibid, 8: 16–20, 21–28.

36   Ibid, 9: 1–7.

37   Ibid, 9: 13–35.

38   Ibid, 10: 1–20.

39   Ibid, 10: 21–29.

40   Ibid, 11: 4–8; 12: 29–32.

41	Ibid, 25, 27b, 30–31. The crossing of the Sea of Reeds.
42	Ibid, 19: 3b–8.
43	Ibid, 24: 3–8.
44	Ibid, 19: 4. *Deuteronomy* 11: 7; 1: 31.
45	*Joshua* 24: 5.
46	*Deuteronomy* 11: 3; 29: 1; 6: 21 ff.
47	*Exodus* 10: 1–2.
48	Ibid, 19: 3b–8.
49	Ibid, 24: 3–8.
50	Bloom, *op.cit.*, 292.
51	Ibid, 280–281.
52	Ibid, 281.
53	Ibid, 293.
54	Ibid, 294.
55	*Exodus* 39: 1.
56	Ibid, 39: 6.
57	Ibid, 28: 35.
58	Kaufman, *op.cit.*, 240–241.

Chapter 7 PLAYS OF THE LAND AND THE SEASONS

1	Weber (1967) 187–188.
2	*Genesis* 32: 12.
3	Ibid, 28: 14.
4	La Barre (1972) 562.
5	Weber, *op.cit.*, 189–193.
6	Edwards (1967) 21–35.
7	de Silla Pool (1953) 27.
8	*Exodus* 34: 22.
9	*1 Samuel* 1: 3ff.
10	*Exodus* 23: 14; 34: 23.
11	*Numbers* 28–29.
12	Gaster (1978) 62.
13	Ibid, 7.
14	*Exodus* 14: 13–18.
15	Ibid, 14: 20–31.

16   Ibid, 15: 1–18.

17   Ibid, 15: 20–21.

18   *Joshua* 3: 16, 17.

19   Ibid, 3: 14, 15.

20   *Deuteronomy* 5: 2.

21   Wijngaards (1969) 110.

22   Ibid.: 15.

23   *Psalms* 60: 8–10; 108: 8–10.

24   Wijngaards, *op.cit.,* 18–20.

25   Ibid, 25.

26   Ibid, 27.

27   Ibid, 30.

28   Ibid, 31.

29   *Joshua* 6: 1–21.

30   Gaster (1969) 411–413.

31   *Joshua* 6: 26.

32   Gaster *op.cit.,* 413–414.

PART THREE: ROYAL RITUAL DRAMA

Chapter 8 FROM JOSHUA TO DAVID

1   Freedman (1980) 84.

2   Ibid, 143.

3   *Judges* 5.

4   Freedman, *op.cit,* 153.

5   Gottwald (1979) 493–497; Lemche (1985) 430.

6   Flanagan (1975) 165.

7   Ahlstrom (1986) 40; Ahlstrom and Edelman (1985).

8   See *1 Chronicles* 13; 15; *Psalm* 132.

9   McCarter (1980) 62.

10   *1 Samuel* 1: 1.

11   Ibid, v. 37.

12   Ibid, vv. 19–20.

13   *1 Samuel* 19.

14   Ibid, 28.

15   Ibid, 3: 3.

16   Ibid, 8–10.

17   Rosenberg (1986) 1–46.

18   *1 Samuel* 15: 22.

19   *Deuteronomy* 14: 1.

20   *Exodus* 5: 3; 8: 27.

21   *Hosea* 6: 2. *Joshua* 3: 3. *Exodus* 19: 11.

22   Wijngaards, *op.cit.*, 28.

23   Pallis (1926) 251 fn.

24   *Judges* 11: 30–40.

25   Gaster (1969) 430–432.

26   *1 Samuel* 18: 1–4.

27   Ibid, 20–26.

28   Ibid, 17.

29   Ibid, 18.

30   Ibid, 24; 26.

31   *2 Samuel* 1.

32   Ibid, 9; 21: 7.

33   *1 Samuel* 18–19.

34   Ibid, 25: 45.

35   McCarter, *op.cit.*, 400.

36   *2 Samuel* 3: 12–16.

37   Ibid, 6.

38   Ibid, 21.

39   The dramatic metaphor became the focus of Shakespeare ("All the world's a stage," and "We are such stuff As dreams are made on"), as well as Cervantes, Montaigne and Sterne; Pirandello, Sartre, Buber, and Kenneth Burke.

40   Flanagan (1988).

41   *2 Samuel* 9: 12; cf. *1 Chronicles* 8; 9.

42   Service (1962) 162.

43   *2 Samuel* 3: 2–5.

44   *1 Samuel* 20: 31.

45   *2 Samuel* 6: 22.

46   Ibid, 17: 24–26.

47   Ibid, 11; 12: 24–26.

48   Ibid, 3: 2–5; 5: 13–16.

49   Ibid, 20.

50   Ibid, 19: 45.

51   Flanagan (1976).

52   Flanagan (1988).

53   *2 Samuel* 20.

54   Ibid, 21.

55   Ibid, 22.

56   Ibid, 23.

57   Ibid, 24.

58   McCarter, *op.cit.*, 512–514.

59   *Deuteronomy* 1–4.

60   *2 Kings* 22.

61   Ibid, 23.

62   *Joshua* 24; *1 Samuel* 12; *2 Samuel* 7; cf. McCarthy (1965) 137, etc.

63   *Deuteronomy, Joshua, Judges, 1 Samuel* 1–2, *II Samuel* 5.

64   *Judges* and *1 Samuel.*

65   From *2 Samuel* 8 to *1 Kings* 11.

66   *1 Kings* 12 to the end of *2 Kings.*

67   *Deuteronomy* 10: 1–9.

68   Ibid, 31: 9–13, 25–26.

69   *Joshua* 3–8.

70   Flanagan, *op.cit.*

71   Cf. Jobling (1986) 107–119.

72   Idelsohn (1972) Chap. 1.

73   Ibid, Chap. 2. See also Wright and Fuller (1960) 124.

74   *Leviticus* 9: 22. *Numbers* 6: 24–27.

75   Winter (1973) 51.

76   *1 Samuel* 13: 32–33.

77   Gaster, *op.cit*, 455–457.

78   Ibid. 456.

79   *1 Samuel* 10: 6.

80   *2 Kings* 9: 11.

81   *1 Samuel* 19: 24.

82   Ibid, 10: 10.
83   Barton (1961) 84.
84   *1 Kings*: 8.
85   Josephus (192530).
86   Weber (1967) 222.
87   *Judges* 20: 27.
88   *2 Samuel* 4: 1–7: 1.
89   *1 Samuel* 14: 18.
90   McCarter, *op.cit.*
91   Flanagan (1983b).
92   *1 Chronicles* 1–9.
93   Ibid, 22: 15, 37; 19: 17.
94   Williamson (1977); (1982) 45.
95   *1 Chronicles* 10: 14.
96   Ibid, 13–16; 21–27.
97   Williamson (1982) 27.
98   Williamson (1977).
99   *2 Chronicles* 10: 1.
100   Ibid, 9: 1.
101   Ibid, 18: 8.

Chapter 9 THE JUDEAN ROYAL DRAMA

1   Bloom (1990) 37–38.
2   Made by Yahweh through Nathan to David in *2 Samuel* 7:12–16. It has to be made, interestingly, through an intermediary.
3   Bloom, *op.cit.*, 285–286.
4   Ibid, 291.
5   Ibid, 37.
6   Ibid, 42–43.
7   Ibid, 43–44.
8   The Shakespearean parallel is *Henry VIII*: J looks back from the reign of James I (Rehoboam) through Elizabeth I (Solomon), Henry VIII (David) and Henry VII (Saul) to the time of Henry V (Moses). A comment by Bloom.
9   Leach (1969) 81.
10   Flanagan (1988).

11   Flanagan (1976) 177–180.
12   Turner (1974) 35.
13   Noth (1967).
14   *2 Samuel* 6: 20–23.
15   Flanagan (1988).
16   Ibid.
17   Cf. von Rad (1965) 201.
18   *2 Samuel* 16: 3.
19   Ibid, 15: 16.
20   Ibid, 16: 21.
21   Ibid, 19: 2. House is mentioned in each reference and three more times in a single verse, without mentioning the Ark or its habitation (*2 Samuel* 20:3).

Chapter 10 THE DAVID PLAY

1   Flanagan (1972).
2   *2 Kings* 22: 2. Von Rad (1953) 88. Flanagan (1975).
3   *1 Kings* 3: 3; 15: 11; *2 Kings* 14: 3; 16: 2; 18: 3; 22: 2.
4   *1 Kings* 9: 4; 11: 4, 6, 33, 38; 15: 3, 5.
5   Ibid, 5: 17; 8: 17; *2 Kings* 21: 7.
6   *2 Samuel* 7.
7   Gunn (1978) 61.
8   *Psalms* 78: 70; 89: 4, 36, 50; 122: 5; 132: 10; 144: 10.
9   Flanagan (1972).
10   *2 Samuel* 21–24.
11   Ibid, 2: 12–16.
12   Ibid, 3: 1.
13   The same issue arises again with Sheba's rebellion in *2 Samuel* 20 and is not finally resolved until the Schism.
14   *2 Samuel* 3: 6–69.
15   *1 Samuel* 25: 44.
16   *2 Samuel* 6: 16–23.
17   Ibid, 4: 1–12.
18   Ibid, 5: 1–5.
19   Ibid, 22: 5–20; *Psalm* 18: 5–20.
20   *2 Samuel* 22: 32–46; *Psalm* 18: 32–46.

21   *2 Samuel* 22: 47–51; *Psalm* 18: 47–51.
22   *2 Samuel* 24: 18–25.
23   *1 Samuel* 1: 19.
24   *2 Samuel* 21: 1–14.
25   Ibid, 21: 15–22.
26   Ibid, 9–20; *1 Kings* 1–2.
27   Perhaps David; cf. Mowinckel (1962) I: 225.
28   Dahood (1968) 319.
29   Cross (1973) 258–259; Dahood, *op.cit.*, 309, 316.
30   *2 Samuel* 1: 17–21.
31   Ibid, 9: 1–13.
32   Ibid, 14: 1–33; cf. Bellefontaine (1987).
33   *1 Samuel* 2: 3, 10; McCarter (1980) 67–71; Freedman (1980) 243–261.
34   *2 Samuel* 2: 19–27.
35   Ibid, 23: 1–7.
36   McCarter (1984) 481.
37   *Psalm* 78: 65–72.
38   Ibid, 122.
39   *2 Samuel* 7: 2.
40   Ibid, 24: 18–25.
41   *Amos* 6: 5.
42   *1 Chronicles* 25.
43   Gaster (1969) 489–490.
44   *Judges* 9: 6. *2 Kings* 11: 14.
45   *1 Kings* 2: 26; 3: 15.
46   Ibid, 6: 19; 8: 3, 5, 7, 9.
47   Ibid, 6: 1–10; 14–18.
48   Ibid, 7: 1.
49   See *1 Chronicles* 17.

Chapter 11 DRAMA IN THE TWO KINGDOMS
1   *1 Chronicles* 14: 8–17; 18; 19; 20.
2   Ibid, 10: 1.
3   *2 Chronicles* 16–17.
4   Ibid, 10: 19.

5   Ibid, 11: 1–3.
6   Ibid, 11: 12.
7   Ibid, 11: 13.
8   Ibid, 11: 23.
9   Ibid, 12: 1.
10   Ibid, 35: 3.
11   Ibid, 34: 1–7.
12   Ibid, 30: 1–27.
13   Williamson (1977) 119–124.
14   *1 Kings* 12: 27.
15   *Psalms* 50, 76, 78, 81, 82, 89, 105, 111, 114.
16   As in *Joshua* 24.
17   *Joshua* 3–4. *Exodus* 13: 18–20.
18   *1 Kings* 18.
19   *2 Kings* 1.
20   *1 Kings* 19.
21   Ibid, 19: 16–21. *2 Kings* 2: 1–15.
22   *2 Kings* 11: 16–18.
23   Ibid, 2: 8.
24   Ibid, 2: 14.
25   This is precisely *not* to echo Lévi–Straus' dualism. The inversion takes place at a *secondary* level. Only when the first play was created (based on similarities) was the second created.
26   Gaster (1969) 504–510.
27   Ibid, 630–631.
28   *Deuteronomy* 28: 69.
29   *Joshua* 1: 11, 3: 3.
30   Ibid, 3: 23.
31   Ibid, 5: 2–9.
32   Wijngaards (1969) 56–63.
33   Ibid, 121.
34   *1 Kings* 14: 23–24.
35   Patai (1978) 38–39.
36   *Isaiah* 7: 14–16.
37   Ibid, 17: 10.

38   Ibid, 24: 21–23.
39   Ibid, 27: 1.
40   Ibid, 53.
41   *2 Kings* 21: 3, 6.
42   *Nahum* 1; 2: 3–8.
43   Ibid, 3: 3–4.
44   Ibid, 1: 20.
45   Ibid, 3: 5.
46   *Jeremiah* 16: 6; 48: 37; 22: 18.
47   *Psalm* 24.
48   Ibid, 68: 24–25; 118: 27.
49   Ibid, 149: 3.
50   Ibid, 89: 15.
51   Based on the events in *2 Samuel* 6, 7.
52   *Psalms* 46, 48, 76, 84, 87, 112.
53   Ibid, 2, 20, 21, 45, 72, 11 0.
54   Gaster, *op.cit.*, 780–781.
55   *Psalms* 47, 93, 96, 97, 98, 99.
56   Anderson (1966) 478–484.

Chapter 12 THE EXILE AND AFTER
1   *Jeremiah* 44: 17–18.
2   *Ezekiel* 4: 4–8.
3   Ibid, 5: 1–12.
4   Ibid, 7–9.
5   *Jeremiah* 29: 12–14.
6   *Deuteronomy* 4: 27, 29.
7   *Psalm* 137: 1.
8   E.g., *Psalm* 130.
9   Anderson (1966) 389–390.
10   *1 Chronicles* 3: 19.
11   *Ezra* 7: 6.
12   Ibid, 7: 12, 21.
13   *Nehemiah* 8: 1.
14   Ibid, 8: 1–8.

15   Ibid, 8: 13–18.

16   Ibid, 9: 38; 10.

17   *Isaiah* 51: 9–10.

18   *Psalm* 74: 13–14.

19   *Ezekiel* 29: 3–5.

20   Idelsohn (1972) 20.

21   *1 Kings* 22: 39.

22   Patai (1978) 85–86.

23   Ibid.: 86.

24   Gaster (1978) Chap. 10; Gaster (1969) 829–834.

25   Gaster (1961) 71–75.

Conclusion THE PLAY OF THE JEWS

1   Scholem (1961) 7–8.

BIBLIOGRAPHY

Ahlstrom, Gosta W. (1986). *Who Were the Israelites?* Winona Lake, Indiana: Eisenbrauns.

Albright, William F. (1932, 1938, 1943). *The Excavation of Tell Beit Mirsim.* 3 vols. Cambridge, Mass.: American Schools of Oriental Research.

_____ ([1940] 1957). *From the Stone Age to Christianity.* 2nd ed. Garden City, New York: Doubleday.

_____ (1945). "The Chronology of the Divided Monarchy of Israel,". *Bulletin of the American Schools of Oriental Research*: 16–22.

_____ (1964) . *History, Archaeology and Christian Humanism.* New York: McGraw-Hill.

_____ (1966). *Archaeology, Historical Analogy, and Early Biblical Tradition.* Baton Rouge: Louisiana State University.

_____ (1969). *Archaeology and the Religion of Israel.* 5th ed. Garden City, New York: Doubleday.

Anderson, Bernhard W. (1966). *Understanding the Old Testament.* 2nd ed. Englewood Cliffs, New Jersey: Prentice-Hall.

Augé, Marc (1982). *The Anthropological Circle.* Cambridge: Cambridge University Press.

Ball, Edward (1982). "Introduction." in Leonhard Rost, *The Succession to the Throne of David*, trans. M.D.Rutter and D.M.Gunn. Sheffield: Almond.

Barton, G.A. ([1928] 1961). *The Religion of Ancient Israel.* New York: A.S. Barnes.

Bellefontaine, Elizabeth (1987). "Customary Law and Chieftanship: Judicial Aspects of *2 Samuel* 14: 4–21," *Journal for the Study of the Old Testament.*

Black, Matthew (1961). *The Scrolls and Christian Origins*. New York: Scribner's.

Bloom, Harold (1990). *The Book of J*, trans. David Rosenberg. Toronto: General Publishing.

Bowle, John (1977). *Man Through the Ages*. New York: Atheneum.

Buber, Martin (1958). *Moses: The Revelation and the Covenant*. New York: Harper and Row.

Campbell, Joseph ([1959]1975). *The Masks of God*. 4 vols. Harmondsworth: Penguin.

Courtney, Richard (1987). *Lord of the Sky: A Ritual Drama of Ancient Egypt*. Salt Spring Island, B.C.: Bison Books.

Cross, Frank Moore (1973). *Canaanite Myth and Hebrew Epic*. Cambridge, Mass.: Harvard University Press..

Dahood, Mitchell (1968). *Psalms II*. Garden City, New York: Doubleday.

de Silla Pool, D.and T.(1953) [eds.]. *The Haggadah of the Passover*. New York: Block.

Dever, William G. (1977). "Palestine in the Second Millenium BCD: the Archeological Picture," in John H. Hayes and J. Maxwell Miller (eds.). *Israelite and Judaean History*. Philadelphia: Westminster.

Drennan, Robert D. (1976). "Religion and Social Evolution in Formative Mesoamerica," in Kent V.Flannery (ed.). *The Early Mesoamerican Village*. New York: Academic.

Edwards, Ralph (1967). *Erotica Judaica: A Sexual History of the Jews*. New York: The Julian Press.

Eliade, Mircea (1979). *A History of Religious Ideas* Vol. I. London: Collins.

Fairman, H.W. (1974). *The Triumph of Horus: An Ancient Egyptian Sacred Drama.* London: Batsford.

Flanagan, James W. (1972). "Court History or Succession Document? A Study of 2 Samuel 9–20 and 1 Kings 1–2." *Journal of Biblical Literature*, 91: 172–181.

_____ (1975). "Judah in All Israel," in James W. Flanagan and Anita W. Robinson (eds.). *No Famine in the Land.* Missoula, Mt.: Scholars: 165.

_____ (1976). "History, Religion, and Ideology: The Caleb Tradition." *Horizons* 3: 175–185.

_____ (1983). "Social Transformation and Ritual in 2 Samuel 6," in Carol Meyers and Michael P. O'Connor (eds.). *The Word of the Lord Shall Go Forth.* Winona Lake, Indiana: Eisenbrauns.

_____ (1988). *David's Social Drama.* Sheffield: Almond Press.

Frankfort, Henri ([1948] 1978). *Kingship and the Gods: A Study of Ancient Near Eastern Religion as the Integration of Society and Nature.* Chicago: University of Chicago.

Frazer, James George ([1919] 1975). *Folklore in the Old Testament.* 3 vols. New York: Hart.

Friedman, Richard (1987). *Who Wrote the Bible?* New York: Summit Books.

Frye, Northrop (1982). *The Great Code.* Toronto: Academic Press.

Gaster, Theodor H. ([1950] 1961). *Thespis: Ritual, Myth and Drama in the Ancient NearEast.* New York: Doubleday.

_____ (1969). *Myth, Legend and Custom in the Old Testament.* New York: Harper and Row.

_____ (1975). *The Dead Sea Scriptures.* 3rd ed. New York: Doubleday.

_____ (1978). *Festivals of the Jewish Year.* New York: William Morrow.

Gilkes, A.N. (1962). *The Impact of the Dead Sea Scrolls.* London: Macmillan.

Gonen, Rivka (1984). "Urban Canaan in the Late Bronze Age," *Bulletin of the American Schools of Oriental Research*: 70.

Goody, Jack (1976). "Introduction." in Jack Goody (ed.). *Succession to High Office.* Cambridge: Cambridge University Press.

_____ (1977). "Production and Polity in Voltaic Region," in J.Friedman and M.J.Rowlands (eds.). *The Evolution of Social Systems.* London: Duckworth.

Gottwald, Norman K. (1979). *The Tribes of Yahweh.* Maryknoll, New York: Orbis.

Gray, John (1964). *The Canaanites.* London: Thames and Hudson.

_____ (1969). *Near Eastern Mythology.* London: Hamlyn.

Greenberg, Raphael (1987). "New Light on the Early Iron Age at Tell Beit Mirsim." *Bulletin of the American Schools of Oriental Research*: 76.

Gunn, David M. (1978). *The Story of King David.* Sheffield: JSOT.

Gurney, O.R. (1981). *The Hittites.* Harmondsworth: Penguin.

Halpern, Baruch (1983). *Emergence of Israel in Canaan.* Chico, Calif.: Scholars.

Harrelson, Walter (1969). *From Fertility Cult to Worship: A Reassessment of the Worship of Ancient Israel.* New York: Doubleday.

Harris, Marvin (1979). *Cultural Materialism.* New York: Random House.

Hooke, S.H. (1963). *Middle Eastern Mythology*. Harmondsworth: Penguin.

Idelsohn, A Z. (1972). *Jewish Liturgy*. New York: Schocken.

Jacobsen, Thorkild (1976). *The Treasury of Darkness: A History of Mesopotamian Religion*. New Haven: Yale University Press.

Jobling, David (1986). *The Sense of Biblical Narrative*: II. JSOT Supplement Series, 39. Sheffield: JSOT: 107–119.

Josephus, Flavius (1925–30). *Works*. 4 Vols. London: Loeb.

Kaufman, Yehezkel (1972). *The Religion of Israel from its Beginnings to the Babylonian Exile*, trans. Moshe Greenberg. New York: Schocken.

Kraus, H-J. (1966). *Worship in Israel*. Richmond, Va.: John Knox Press.

LaBarre, Weston (1972). *The Ghost Dance*. London: Allen and Unwin.

Leach, Edmund (1969). *Genesis as Myth and Other Essays*. London: Cape.

_____ (1982). *Social Anthropology*. New York: Oxford University Press.

_____ (1983a). "Anthropological Approaches to the Study of the Bible during the Twentieth Century," in Edmund Leach and D.A. Aycock (eds.) *Structuralist Interpretations of Biblical Myth*. Cambridge: Cambridge University Press: 8–23.

_____ (1983b) "Against Genres," ibid, 97–109.

Lemche, Niels P. (1985). *Early Israel*. Supplements to Vetus Testamentum, 37. Leiden: Brill: 430.

Lovejoy, P.E. (1983). *Transformations in Slavery*. Cambridge: Cambridge University Press.

Malamat, Abraham (1976), in Ben-Sasson, H. H. (ed.). *A History of the Jewish People*. Cambridge, Mass.: Harvard University Press: 3–87.

Marfoe, Leon (1979). "The Integrative Transformation: Patterns of Sociopolitical Organization in Southern Syria," *Bulletin of the American Schools of Oriental Research.*

Marshack, Alexander (1972). *The Roots of Civilization.* New York: McGraw-Hill.

McCarter, P. Kyle, Jr. (1980, 1984). *1, II Samuel.* Garden City: Doubleday.

McNutt, P.M.(1983). An Inquiry into the Significance of Iron Technology in Early Iron Age Palestine. Master's Thesis, Missoula, Mt: Univesity of Montana.

Mendenhall, George E. ([1954] 1970a). "Ancient Oriental and Biblical Law," in E.F.Campbell and D.N.Freedman (eds.). *Biblical Archaeologist Reader, 3.* Garden City, New York: Doubleday: 3–24.

_____ (1970b). "Covenant Forms in Israelite Tradition,": ibid: 25–53.

_____ (1970c). "The Hebrew Conquest of Canaan," ibid: 100–120.

Moran, William L. (1975). "The Syrian Scribe of the Jerusalem Amarna Letters," in Hans Goedicke and J. J. M. Roberts (eds.). *Unity and Diversity.* Baltimore: Johns Hopkins University Press: 146–166.

Mowinckel, Sigmund (1962). *The Psalms in Israel's Worship*, trans. D.R. Ap-Thomas. 2 vols. New York: Abingdon.

Noth, Martin (1967). *The Laws of the Pentateuch.* Philadelphia: Fortress.

Pallis, S.A. (1926). *The Babylonian Akîtu Festival.* Copenhagen: A.F.Host.

Patai, Raphael ([1967], 1978). *The Hebrew Goddess.* New York: Avon

Posner, Raphael, Uri Kaploun, and Shalom Cohen (1975) [eds.]. *Jewish Liturgy: Prayer and Synagogue: Service through the Ages.* New York: Leon Amiel.

von Rad, Gerhard ([1962] 1965). *Old Testament Theology*, trans. D.M.G. Stalker. 2 vols. New York: Harper and Row.

_____ ([1958], 1966) "The Beginnings of Historical Writing in Ancient Israel," in Gerhard von Rad. *The Problem of the Hexateuch and other Essays*, trans. E.W.Trueman Dicken. New York: McGraw-Hill: 166–204.

Rappaport, Roy A. (1979). *Ecology, Meaning and Religion*. Richmond, Calif.: North Atlantic Books.

Redford, Donald B. (1985). "The Relations between Egypt and Israel from El-Amarna to the Babylonian Conquest," in Janet Amitai (ed.). *Biblical Archaeology Today*. Jerusalem: Israel Exploration Society: 195–197.

Rosenberg, Joel (1986). *King and Kin*. Bloomington: Indiana University.

Rost, Leonhard (1982). *The Succession to the Throne of David*, trans. Michael D.Rutter and David M.Gunn. Sheffield: Almond.

Sarmela, Matti (1982). "Death of a Bear: An Old Finnish Hunting Drama," *The Drama Review*, 26, 3 (Fall): 57–66.

Schauss, Hayyim (1977). *The Jewish Festivals*. New York: Schocken.

Scholem, Gershom G. (1961). *Jewish Mysticism*. New York: Schocken.

Smith, William Robertson ([1889], 1927). *The Religion of the Semites*. 3rd ed. New York: Harper & Bros.

Solecki, Ralph S. (1972). *Shanidar: The Humanity of Neanderthal Man*. Harmondsworth: Penguin.

Turner, Victor W. (1957). *Schism and Continuity in an African Society*. New York: Manchester University Press.

_____ (1974). *Dramas, Fields, and Metaphors*. Ithaca: Cornell University.

_____ (1977). "Process, System, and Symbol: A New Anthropological Synthesis," *Daedalus*.

_____ (1980). "Social Dramas and Stories about Them." *Critical Inquiry*: 152.

_____ (1985a). *The Ritual Process*. Ithaca: Cornell University Press.

_____ (1985b). *On the Edge of the Bush*, edited by Edith Turner. Tucson: University of Arizona Press.

_____ (1978) and Edith Turner. *Image and Pilgrimage in Christian Culture*. New York: Columbia University Press.

van Gennep, Arnold (1960). *Rites of Passage*. London: Routledge and Kegan Paul.

Van Seters, John (1975). *Abraham in History and Tradition*. New Haven: Yale University Press.

Vawter, Bruce (1977). *On Genesis: A New Reading*. London: Geoffrey Chapman.

Vermes, G. (1975). *The Dead Sea Scrolls in English*. 2nd ed. Hardmondsworth: Penguin.

Weber, Max (1967). *Ancient Judaism*. New York: The Free Press.

Wijngaards, J.N.M. (1969). *The Dramatization of Salvific History in the Deuteronomic Schools*. Leiden: E.J. Brill.

Williamson, H.G.M. ([1977] 1982). *Israel in the Books of Chronicles*. Cambridge: Cambridge University Press.

Wilson, Robert R. (1975). "The Old Testament Genealogies in Recent Research," *Journal of Biblical Literature*.

_____ (1977). *Genealogy and History in the Biblical World*. New Haven: Yale University Press.

Winter, Napthali (1973). *The High Holy Days*. New York: Leon Amiel.

Wright, E.G. (1946). "The Literary and Historical Problem of Joshua 10 and Judges 1," *Journal of Near Eastern Studies*, V.: 105–114.

Wright, G.E. (1983a). "What Archaeology Can and Cannot Do," in E.F.Campbell and D.N.Freedman (eds.). *The Biblical Archaeologist Reader, IV.* .Sheffield: Almond: 69.

_____ "The New Archaeology," ibid: 80–83.

_____ (1960) and Reginald H. Fuller. *The Book of the Acts of God*. New York: Doubleday.

General Index

Index: Books of the Bible